MORAY D/

THE BELFRY ʌ

KATHERINE DALTON RENOIR ('Moray Dalton') was born in Hammersmith, London in 1881, the only child of a Canadian father and English mother.

The author wrote two well-received early novels, *Olive in Italy* (1909), and *The Sword of Love* (1920). However, her career in crime fiction did not begin until 1924, after which Moray Dalton published twenty-nine mysteries, the last in 1951. The majority of these feature her recurring sleuths, Scotland Yard inspector Hugh Collier and private inquiry agent Hermann Glide.

Moray Dalton married Louis Jean Renoir in 1921, and the couple had a son a year later. The author lived on the south coast of England for the majority of her life following the marriage. She died in Worthing, West Sussex, in 1963.

MORAY DALTON MYSTERIES
Available from Dean Street Press

MORAY DALTON

THE BELFRY MURDER

With an introduction by Curtis Evans

DEAN STREET PRESS

LOST GOLD FROM A GOLDEN AGE
The Detective Fiction of Moray Dalton
(Katherine Mary Deville Dalton Renoir, 1881-1963)

"GOLD" COMES in many forms. For literal-minded people gold may be merely a precious metal, physically stripped from the earth. For fans of Golden Age detective fiction, however, gold can be artfully spun out of the human brain, in the form not of bricks but books. While the father of Katherine Mary Deville Dalton Renoir may have derived the Dalton family fortune from nuggets of metallic ore, the riches which she herself produced were made from far humbler, though arguably ultimately mightier, materials: paper and ink. As the mystery writer Moray Dalton, Katherine Dalton Renoir published twenty-nine crime novels between 1924 and 1951, the majority of which feature her recurring sleuths, Scotland Yard inspector Hugh Collier and private inquiry agent Hermann Glide. Although the Moray Dalton mysteries are finely polished examples of criminally scintillating Golden Age art, the books unjustifiably fell into neglect for decades. For most fans of vintage mystery they long remained, like the fabled Lost Dutchman's mine, tantalizingly elusive treasure. Happily the crime fiction of Moray Dalton has been unearthed for modern readers by those industrious miners of vintage mystery at Dean Street Press.

Born in Hammersmith, London on May 6, 1881, Katherine was the only child of Joseph Dixon Dalton and Laura Back Dalton. Like the parents of that admittedly more famous mistress of mystery, Agatha Christie, Katherine's parents hailed from different nations, separated by the Atlantic Ocean. While both authors had British mothers, Christie's father was American and Dalton's father Canadian.

Laura Back Dalton, who at the time of her marriage in 1879 was twenty-six years old, about fifteen years younger than her husband, was the daughter of Alfred and Catherine Mary Back. In her early childhood years Laura Back resided at Valley House, a lovely regency villa built around 1825 in Stratford St. Mary, Suffolk, in the heart of so-called "Constable Country" (so named for the fact that the great Suffolk landscape artist John Constable painted many of his works in and around Stratford). Alfred Back was a wealthy miller who with his brother Octavius, a corn merchant, owned and operated a steam-powered six-story mill right across the River Stour from Valley House. In 1820 John Constable, himself the son of a miller, executed a painting of fishers on the River Stour which partly included the earlier, more modest incarnation (complete with water wheel) of the Back family's mill. (This piece Constable later repainted under the title *The Young Waltonians*, one of his best known works.) After Alfred Back's death in 1860, his widow moved with her daughters to Brondesbury Villas in Maida Vale, London, where Laura in the 1870s met Joseph Dixon Dalton, an eligible Canadian-born bachelor and retired gold miner of about forty years of age who lived in nearby Kew.

Joseph Dixon Dalton was born around 1838 in London, Ontario, Canada, to Henry and Mary (Dixon) Dalton, Wesleyan Methodists from northern England who had migrated to Canada a few years previously. In 1834, not long before Joseph's birth, Henry Dalton started a soap and candle factory in London, Ontario, which after his death two decades later was continued, under the appellation Dalton Brothers, by Joseph and his siblings Joshua and Thomas. (No relation to the notorious "Dalton Gang" of American outlaws is presumed.) Joseph's sister Hannah wed John Carling, a politician who came from a prominent family of Canadian brewers and was later knighted for his varied public services, making him Sir John and his wife Lady Hannah. Just how Joseph left the family soap and candle business to prospect for gold is currently unclear, but sometime in the 1870s, after fabulous gold rushes at Cariboo and Cassiar, British Columbia and the Black Hills of South Dakota, among other locales, Joseph left Canada and carried his riches with him to London, England, where for a time he enjoyed life as a gentleman of leisure in one of the great metropolises of the world.

Although Joshua and Laura Dalton's first married years were spent with their daughter Katherine in Hammersmith at a villa named Kenmore Lodge, by 1891 the family had moved to 9 Orchard Place in Southampton, where young Katherine received a private education from Jeanne Delport, a governess from Paris. Two decades later, Katherine, now 30 years old, resided with her parents at Perth Villa in the village of Merriott, Somerset, today about an eighty miles' drive west of Southampton. By this time Katherine had published, under the masculine-sounding pseudonym of Moray Dalton (probably a gender-bending play on "Mary Dalton") a well-received first novel, *Olive in Italy* (1909), a study of a winsome orphaned Englishwoman attempting to make her own living as an artist's model in Italy that possibly had been influenced by E.M. Forster's novels *Where Angels Fear to Tread* (1905) and *A Room with a View* (1908), both of which are partly set in an idealized Italy of pure gold sunlight and passionate love. Yet despite her accomplishment, Katherine's name had no occupation listed next it in the census two years later.

During the Great War the Daltons, parents and child, resided at 14 East Ham Road in Littlehampton, a seaside resort town located 19 miles west of Brighton. Like many other bookish and patriotic British women of her day, Katherine produced an effusion of memorial war poetry, including "To Some Who Have Fallen," "Edith Cavell," "Rupert Brooke," "To Italy" and "Mort Homme." These short works appeared in the *Spectator* and were reprinted during and after the war in George Herbert Clarke's *Treasury of War Poetry* anthologies. "To Italy," which Katherine had composed as a tribute to the beleaguered British ally after its calamitous defeat, at the hands of the forces of Germany and Austria-Hungary, at the Battle of Caporetto in 1917, even popped up in the United States in the "poet's corner" of the *United Mine Workers Journal*, perhaps on account of the poem's pro-Italy sentiment, doubtlessly agreeable to Italian miner immigrants in America.

Katherine also published short stories in various periodicals, including *The Cornhill Magazine*, which was then edited by Leonard Huxley, son of the eminent zoologist Thomas Henry Huxley and father of famed writer Aldous Huxley. Leonard Huxley obligingly read over--and in his words "plied my scalpel upon"--Katherine's second novel, *The Sword of Love*, a romantic adventure saga set in the Florentine Republic at the time of Lorenzo the Magnificent and the infamous Pazzi Conspiracy, which was published in 1920. Katherine writes with obvious affection for *il bel paese* in her first two novels and her poem "To Italy," which concludes with the ringing lines

> Greece was enslaved, and Carthage is but dust,
> But thou art living, maugre [i.e., in spite of] all thy scars,
> To bear fresh wounds of rapine and of lust,
> Immortal victim of unnumbered wars.
> Nor shalt thou cease until we cease to be
> Whose hearts are thine, beloved Italy.

The author maintained her affection for "beloved Italy" in her later Moray Dalton mysteries, which include sympathetically-rendered Italian settings and characters.

Around this time Katherine in her own life evidently discovered romance, however short-lived. At Brighton in the spring of 1921, the author, now nearly 40 years old, wed a presumed Frenchman, Louis Jean Renoir, by whom the next year she bore her only child, a son, Louis Anthony Laurence Dalton Renoir. (Katherine's father seems to have missed these important developments in his daughter's life, apparently having died in 1918, possibly in the flu pandemic.) Sparse evidence as to the actual existence of this man, Louis Jean Renoir, in Katherine's life suggests that the marriage may not have been a successful one. In the 1939 census Katherine was listed as living with her mother Laura at 71 Wallace Avenue in Worthing, Sussex, another coastal town not far from Brighton, where she had married Louis Jean eighteen years earlier; yet he is not in evidence, even though he is stated to be Katherine's husband in her mother's will, which was probated in Worthing in 1945. Perhaps not unrelatedly, empathy with what people in her day considered unorthodox sexual unions characterizes the crime fiction which Katherine would write.

Whatever happened to Louis Jean Renoir, marriage and motherhood did not slow down "Moray Dalton." Indeed, much to the contrary, in 1924, only a couple of years after the birth of her son, Katherine published, at the age of 42 (the same age at which

P.D. James published her debut mystery novel, *Cover Her Face*), *The Kingsclere Mystery*, the first of her 29 crime novels. (Possibly the title was derived from the village of Kingsclere, located some 30 miles north of Southampton.) The heady scent of Renaissance romance which perfumes *The Sword of Love* is found as well in the first four Moray Dalton mysteries (aside from *The Kingsclere Mystery*, these are *The Shadow on the Wall*, *The Black Wings* and *The Stretton Darknesse Mystery*), which although set in the present-day world have, like much of the mystery fiction of John Dickson Carr, the elevated emotional temperature of the highly-colored age of the cavaliers. However in 1929 and 1930, with the publication of, respectively, *One by One They Disappeared*, the first of the Inspector Hugh Collier mysteries and *The Body in the Road*, the debut Hermann Glide tale, the Moray Dalton novels begin to become more typical of British crime fiction at that time, ultimately bearing considerable similarity to the work of Agatha Christie and Dorothy L. Sayers, as well as other prolific women mystery authors who would achieve popularity in the 1930s, such as Margery Allingham, Lucy Beatrice Malleson (best known as "Anthony Gilbert") and Edith Caroline Rivett, who wrote under the pen names E.C.R. Lorac and Carol Carnac.

For much of the decade of the 1930s Katherine shared the same publisher, Sampson Low, with Edith Rivett, who published her first detective novel in 1931, although Rivett moved on, with both of her pseudonyms, to that rather more prominent purveyor of mysteries, the Collins Crime Club. Consequently the Lorac and Carnac novels are better known today than those of Moray Dalton. Additionally, only three early Moray Dalton titles (*One by One They Disappeared*, *The Body in the Road* and *The Night of Fear*) were picked up in the United States, another factor which mitigated against the Dalton mysteries achieving long-term renown. It is also possible that the independently wealthy author, who left an estate valued, in modern estimation, at nearly a million American dollars at her death at the age of 81 in 1963, felt less of an imperative to "push" her writing than the typical "starving author."

Whatever forces compelled Katherine Dalton Renoir to write fiction, between 1929 and 1951 the author as Moray Dalton published fifteen Inspector Hugh Collier mysteries and ten other crime novels (several of these with Hermann Glide). Some of the non-series novels daringly straddle genres. *The Black Death*, for example, somewhat bizarrely yet altogether compellingly merges the murder mystery with post-apocalyptic science fiction, whereas *Death at the Villa*, set in Italy during the Second World War, is a gripping wartime adventure thriller with crime and death. Taken together, the imaginative and ingenious Moray Dalton crime fiction, wherein death is not so much a game as a dark and compelling human drama, is one of the more significant bodies of work by a Golden Age mystery writer—though the author has, until now, been most regrettably overlooked by publishers, for decades remaining accessible almost solely to connoisseurs with deep pockets.

Even noted mystery genre authorities Jacques Barzun and Wendell Hertig Taylor managed to read only five books by Moray Dalton, all of which the pair thereupon listed in their massive critical compendium, *A Catalogue of Crime* (1972; revised and expanded 1989). Yet Barzun and Taylor were warm admirers of the author's writing, avowing for example, of the twelfth Hugh Collier mystery, *The Condamine Case* (under the impression that the author was a man): "[T]his is the author's 17th book, and [it is] remarkably fresh and unstereotyped [actually it was Dalton's 25th book, making it even more remarkable—C.E.]. . . . [H]ere is a neglected man, for his earlier work shows him to be a conscientious workman, with a flair for the unusual, and capable of clever touches."

Today in 2019, nine decades since the debut of the conscientious and clever Moray Dalton's Inspector Hugh Collier detective series, it is a great personal pleasure to announce that this criminally neglected woman is neglected no longer and to welcome her books back into light. Vintage crime fiction fans have a golden treat in store with the classic mysteries of Moray Dalton.

The Belfry Murder

THE Russian Revolutions of February and October 1917 saw respectively the abdication of Tsar Nicholas II from his throne and the seizure of power by Vladimir Lenin's Bolshevik Party, a violent radical organization committed to establishing, though the systematic use of brutal force known as the "Red Terror," the supremacy of Communism in Russia. Thus was launched a cataclysmic six-year civil war which resulted, before the Communists finally emerged victorious, in the deaths of millions, including many of those who formerly had stood at the privileged apex of Russian society: aristocrats and members of the imperial family. The Tsar and Tsarina were themselves viciously exterminated, along with their five young children, in a sickening hail of gunfire and brandishing of bayonets at the basement of a house in Ekaterinburg in July 1918, while eleven of their Romanov relations met similar ghastly fates at the hands of remorseless revolutionaries that same year. As for the aristocrats, a *New Republic* review of Douglas Smith's prizewinning 2012 book *Former People: The Final Days of the Russian Aristocracy* grimly recounts that they were "murdered by mobs, arrested repeatedly, tortured and starved, shot and shot and shot (how many times does that word appear in this book?)," unless they managed to escape from their native country, preferably with some of the family jewels cunningly stashed away somewhere. "Even if their estates were looted or pillaged," notes the reviewer, "one necklace, stitched into the lining of a child's teddy bear, could fund life abroad."

Lost or stolen Russian gems are, like Chinese opium dens and Argentine white slavery rings, one of the wellsprings of British crime thrillers in the Twenties and Thirties. They feature as well as plot devices in mainstream media from the period, like the acclaimed satirical 1939 Greta Garbo film *Ninotchka*, in which three bumbling Soviet agents travel to Paris to raise money for the Communist government by selling jewelry confiscated from exiled aristocrats, dubbed "enemies of the people." Similarly, the impecunious White Russian émigré, calculatedly trading on little else but an ample stock of grace and charm, is a familiar figure in between-the-wars film and fiction, such as Edith Wharton's aptly titled and drolly engaging 1934 short story "Charm, Incorporated." Elements of Moray Dalton's lost Russian gems mystery, *The Belfry Murder* (1933), recall an altogether more somber tale, however, which preceded it into print by a year: *The Ostrekoff Jewels*, a 1932 thriller by the bestselling "Prince of Storytellers," E. Phillips Oppenheim. However, in her own crime embroidery Dalton cunningly stiches these basic thematic elements into an appealing pattern which is all her own.

The Belfry Murder, Dalton's third Inspector Hugh Collier mystery (published after *One by One They Disappeared* and *The Night of Fear*, both previously reprinted by Dean Street Press), concerns the avid pursuit by various parties, nefarious and otherwise, of the "Eye of Nero." This storied treasure is a great pendant-set emerald, said to be the largest in the world, which had formerly been owned by the Russian imperial family, having once belonged to no less than Empress Catherine the Great and, reputedly, the infamous Roman emperor Nero, who according to ancient accounts used an emerald as a lens though which to view gladiatorial contests. One is reminded, presumably with the author's intent, of Catherine's fabulous Orlov Diamond, allegedly stolen from a Hindu temple--see Wilkie Collins' landmark mystery *The Moonstone*--and bestowed upon her by her advisor and lover Count Grigory Orlov (though in fact the huge gem was surreptitiously purchased by the Empress herself.).

The Eye of Nero, we learn as *The Belfry Murder* progresses, was the greatest of the jewels which Tsarina Alexandra, while interned with her family at the Alexander Palace at Tsarkoe Selo in the summer of 1917 by the provisional government, entrusted to Nadine, the lovely daughter of a Russian noble family and friend of the Tsarina's daughters, the Grand Duchesses Olga, Tatiana, Maria and Anastasia. The Tsarina had implored Nadine to get the jewels to England, where they could be sold to support her children, should they make it to England themselves. Unhappily, Nadine and her parents later were "shot down in the ball-room of their great house on the Nevski Prospect," but before that the beautiful young noblewoman had passed the jewels on to her "dear old English governess," Mary Borlase, to carry them out of the country. The dutiful Mary just made it to England, to the London home of her brother John Borlase, secondhand furniture and book dealer, and his young daughter, Anne, before herself expiring from pneumonia. Now, over a dozen years later, various parties suddenly are showing rather disquieting interest in the Borlases' seemingly unremarkable backwater curio shop.

Thus opens a sweeping tale of intrigue and murder which eventually engulfs not only the Borlases, father and daughter, but also such parties as Stephen and Martin Drury, grandsons of the "old squire" in Ladebrook, Sussex who now reside at the Dower House and eke out a precarious living at poultry farming (the elder brother, Stephen, prior to the war had served as an attaché at the English Embassy in Saint Petersburg); Israel Kafka, a humbly born yet now bountifully wealthy art dealer and collector, and his "slim, dark, and good looking" son, Maurice, a polished and sophisticated product of Winchester College and Oxford University who, groomed for great things, is secretary to politician and lawyer Lord Bember and the fiancé of Lord Bember's rather hard-boiled daughter, Lady Jocelyn Vaste; Lady Jocelyn's weakling brother, Bertie, a student at Reverend Stephen Henshawe's school for "difficult" privileged boys ("They're all rotters, and they'd be at Borstal if their parents weren't rich. . . . I've seen them slouching about the village in jazz pull-overs and trailing scarves, with gaspers stuck to their underlips."); darkly brooding Sussex doctor Doctor Henry Clowes, who has been utterly beguiled by Lady Jocelyn's charms; and, of course, Inspector Hugh Collier of Scotland Yard.

It is truly an "extraordinary case" that gets handed to the upright and zealously do-gooding Inspector Collier, along with his politically restrained and reluctant colleagues Chief-Inspector Cardew and Assistant Commissioner Sir James Mercer. Once again Inspector Collier has to persist in the face not only of the devious machinations of the most deep-dyed of villains, but of the hesitations of his superiors, who are fearful of the consequences of inconveniencing the rich and powerful. *The Belfry Murder* is an uncommonly rich and engrossing tale of crime and assorted dastardly evildoing, enhanced by the author's portrayal, uncommonly thoughtful for its time and place in my view, of its Jewish characters, the Kafkas. In Dalton's depiction of not only how others see them, but of how the Kafkas, father and son, see themselves, we learn something about social attitudes of that day. Readers will judge for themselves, but in my reading of *The Belfry Murder* I find that the author's handling of the subject is unusually nuanced compared with efforts from such better-known contemporary mystery writers of her day as Agatha Christie, Freeman Wills Crofts and Anthony Berkeley.

Speaking of Agatha Christie, her admirers should be struck by this passage from *The Belfry Murder*, wherein Inspector Collier reflects on the regrettable lack of support for his investigation into the Eye of Nero affair which he is receiving from his timid superiors:

> He could not blame the authorities for leaving him to make his preliminary investigations alone. Quite recently a considerable amount of public money had been wasted and a number of officers had been employed for days in searching for a woman whose disappearance had proved to be voluntary and in the nature of a practical joke. Naturally the result had been to make the police afraid to commit themselves too far with what might turn out to be a similar case.

Could Moray Dalton be referring here, rather caustically, to Agatha Christie's notorious eleven-day disappearance in December 1926 (about a half-dozen years before the publication of *The Belfry Murder*), which many members of the press and public believed (erroneously) to have been a cynically calculated publicity hoax on Christie's part? It might seem so to the devoted mystery fan, but more probably Dalton is recalling the case of famed American evangelist Aimee Semple McPherson, who likewise disappeared in 1926, for five weeks, during which time she claimed, upon her reappearance, to have been kidnapped. McPherson's story was viewed dubiously by authorities in California, who in 1927 prosecuted her, unsuccessfully, for conspiracy, perjury and obstruction of justice. The McPherson imbroglio helped inspire another 1933 mystery novel, American journalist Nancy Barr Mavity's *The Fate of Jane McKenzie*.

Curtis Evans

PROLOGUE

IT WAS the slack time in the Caffè della Dea and the waiter had shuffled wearily up the steep flight of dirty steps from the basement and crossed the road to sit on the seat under the pepper tree. Sea and sky were intensely blue and the walls of the villas on the hillside dazzlingly white in the blazing sunlight. The waiter, pallid and unshaven in his greasy dress suit, looked like one of the noisome insects that live in darkness under the stones as he sat staring vacantly with bleared eyes at the shipping in the harbour, a forest of masts and funnels. Actually he was more observant than he seemed and he had already noticed a stranger who leaned against the wall of the quay a few paces away. The stranger was smoking a cigarette. He was well dressed. The waiter, whose name was Ivan, had seen men of all nations, and he decided that this was an Englishman. He might have come ashore from one of the yachts in the harbour, or from the liner that would be leaving in a few hours. His Panama hat was tilted over his eyes, shading his face.

An itinerant vendor of the local jewellery sidled up to him, opened the case slung from his shoulders by a leather strap, and displayed coral necklaces, tortoiseshell combs, and brooches made of lava and of mosaic. The stranger entered into conversation, picked out some ornament and paid for it with a bundle of notes taken from his pocket-book. Then the peddler shut his case with the air of a man in a hurry and shambled rapidly away.

Ivan, gazing after him, regretted his weak eyesight. There had been something furtive about the transaction that aroused his interest. He got up and went to lean on the quay wall next to the stranger.

"A fine day, sir," he said, speaking English.

The stranger answered curtly, "Very."

The stranger looked bored. He was perhaps waiting for somebody and found the time hang heavy on his hands.

"Pretty things made out of coral," said Ivan.

"Very."

"The people here think the branched coral is useful. Against the mal occhio, you know. The evil eye. Did you ever hear of the Eye of Nero?"

The question had the effect intended. The stranger turned his head and looked at Ivan, abandoning his evident intention of walking away.

"Yes. What about it?"

"I could tell you a story about it, a very interesting story," said Ivan. "I was not always a waiter in the Caffé della Dea."

The stranger gave him a measuring glance. The sagging paunch and the flat feet, the dirty, ill-fitting clothes, still left a few traces of the man's former good looks. He had been a fine, well set up young fellow once.

"Russian?" said the stranger.

"Yes."

"The Army?"

"No. I was a servant in the Imperial household. I was one of the few who remained at the Tsarskoe Selo until the Romanoffs were taken to Siberia. They had an Aladdin's cave of jewels, and what became of them? I ask you?"

The stranger shrugged his shoulders. "What becomes of the pebbles on the mountain path after the avalanche has carried it away?"

"Yes," said the seedy waiter, "but not the Eye of Nero. I know what became of that. I even planned to go after it. But I was arrested and thrown into prison. I was treated with the basest ingratitude. I tried to buy my freedom by telling them what I had overheard. I tell you I heard it, the Tsarina herself and the little countess—but they wouldn't believe me. The Eye of Nero! Why, some said it was the biggest emerald in the world. And it's historic. Nero looked through it at Peter, head downwards on his cross."

"I know all that," said the stranger. "I happen to be interested in jewels. Tell me what I don't know, and quickly."

He took a couple of notes from his case. Ivan shook his head.

"More."

The stranger added another. "That's all you'll get. Take it or leave it."

Ivan had an uneasy feeling that the information he was about to impart was worth a good deal more. On the other hand many years had gone by. The scent had grown cold. Nothing had been heard of that famous stone, that translucent green loveliness, since it had passed from the Tsarina's keeping. It was almost certainly lost for ever. So he clutched the proffered notes and crammed them into his greasy trouser pocket.

"This is what happened—" he began.

He talked earnestly for ten minutes, and the stranger listened with equal earnestness, but at the end he only laughed.

"The needle and the haystack."

"But the name is unusual," said Ivan, "that should be a help."

"Well, I shouldn't tell that tale again if I were you," said the stranger. "I warn you for your own sake."

Ivan cringed, not so much at the words as at the tone. What little spirit he had ever possessed had been broken long ago.

"What do you mean?" he quavered.

"Well, you aren't in Russia now, but there are agents of that Government in other countries. They wouldn't buy your story, they'd wring it out of you. That's why I advise you to forget it after this."

Ivan looked after him as he strolled away in the direction of the harbour, and then, hearing a clock striking the hour, trudged back to his steaming underground kitchen. He was not impressed by the stranger's warning. If the Bolsheviki wanted his story they could have it; he had told it often enough in the past to half drunken listeners who thought he was lying, but he had never been paid for it before, and he was elated by his success. When some Russians from a tramp steamer discharging a cargo of timber spent a riotous evening in the Caffé della Dea soon afterwards he repeated his performance for a fifty lire note and half a bottle of the padrone's worst vermouth. The next day he disappeared.

A week later a man's body was washed up on the beach some miles farther down the coast. The padrone read about it in the paper and thought he might be able to identify it, but his wife persuaded him not to go to the mortuary. It was better not to get mixed up in such an affair, and when, the next day, he heard that there had been a knife thrust between the shoulder blades, he was glad he had taken her advice. Ivan, ex-servant, ex-traitor, ex-spy, was gone, but the emerald he had seen twice in his life, first at a State Ball, gleaming on the breast of an Empress, and next, through a keyhole, lying in the palm of her hand, shone still, like a baleful star, in other minds.

CHAPTER I
THE FIRST MOVE

ELMER Passage was an alley leading down to the river which, since the boat builder's yard at the end had become derelict, was practically a cul-de-sac. As there were no chance passers-by there were no chance customers at the second-hand furniture and book shop that was wedged in there between the high blank walls of warehouses, but old John Borlase, who had inherited the business from his grandfather, had an enviable reputation with that fairly numerous class of small collectors who like to feel sure that they are not being cheated. He did not belong to the ring of furniture and art dealers, and, perhaps owing to that fact, had never been very prosperous, but the shop with the house and the yard at the back were his own property, and since Anne, his only child, had left school and was helping him in the shop he had not to pay the wages of an assistant. He suffered a good deal from sciatica, and sometimes lately she had gone in his stead to sales and auctions all over the country. The big dealers, those swarthy men with guttural voices and fur-lined coats, who smoked expensive cigars and travelled in huge glittering cars, regarded her with good-natured amusement. She was so small and so fearless that they nicknamed her the robin, and she was allowed to pick up the crumbs they let fall, so that often she came home in triumph in her aged and battered Ford with a Victorian firescreen or some scraps of old lace, or a bundle of books acquired for a few shillings.

Anne was alone in the shop one afternoon in October when a woman came in and asked for Russian embroideries. She was a big woman with a deep, hoarse voice. Her face was thickly powdered and her big mouth was smeared with streaks of red. She wore a fox fur wound round her throat, and a black coat, and a black velvet beret pulled well down to her eyes. Anne thought she was the most repulsive-looking person she had ever seen.

"Russian, madam? I'm afraid not. I have a strip of Flemish lace." She unfolded a roll of the cobweb stuff carefully on the counter. "Isn't that lovely?"

The strange customer touched the lace with a black gloved forefinger. Anne noticed that she had enormous hands.

"Yes," she said, but she did not seem really interested. She was darting glances here, and there into the dark recesses of the shop. "You are Miss Borlase?"

"Yes."

"I saw the name of Borlase over the shop front. It is an unusual name, is it not?"

"Perhaps it is."

"You live here all alone with your father?"

"Yes." Anne was beginning to resent this cross-examination.

"And your aunt?" The woman in black seemed to attach importance to Anne's answer, for she leaned towards her across the counter.

Anne shrank a little instinctively.

"Aunt Mary? She died years ago."

"Here?"

"Yes, she'd only just come back to England. Why do you—"

She broke off as the shop door bell rang again and another customer came in. This time it was an old gentleman well known to her. who had picked out some books from the shelves a week before and had now returned to pay for them. The woman put down the lace quickly and with a murmured "Thank you. Good afternoon," left the shop. Anne, relieved by her departure, took the old gentleman's money, receipted his bill, and, after the usual interchange of remarks about the weather, which was cold and wet, saw him off the premises. Big Ben, across the river, was striking six. Anne locked the shop door and drew down the blinds. Then she went into the living-room at the back of the house where her father was making toast for tea.

"Who was that just now, Anne?"

"Mr. Belsize."

"I heard him too. Before that."

"A woman. She asked for Russian embroideries. And then she asked for Aunt Mary. Mind, Father, the toast is burning."

"Dear me!" said John Borlase. "Your aunt had lived so long in Russia that she had no friends left in England. In all these years not a soul has enquired after her. I wish I had seen this lady. Was she Russian, do you think?"

"I don't know. She kept asking questions, and then Mr. Belsize came in, and she left. I wasn't sorry. There was something funny about her. Mr. Belsize has taken that copy of Eothen. Will you be wanting me to go to the library to change your novel?"

"No. I haven't finished the last one yet. But you ought to go out and get a breath of fresh air, my dear. I don't like you being shut up in this musty dark little shop day after day. It's all very well for an old man like me, but not for a pretty young girl."

Anne laughed. "Thanks for the bouquet, but I'm all right. I love my job. Don't worry, darling."

Anne made the tea and they sat down to their evening meal. The living-room was dark for there was only one window facing the yard, and the yard was surrounded by the high walls of warehouses, and it was too full of furniture, but the fire burning in the old-fashioned grate made it seem cosy, and Anne had covered her father's armchair with bright flowered chintz. John Borlase was small and frail and bent, with eyes brown as Anne's, but tired and faded. His daughter looked at him with veiled anxiety as she passed him his cup.

"How are you now, Father?"

"Better, my dear, much better. I shall be well enough to look after the shop tomorrow."

"Then I can go to that sale at Horsham. We'll see."

When they had finished their tea the old man turned to his chair by the fire and lit his pipe. "About that woman," he said, "Was she a foreigner?"

"I thought there was something foreign about her," said Anne. She added in her downright way—"I didn't take to her."

She went out to the scullery to wash the tea things. When she came back she noticed that her father, who usually was an inveterate reader, had laid aside his book and was gazing thoughtfully at the fire. He glanced up as she entered.

"You haven't forgotten your Aunt Mary?"

"I was only ten when she came back from Russia, Father, but I do remember it quite well. She arrived after dark one evening in the autumn of 1918. I can see her sitting where you are sitting now, shaking with cold and clutching a bundle. Her clothes were sticky with sea water. The charwoman had gone home and I had to get the spare room ready for her and heat some milk for her to drink. I remember feeling very excited and important. But it was the end of my holidays and I had to go back to school the next day. And ten days later you wrote to tell me she had died of pneumonia."

John Borlase drew at his pipe. "Aye. The doctor called it that. Myself, I think she died of fright."

Anne's eyes opened very wide. "What was she frightened of?"

"That's what I don't know," he said. "I fancied at the time that she was delirious. She was very ill, poor thing. She'd suffered great hardships. I never knew how she got out of Russia. She had been first nursery governess and then maid companion to a young Russian lady belonging to one of the great land-owning families, who was maid of honour to the Tsarina. Nadine her name was, and Mary said she was a lovely girl. Mary told me the revolutionaries broke into their house on the Nevski Prospect and lined the whole family up against the wall in the ball-room and shot them. Mary, poor soul, seemed to imagine she was in danger even here. She made me promise not to let anyone into the house. She didn't want me to fetch the doctor. The second night she got out of bed and went down to the shop. I found her lying there in her nightgown when I went to look for her. She was unconscious, but when she came to she kept on about taking messages to somebody. It was terribly important, she said, but it was all muddled up and I couldn't make head or tail of it."

"And she died without explaining?" said Anne, who was deeply interested.

"Yes. She kept on trying to the very end, clinging to my hand with her weak fingers, and her lips moving, but she couldn't make a sound. I expect it was just feverish fancies, Anne. Nothing in it. But this woman coming has brought it all back to my mind. A bit of a mystery, but it never will be solved now."

"What had she got in that bundle? I remember she wouldn't let you take it from her."

"Nothing much," he said. "Old clothes, a brush and comb, a pair of shoes. Everything she'd been able to bring away with her. I was so upset about it all that I shoved the things away in a drawer where they've been ever since."

"Might I have a look at them, Father?"

"You can if you like," he said. "The bottom drawer in the chest in the spare room. We don't have visitors, Anne, and no one has slept there since. Bring the stuff down here."

Anne ran upstairs and came down again presently with an untidy bundle of clothing.

"Moth has got into the woollen things, Father. They ought not to have been left there so long. If I had known—"

The old man watched her sorting out ragged vests and black stockings green with age. A moth flew up and Anne caught it. There was an ivory-backed brush with the initials M.B. on it in tarnished silver.

"Mary told me the little countess Nadine gave her that."

He leaned forward. "What is it, Anne?"

There was one dress in the bundle, an old-fashioned black cloth dress with a lined bodice. Anne held it up for him to see. The moths, eating into the material, had made a large hole under one arm.

"Look, Father, there's paper between the stuff and the lining! Wait a minute." She fetched her scissors from her work basket, enlarged the hole, and drew out an envelope. "It's addressed to Colonel Drury at the Dower House, Ladebrook, Sussex." She turned it over and looked at the seal of blue wax. "An N with a little crown over it. Oh, I suppose it's a coronet. Father," the girl's voice shook with excitement, "this must be the message Aunt Mary was so worried about, and it's been lying in the spare room drawer, undelivered, for fourteen years. Oh, I'm not blaming you, darling, you couldn't possibly know. I'll just go thoroughly through every-thing now."

But there was only that one letter.

"I should slit up every seam," advised Borlase.

"All right, Father." She snipped away busily. "But what else could there be?"

"Well—you never know. I wish now that I had listened more carefully to her wandering talk, but I had my hands full with the shop to mind and all. That was the dress she was wearing. I dare-say she was searched more than once on frontiers on her way across Europe. To think they never found that letter."

Anne rolled up the heap of shredded clothing in a newspaper.

"No use keeping this," she said. "I'll burn it in the copper next time it's lit. The moth might get into something else. Father, do you know what I'll do? I'm going into Sussex to that sale to-mor-row. I'll take this letter and deliver it myself on my way home."

"Not a bad idea. Then you can explain the delay."

"A letter from the dead," said Anne slowly. "That N must stand for Nadine. I wonder who this Colonel Drury is."

"You may not find him," said Borlase. "Fourteen years is a long time. He may have left the neighbourhood. Whereabouts is Lade-brook? I never heard of it."

Anne got a map from the bookcase and pored over it.

"Here it is," she said presently. "If I take the Petworth road from Pulborough and branch off here I ought to get to it. I must allow plenty of time. Poor Aunt Mary! She said it was terribly important, didn't she? I wonder if it is still. It's funny how things happen. If that woman had not come into the shop this afternoon we might never have found this letter."

"No," said her father. He was frowning a little. "I rather wish we hadn't. I don't like mysteries."

"Oh, Father!" The girl's face was flushed and eager. "I think it's awfully thrilling. It's quite an adventure."

He smiled faintly at her enthusiasm. "Yes. I suppose I'm old and unenterprising. But I can't help remembering that Mary was afraid."

"But, Father," Anne argued, "that was the war and the revolution. I daresay she went through a lot, poor dear, but that's all over long ago. There's absolutely nothing to worry about now. Anyhow, we're bound to deliver this letter if we can, aren't we, and I don't feel like posting it. We're bound to explain how we came by it and that would mean writing pages. Besides, I'm curious. I want to see this Colonel Drury."

"Very well," he said, "but promise you'll be careful."

She laughed. "Of course. If I meet any dragons I'll run away."

CHAPTER II
THE LETTER

ANNE made an early start, reaching Horsham soon after eleven, and slipped into the marquee in which the sale was being held in time to bid for the three lots she had marked in her catalogue. Two were knocked down to her, but she lost the third which was put up just before the lunch interval. As she passed out with the crowd she found herself next to a famous art dealer whose name was almost as well known to connoisseurs all over the world as that of the Duveens.

"Ah, my little chirping friend," his black eyes twinkled good-naturedly as he looked down at her, "still hopping about our feet, eh? How is your good father?"

"Not too well, Mr. Kafka. And I'm not going to thank you for that inlaid tea caddy that was knocked down to me because I know you didn't want it."

He chuckled. "Impudence. But there is a firescreen. I know you like little things that you can carry away without any trouble. You shall have that too."

"Thank you, Mr. Kafka, but I'm going now."

"So early? That is foolish."

"I can't help it. I'm going somewhere else. We're blocking the way."

Some men behind were laughing. Old Kafka talking to the little Borlase girl reminded them of a liner with a dinghy in tow.

Kafka's huge bulk was increased by his fur-lined coat. His size was portentous, but mind still ruled matter. Nothing escaped him.

"They laughed; let them laugh," he said equably. "Good-bye, little birdkin."

She slipped by him and went to find the auctioneer's clerk and collect her stuff. Her shabby Ford was at the end of the row in which Mr. Kafka's magnificent Rolls was the most conspicuous object. She ate her sandwiches and drank the coffee she had brought with her in a Thermos flask before she started. Once she had left the narrow winding streets of the old town behind her she began to enjoy herself. It was a fine day, with fleecy white clouds drifting slowly northward over the Downs, and the air was warm for October. Anne, who loved the country and was obliged to live in London, felt her spirits rising.

After she left the main road at Pulborough she met very little traffic. She became involved in a maze of lanes winding between high tree-crowned banks and crossed a heath and entered a densely wooded valley.

At last she saw a finger-post.

Ladebrook, three miles.

The woodlands evidently were private property for the road she followed now was bordered on one side by chestnut palings and on the other by a high stone wall. Presently the palings stopped and gave place to a privet hedge. She saw a row of hencoops on a patch of ground that had been cleared of trees and undergrowth, and a number of white fowls following a young man who was wheeling a barrow. She stopped her car and got out at the gate of the field. The young man left his barrow and came towards her. He was in his shirt sleeves and his sunburned throat and arms were bare. He had a pleasant freckled face with steady grey eyes. The fowls still followed him with excited cluckings.

"What can I do for you?"

"Can you tell me the way to the Dower House, Ladebrook?"

He pointed to a long roof of Horsham stone just visible over a bank of flowering shrubs and a high hedge of clipped yew adjoining the field. "That's the Dower House. I live there." He glanced towards her car. "If you're selling vacuum cleaners it's no use. We're very old-fashioned."

"I'm not. Does Colonel Drury live here still?"

"My brother. Yes. What do you want with him?"

"Can I see him?"

"It depends. He's an invalid. Perhaps you can tell me what it's all about."

The young man was smiling. Anne amused him. She was so small and so determined. He still thought that she was probably trying to sell something. Perhaps, if she was not too persistent, she would be good for Stephen. The poor chap was apt to brood.

"I'd like to see him, if possible," said Anne. "I've got a letter for him and I want to explain why it wasn't delivered years ago." She hesitated. "Is his heart weak, or anything? It may be rather upsetting," she added.

Martin Drury's smile had faded. "His heart is all right, but his back was injured when the trench he was in was blown up. He can move from room to room on crutches but he spends most of his days on a spinal couch. I certainly don't want him to be worried unnecessarily."

"I'm sorry," said Anne gently. "I'm so sorry if this is going to hurt him, but I think he ought to have the letter. It comes from Russia."

"Russia? My brother was an attaché at the English Embassy until just before the War broke out. He had friends there, but they all belonged to the class that was wiped out during the revolution." Martin reflected a moment. "All right," he said finally, "I'll take you in to him, but you must just wait while I feed the chickens."

Anne waited at the gate while he scattered the contents of a big bowl of meal in two netted enclosures. The birds, crowding after him, rushed for the food.

"It's like a bus stop at the rush hour," said the girl. "Are they always as hungry as that?"

"Always." He came into the road, closing the gate after him.

"Your car will be safe here if you like to leave it. We don't get much traffic this way. I could have taken you in through the field, but it's rather muddy. By the way, my name's Martin Drury."

"Mine is Anne Borlase."

The entrance gate to the Dower House was only thirty yards farther along the lane, a tall, wrought-iron gate hung between crumbling stone pillars. An aberdeen terrier was poking his shiny black nose through the bars. He grumbled at the sight of Anne but stopped when Martin spoke to him.

"He's not used to strangers. We don't often have visitors. Are you afraid of dogs?"

"Not a bit. I love them."

The girl stooped, holding out her hand. The dog approached cautiously, sniffed her fingers, and signified approval in the usual manner by wagging his stumpy tail before he trotted before them up the curving drive that led, between high walls of clipped yew, to the front door.

"Mac is my brother's dog," said Martin, "and absolutely devoted to him. We've got a housekeeper, a dear old thing, but I attend to the poultry farm and the garden, and that means that Stephen is left alone rather a lot. If he needs me he tells Mac to fetch me and the little chap understands perfectly."

They reached the house, which had been hidden from the road by the yew hedges. Anne looked up at the timbered front, the lattice windows under the deep eaves, and the date on the lintel, 1609.

"What a lovely old place!"

"Not too bad," Martin's under statement did not conceal his immense affection for every stick and stone in the little demesne. "There have always been Drurys at Ladebrook, but my great-great-grandfather was an old rip, in the Prince Regent's set, and ruined himself, and had to sell the Abbey. This was used sometimes for the steward and sometimes as a dower house, and he managed to save it from the wreck. Will you wait in the hall a minute while I speak to my brother?"

He pulled out a chair from the wall but Anne preferred to stand. An oak staircase with shallow treads worn in the middle by over three hundred years of use, rose on her left. She noticed the silvery grey linenfold panelling on the walls. There was a blue lustre bowl of Michaelmas daisies on a gate-leg table. Only the ticking of a clock broke the silence. The house had a peaceful atmosphere. Anne wondered uneasily if her coming would disturb it. Perhaps her father had been right and the letter would do harm. But since she had found it she had had no choice.

Martin came back. "My brother will see you, Miss Borlase. This way."

She followed him into a large room whose walls were lined with books except where an oil painting of a man in a blue satin coat hung over the mantelpiece. There was a french window opening on to the garden at the back, and lying on a wheeled couch near the window was a figure swathed in rugs that turned its head at Anne's timid approach and extended a sinewy and powerful hand.

"How do you do, Miss Borlase, Martin tells me you have brought me a letter. Very good of you. Won't you sit down?"

His voice was very like his brother's, but he was considerably older. Anne was prepared for that. A man who was attaché at an Embassy before 1914 must be at least forty in 1932. Martin, she thought, must be still in his twenties. There was a charming touch of deference in his manner when he spoke.

"Shall I leave Miss Borlase with you, Stephen?"

"No. I don't know what it's all about, but I'd like you to stay."

They both looked at her, waiting for her to begin. The terrier had jumped up on the couch and lain down where his master's long fingers could reach his shaggy little head.

Anne was nervous now, fearing that she was about to inflict a wound. She had been startled by Stephen Drury's extraordinarily good looks. As a young man, she thought, he must have been quite irresistible.

She realised that the silence had lasted long enough and rushed into speech.

"I've got to go back a long way. My aunt was first governess and then a sort of companion to a Russian girl of good family who was maid of honour to the Tsarina. After the revolution my aunt managed to escape from Russia. She came to us. My father is a dealer in antiques. We live over the shop. My aunt was ill when she arrived and she died a few days later. Father put her clothes away in a drawer. Yesterday a woman came into the shop and enquired after her. I don't know who she was and she went without leaving her name. Afterwards I told my father and we got talking of my aunt and presently I fetched her clothes and looked them over, and I found a letter sewn between the lining and the stuff of the dress she had worn. It is addressed to you, Colonel Drury. I was coming down to Horsham anyway to attend a sale so I thought I would bring it to you."

She took the letter from her handbag and gave it to him.

He took it without a word and lay for a while gazing at the delicate sloping writing.

"Nadine," he whispered at last, and his brother looked at him anxiously, for there was agony in his utterance of a name that had not passed his lips for many years. "When—how long have you had this, Miss Borlase?"

"I found it yesterday. My aunt brought it with her from Russia. I don't know when she left but I think she was a long time on the way."

The thin foreign paper crackled as he tore open the envelope.

Anne dared not look at him and his brother had turned away and was standing at the window.

There was a rather long silence before Stephen Drury spoke again.

"There was nothing else?"

"Nothing but a change of linen and a brush and comb."

"She was ill when she arrived, you say, and died a few days later."

"Yes. I don't really remember much. I was only ten and I was going back to school the next day. I know she was frightened. She thought she was being followed. Father had to nurse her. She dreaded seeing strangers. Father thought the hardships she had been through and all the horrors had affected her mind."

"I should like to see your father, Miss Borlase. I am a fixture here unfortunately. I wonder if he would be so kind as to come down one day?"

Anne thought a moment. "I could drive him down next Sunday if that would suit you," she said. "We can't leave the shop together on week days, and he can't drive himself."

"We should be delighted to see you both," he said. "We shall expect you in time for lunch. I remember your aunt. When Martin told me your, name just now I thought it was familiar. She lived with the Sariatinskis. She was Nadine's governess and absolutely devoted to her." She saw his painful hesitation. "I—I have never heard what became of the family—"

Anne had been dreading this moment. Her father had warned her.

"If this Colonel Drury was a friend of Mary's employers it will be a shock—" he had said.

Was she to repeat all the horrid details her father had learned from his sister and repeated to her last night when they had sat up late talking things over? The fusillade of shots, the crash of shattered glass, the screams and the shouts of laughter. No.

"The house was invaded by the mob. Someone pushed my aunt into a cupboard and locked her in. After nightfall one of the servants crept back and let her out. They—the little countess and her parents—were in the ball-room. They'd been shot. They—they were—I mean—nobody could hurt them any more."

Anne was trembling. She felt as if she had killed something. Had he been hoping all these years that the girl he had loved had survived the cataclysm? Martin, standing with his back to the room, looking out at the garden, shifted his feet uneasily.

"Martin," the elder man's self-control was perfect, "I should like to be alone for a while. "Will you look after Miss Borlase? I expect she would like some tea before she goes."

"All right, Stephen."

When they had left him Stephen Drury re-read his letter. Fourteen years since they had murdered her, but as he lingered over the simple phrases so characteristic of that faithful heart it seemed to him that she lived still.

"Father and mother are sorry, now that it is too late, that they did not let me marry you. They did not realise that I meant what I said when I told them I should never look at another man. And, as poor mother said to-day, I should have been safe now in England. But you—where are you, my darling—how is the fighting going on the Western front? We hear nothing now. Those I serve and love are prisoners at the Tsarskoe Selo. I have tried, but I am not allowed to see them. There is just a chance that

Mary, being English, may be able to leave this unhappy country. If I can persuade her to try she will take this letter and the packet entrusted to me—"

He read on to the end before he returned the closely-written sheets to the envelope and slipped it into his pocket-book. Then, for a while, he lay so still that Mac, with bright eyes fixed on his master's face, grew anxious, and, creeping a little closer, began to lick his hand.

CHAPTER III
THE SECOND MOVE

IT WAS after dark when Anne reached home. She backed her aged Ford down the passage into their yard, shut the gate, and let herself in by the side door. The shop was closed at seven, and her father was smoking his pipe by the fire in the back room. They sat down to their frugal supper of bread and cheese and cocoa and she related her adventures.

When she had done the old dealer shook his head. "It's as I feared. I wish we'd burnt the letter with poor Mary's clothes."

"We couldn't have done that, Father."

"Perhaps not. But I've a sort of foreboding." Anne's bright face clouded. "Don't you want to go down next Sunday? I promised we would. The Colonel seemed to think you might be able to tell him more than I could."

Borlase had finished his supper. He went back to his chair by the fireside. "She did say something about a packet. But whether it was posted before she came here, or lost on the journey, or what, I can't tell you. It was just at the last when she was too weak to raise her voice. I told you she got up one night and crept down to the shop. I found her lying unconscious on the floor. I've got a lot of stuff in stock that was in the shop then. The big pieces that are practically unsaleable these days, sideboards and bookcases."

"We ought to go through it all, I suppose," said Anne. "We've never had a real turn out. Mr. Drury, the younger brother, gave me a basket of eggs. He runs a little poultry farm. They are quite poor,

I think, though they've got a lovely old house and furniture. I got what I wanted at Horsham. Mr. Kafka spoke to me. He's rather a lamb, I think. I wonder what his son is like. I've heard he simply idolises him."

"Very likely. Old Kafka started without a penny they say, but his boy has had every advantage. A good public school, and Oxford. I saw him once at a country sale with his father. Rather a striking appearance, and very pleasant manners. Did you think of having this turn out before you go down again to Sussex?"

"I'm not looking forward to it," she said. "Mrs. Bates never dusts behind anything. It will be an awful business. It's your fault, darling. You accumulated tons of rubbish before I left school."

"Did I?" he said placidly. "Don't forget that the rubbish of to-day is the antique of to-morrow. I'm glad Kafka notices you. The Jews are a wonderful people, Anne. They have their faults, but think of the way they've been treated."

"We're not a match for them in the auction room," she said rather ruefully. "If it was not for Mr. Kafka I shouldn't get a chance. He won't let them run up the prices when I'm bidding. He really is a dear."

"A man like that can be a very good friend. I shan't always be here, and I wonder sometimes what will become of you, child. You couldn't run this shop by yourself. It's not a fit place for a woman alone, but we can't very well move. We'd lose our old customers and we might not get new ones. And we live here rent free."

"Don't worry, dear," said his daughter. She was clearing the table, carrying the tray out into the scullery, whisking the cloth off the table. Though she was quick in her movements she never clattered. She did what had to be done, but clearly her thoughts were elsewhere.

"We'll have real fresh eggs for breakfast," she said. "I love the country, and especially Sussex. Bed time," she leaned over the back of his chair and kissed the top of his head. And then— perhaps she was overtired, perhaps the veil that hides the future from our eyes was lifted for an instant—she felt her heart sink.

"Father—"

"Yes, my dear?"

"Nothing. It's been a long day. Good night."

They had their breakfast as usual at eight. A letter addressed to Mr. Borlase, had come by the first post. He read it and passed it over to Anne

She read the letter aloud.

> "The Laurels
>
> "Near Capel, Surrey
>
> "DEAR SIR,
>
> "I have a very curious set of chessmen and a few other odds and ends of lacquer to dispose of. You can have the lot very cheaply if you will take them now. I am going abroad and wish to dispose of them at once. I will meet the 9.27 train from Victoria at Dorking to-morrow, Wednesday.
>
> "Yours faithfully,
>
> "F. BROWN."

"I suppose I had better go," she said. "It's early closing so you'll be able to get on with sorting those stamps into sixpenny packets."

"I'm not very keen," he said. "We don't want to be landed with the proceeds of a burglary."

"Aren't there regular fences?" she asked, smiling. "I shan't take the stuff if I don't fancy it. You feel all right this morning, don't you, Father? You won't mind being left. I'll be home earlier than I was yesterday."

"I'm perfectly all right. Only be careful."

Anne laughed. "I wasn't born yesterday. I shan't have time to clear away the breakfast. It's a good thing it's Mrs. Bates' morning. Remind her to sweep down the stairs. I must run and change my dress."

"Be careful," he repeated when she came down with her hat and coat on. "We know nothing of this man. Beware of faking." He would have liked to say "Don't go!" but he thought another day out of London would be good for her. She was young and needed change of scene. But, just at the last, she betrayed an unaccountable reluctance.

"For two pins I'd stay at home. We can do without his old chessmen. I don't like running off like this two days running. Take care of yourself, Daddy dear."

"I shall do famously," he assured her.

He stood at the shop door and watched her run up the passage and turn into the street at the end, her slight, alert figure dwarfed by the towering walls of the warehouses on either side. Then he went back into the shop and pottered around with a duster before settling down to the job of sorting out a heap of foreign stamps. It did not trouble him much that there were no customers. Business had been slack for some time. Mrs. Bates came in at twelve to get her money. She was a good-natured, garrulous woman with an unsatisfactory husband whom she defended from adverse comment with the pathetic loyalty of her type.

"You're wondering how I got this black eye, Mr. Borlase. Fell over me pail. Silly, aren't I!"

Anne would have noticed the bruise. Anne was very quick to notice. Her father had not, but he was vaguely sympathetic and produced an extra shilling. "Buy some arnica or something."

She left, and he went on with his work. He wondered how Anne was getting on. Strange that they should have found that letter after all these years that poor Mary's things had been lying forgotten in the spare room drawer. It was that woman asking for her that had reminded him. Who was that woman? That was queer, too. Someone Mary had known long ago in Russia, perhaps. Anne had said she was like a man dressed up as a woman, but that, of course, was absurd. It might be as well to tell the Colonel about her. The Colonel had known Mary. Anne seemed to think he had been in love with the little countess, Mary's pupil. Probably they would hear more when they went down to Ladebrook on Sunday. It was a long time since he had had a country jaunt and he was looking forward to it. Anne seemed quite taken with the younger brother. It was kind of him to give her those eggs.

The stamps were all sorted. Borlase looked at his watch. Ten minutes to one. He might as well shut up for the day. But the door bell rang just as he was getting up, and a man came in. The old dealer came forward, shuffling in his carpet slippers, and rubbing his fine sensitive hands together in the nervous fashion that was habitual with him when he had to cope with a stranger.

"What can I do for you, sir?"

The other answered brusquely. "I won't waste your time or my own, Mr. Borlase, but come to the point at once. I'm an Inspector from the Yard. My information is that you have some stolen property, precious stones, hidden on the premises."

John Borlase was profoundly shocked by this accusation. His reply was emphatic. "You are mistaken."

"Come, come. You had far better admit it. You've a good character hitherto and we shan't be hard on you if you own up. Save us trouble and we save you trouble. See?"

There was a veiled threat in the words and something definitely unpleasant in the Inspector's manner. Borlase's indignation was tinged now with fear. He wished his daughter had been there to come to his support. She was young and her nerves were stronger than his.

"I would always help the police if I could," he said with an attempt to speak firmly, "but I haven't any precious stones. Only some old paste that you can see in the window."

The other stared at him with hard eyes. "It is my duty to warn you that you are in danger. We can afford you protection, but only if you are frank with us. We know that your sister brought some jewels belonging to the Russian crown, including the emerald pendant of the Empress Catherine, over to England, and that they have remained in your possession. If you are wise you will hand them over to me now."

John Borlase's lips moved but no sound came from them. At last he was able to utter. "I assure you, Inspector, that I know nothing whatever about this. My sister escaped from Russia with practically nothing but the clothes she stood up in. She was months on the way and suffered great hardships. If any valuables were entrusted to her she lost them, or they were taken from her before she landed in England."

His interlocutor smiled, and his smile was not reassuring. "That's not in accordance with our information. We shall have to search your premises."

The old man was trembling with agitation. "You can't do that without a warrant," he said.

A police inspector had been once to his shop about some contravention of the lighting regulations during the War. He had been very different to this man.

The stranger was looking red and angry now, his hard eyes squinting a little as he leaned across the counter. "That is enough," he said harshly. There was something unfamiliar about the words he uttered. "He doesn't sound English—" thought Borlase.

At that moment the door bell rang and a second man entered. Borlase looked towards him hopefully, but hope died as he realised that they were known to each other.

"You aren't the police. Help! Help!"

He darted round the counter and tried to reach the shop door, but they were too quick for him.

When the constable on the beat came down Elmer Passage an hour later the shop was closed and the blinds drawn down as usual on a Wednesday afternoon. He tried the door and found it locked before he passed on, his footfalls echoing between the high walls.

CHAPTER IV
THE BIRD AND THE FOWLERS

ANNE was met by a young man wearing the dark blue uniform and leather leggings of a chauffeur. He approached her as she waited on the platform at Dorking.

"Is it Miss Borlase, Miss? Mr. Brown thought you might come instead of your father. He's sorry he was not able to meet you himself. The car's outside."

Anne followed him into the yard where a black saloon car was waiting.

"Is it far to go?"

"A goodish way, Miss."

The chauffeur closed the door on her and got into the driving seat. It was quite a coincidence, Anne thought, that she should be passing through Dorking again. For a few miles the road they followed seemed quite familiar to her, but after a while they diverged and she lost her bearings. It certainly was a long way from Dorking. She began to wonder if some other station would not have been more convenient. And was it really necessary to drive so fast? They missed a farm waggon by inches as it turned out of a field and left a frightened boy trying to pacify a plunging horse. Anne heaved a sigh of relief when they stopped at last. The chauffeur got down and unlocked a high gate of wrought iron. They went up a long weed-grown avenue, after passing a lodge whose windows were boarded up. Anne saw a large white house standing on the crest of a long slope of park land. It had a neglected and derelict appearance. They stopped at the foot of a dirty and moss-grown flight of steps leading up to a pillared portico. The chauffeur got down and opened the door for his passenger.

Anne got out with a certain reluctance.

"Is this where Mr. Brown lives?"

"Well, he's here now, Miss. But the place has been shut up for years."

"I see."

The chauffeur was a big young man, heavily-built. He reminded Anne of a bull. He was looking at her rather oddly. She was conscious of a thrill of something like fear. It was all so queer and unexpected. Why did he stare at her like that?

He went up the steps before her, unlocked the front door and stood aside to allow her to pass in. Her heart sank as she crossed the threshold. The air was clammy and cold and smelt of mildew and decay. She found herself in a large circular hall. A little light filtered down from a window on the first landing and revealed the shabby pseudo-classic decoration of columns and niches, only one of which still contained a battered plaster replica of a statue of Niobe clasping two of her doomed children. An uncarpeted flight of stairs on the left led, presumably, to the upper floors. There was a baize-covered door to the servants' quarters, with the baize gnawed by rats and hanging in strips, and other doors, all closed.

The chauffeur knocked on a door on the right. A voice said, "Come in."

"It's Miss Borlase, sir, from the antique shop."

Entering, Anne received another shock. This room, too, was unfurnished, though several packing cases were stacked along the wall and there was some straw scattered over the dirty parquet floor, and its occupant, standing by one of the long french windows opening on the terrace, turned towards her a face that was a terrifying featureless blank. After a second of sheer panic she realised that he was wearing a white linen mask that covered his whole face and head, which, with the long white overall which came down to his knees, gave him a spectral appearance. But his voice, cultured and pleasant, was reassuring.

"Did I frighten you? I'm awfully sorry. My man should have prepared you. I had an accident with some broken glass which had made rather a nasty mess of me. That's why I didn't come myself to meet you. I hope you'll forgive us for being in such an awful muddle. I haven't even a chair to offer you, nothing but a packing case, and I'm afraid I shall have to keep you waiting. The stuff I hoped you'd buy is in a van which hasn't yet arrived. It ought to be here any time now. Shall you mind being left here for a bit? I've got a supply of sandwiches. Here they are on this case. I'm sorry there's nothing to read."

"I've got a book I was reading in the train," she said. "I suppose I'd better wait as I've come so far, Mr. Brown, but I can't stay indefinitely, you know. I shall have to rely on you to get me back to the station."

"We shall do that, of course. I hope you won't be bored stiff, but it can't be helped." He went out quickly, shutting the door after him, before she had time to ask any questions.

She would have preferred to wait outside on the terrace in the sunshine than in that dusty airless room, but he had given her no choice, and when she tried the windows she found that they would not open. She went back to the packing case he had indicated and sat down. The sandwiches proved satisfactory; though they were small and cut very thin there were enough of them to satisfy her healthy appetite. When she had finished she opened her book and began to read. It was an interesting story and she became absorbed in it so that the time passed unnoticed. When, at last, she laid her book down she was startled, on looking at her watch, to find how late it was.

She had accepted Mr. Brown's explanation, but, as she had told him, she could not wait for ever. The house was very still. As she listened, in vain, for any sound that would prove that she was not alone in it her former doubts and fears recurred. Had Mr. Brown written to her father about the stuff he had to sell before he met with his accident? Would he go abroad in spite of it? Why was a man who could afford to buy or rent a mansion standing in several acres of ground so concerned to sell a few chessmen and some bits of lacquer?

Anne wandered restlessly about the room and finally opened the door a few inches and peeped into the dark and deserted hall. The Niobe, embracing her cowering children, glimmered palely on her dusty niche.

"I ought to be going," the girl thought uneasily. If there was nobody about she might walk out of the house and down the avenue and trust to luck to get a lift on her way back to the station. Then, as she hesitated, she heard the sound of a car driven at a reckless speed, followed by a grinding of brakes. She shut the door, but remained near it. Other doors opened and shut, footsteps crossed the hall.

There were people now talking in the adjoining room. Something, evidently, had gone wrong. They were angry, excited. It sounded like two men shouting at once. Then there was a silence followed by whispering in the hall just outside her door. The whispering went on for a long time.

Anne suddenly lost her temper, and when she was angry she forgot she was frightened. She flung the door open. Mr. Brown was in the hall with another man who went quickly back into the next room as she appeared.

"It's getting late," she said. "I really must go home."

He said nothing, but stood staring down at her through the holes in his linen mask. She got the impression that he was making up his mind to something.

"Of course," he said at last. "Too bad to keep you here all this time, and all for nothing. The van hasn't come. There's been a break-down on the road. Would you like a cup of tea before you start? I've got some in a vacuum flask. I meant to give it you with the sandwiches, but I forgot. Just while my man is bringing the car round."

He vanished and reappeared after a short interval with the flask and a cardboard cup. He filled the cup for her. The tea was steaming hot. Anne, who was very thirsty, took it gratefully. He stood by while she drank and refilled the cup. "It will refresh you," he said. He left her, saying that he would see if the car was at the door.

When he came back she was leaning against the wall. "I—I feel funny," she said. Her small face was colourless and the pupils of her eyes had shrunk to pinpoints. "Please—"

But he stood a little way from her, coldly aloof and observant, as she slid to the floor with a little moan and lay there.

The chauffeur came in and joined him. "You—you haven't—"

"Only doped," said the other curtly. "It was necessary. I must have a breathing space to decide on our course of action. The position is serious, thanks to the bungling of those young fools."

They went back to the adjoining room where three other men were waiting, smoking cigarettes and whispering together. They were silent as Brown entered and looked towards him uneasily.

"Now," he said bitingly, "let's have it again. You, Bill—"

He sat on a packing case while the others remained on their feet. It was obvious from their manner that they regarded him with a mixture of admiration and awe. All, that is, except the youngest, who stood with his hands in his pockets and his eyes fixed sullenly on the floor. He was referred to by his companions as the Kid.

The young man called Bill cleared his throat. "It wasn't our fault. We should have got there before the shop closed if we hadn't had engine trouble, but being late didn't worry us much. We were pretty sure the old chap would be somewhere about. The blinds were drawn over the shop window and the shop door. We knocked on the side door and got no answer. Well, there was no one in sight, and it seemed pretty safe. You know I'm pretty good with locks. I've got a little gadget that's as useful as Open Sesame. We got into a narrow passage with a flight of stairs at the end and a door with glass in the upper part on the left that led into the shop. We just looked in. Gosh darn! You never saw anything like it. The place was wrecked. Bookcases, chairs, cabinets shattered to splinters and the floor strewn with torn books and junk. And that wasn't all."

"Go on," said the masked man harshly.

"There was a lot of blood about, wasn't there, Kid?"

"Yes," said the Kid in a dull voice.

"The Kid was upset."

"He would be," said Mr. Brown with icy contempt. "It comes to this. Someone's got in front of us. I wonder if they found the jewels. I doubt it. They wouldn't have smashed everything. But they've made the place too hot for us as well as themselves, and if you two were seen prowling about you may find yourselves in a very unpleasant and conspicuous position. I refer to the dock."

"We didn't do anything," said Bill.

"No. But who's to prove that? Did you wear gloves?"

"Yes. I'm sorry, but I don't see what we've got to worry about apart from the fact that these other chaps, whoever they may be, have got ahead of us. And of course we shouldn't have hurt the old man."

"Apart from that fact, nothing," Brown said cuttingly. "I agree. If it's nothing to fail."

"I'm sorry we ever went in for this," said the young man who had not yet spoken; "we've done very well with the old stunt. This looks like the hell of a mess to me."

"We've got the girl here on our hands," said the chauffeur. "I came a good fifteen miles out of the way bringing her here, but she might find it again. She'll bring the police down upon us as sure as fate. If the place is in the state you say the first thing she'll do when she gets home will be to rush out to fetch a bobby—"

"Naturally," said Brown. "Your mental processes are slow, but you have now reached the point when you begin to realise that we cannot afford to let her go home."

There was a heavy silence. The chauffeur broke it. "I don't like this," he said. "Len's right. The dope smuggling was profitable enough and I got all the kick I wanted out of it. I don't like being mixed up with murders."

The word dropped like a stone in a well. Nobody spoke for a minute. Then the young man he had called Len said. "They may not have killed the old man. You—you didn't see a body."

"No. But the place felt like death. Awful. Besides—I told you—"

"All right," said the masked man, "it can't be helped now. What's done is done, and we must go forward. We need not take any decisive step for a day or so. The girl will be safe here if she is kept drugged. I only gave her a little just now. She'll be coming round. I've got to be going, but I'll ask her a few questions first. One of you had better come in with me."

He beckoned to the young man called Len who followed him obediently. The other three, left alone, resumed their whispered conversation.

"I don't like it."

"Neither do I much, but the Chief knows best. He's never let the Ten down yet."

"The Kid looks white about the gills. Are you going to be sick, Kid?"

"Let me alone, can't you."

Anne was recovering. She was struggling into a sitting posture.

The man she knew as Mr. Brown was just entering the room with his companion. He bent over her and helped her to rise.

"Better now?" he said easily. "That's right. You fainted."

"Did I? How silly of me. I've never done a thing like that before. But this room's rather close. If the stuff you had to sell hasn't come I'm afraid I must ask you to drive me back to the station. I've left my father longer than I meant to as it is."

"The car will be round in a few minutes. Meanwhile, Miss Borlase, I want to ask you one question. *Why did you visit Colonel Drury yesterday?*"

"Colonel Drury?" she said, startled. "Do you know him?"

"I know of him. When your aunt came back to England—in 1917 or 1918, wasn't it?—she brought over some valuable jewellery which had been entrusted to her. He was to keep it until it was claimed by the rightful owners, and I am their representative."

Anne met the eyes that stared at her through the holes in the linen mask and felt herself growing cold.

"I don't know," she faltered. "I don't know anything about jewellery. I took him a letter."

"Yes," he said smoothly. "That intrigues me. Why communicate with him now, after all these years?"

"A—a woman came into the shop and enquired after Aunt Mary. We—we looked over her clothes afterwards and found the letter. But what business is it of yours? Who are you?"

"I represent the surviving members of the Romanoff family. The jewels entrusted to your aunt belonged to the Tsarina, and should come to them. I rely on you to assist me, Miss Borlase."

"Why don't you go to the Colonel and ask him about it?"

"I have. He, like you, denies all knowledge of the jewels. It is a difficult position, an impasse. But if you have any ideas on the subject, any inkling of where they may be I strongly advise you to tell me now if you want to save your father worry and anxiety."

"Father? He doesn't know anything either. I tell you we only found the letter, sewn up in the lining of Aunt Mary's dress, the day before yesterday. I took it to the Colonel the next day. I don't know what was in it." She stared at him. "Then the chess men—your letter—it was just to bring me here, to find out what you could. That woman who came into the shop. She looked like a man dressed up. Was it one of you?"

"No. It wasn't," said Brown. "I'd very much like to know who it was. A sudden burst of interest in you and your affairs, eh, Miss Borlase? A curious coincidence."

"She was foreign," said Anne slowly. "But you're English."

She was trying to think but it was difficult while he stood so close to her, blocking her way to the door, trying to wear her down.

Instinctively she felt that he enjoyed her terror and confusion. She remembered the avenue, fully half a mile long, that led from the road to the house. No one would hear her if she called for help. She was entirely at his mercy.

"I am waiting," he said.

"It's no use bullying me," she answered with a sudden flash of spirit,

He laughed. "Isn't it, by Gad?" He gripped her left arm and gave it a sharp twist. She screamed and he released her at once.

His companion moved uneasily. "I say—must you do that?" he muttered.

Brown turned on him savagely. "Leave this to me, please. I can deal with her. I don't think much of your pose of ignorance, Miss Borlase. These jewels are immensely valuable. You and your father may have planned to hold on to them, but I warn you that you won't get away with it. You'll find yourself in a very serious position. Very serious."

"I don't know anything," she repeated.

"Very well. Time's passing. This way." He stood aside to allow her to pass. She started forward and he caught her.

"Hold her wrists, Len. Don't be squeamish, you fool. Our lives depend on it. I've got the hypodermic. Push up her sleeve. Good." She struggled frantically but he held her fast and after a minute her resistance was at an end. Breathing heavily he flung her down on the heap of mouldy straw between two packing cases. "She'll do now for some time. This business needs careful handling. That emerald must be somewhere. Its history goes back two thousand years. I'm inclined to think Drury has it. We shall see. It's quite an amusing little problem. With a spice of danger, Len. Blood has been shed. Not by any of us—but it would be hard to prove our innocence, and I don't think we had better try. I can't say I'm sorry. The dope smuggling was getting dull."

"You make the plans," said Len, "but I can't help wishing you hadn't brought her here. It's—it's pretty serious really." His voice shook as he gave utterance to his fears. "Was it necessary?"

"I think so," said Brown coolly. "In any case, here she is, and we must make the best of it. *De l'audace, et toujours de l'audace.* There's just one point—" he picked up Anne's handbag and opened it. "Splendid. Here's the letter that brought her here. Keep the shutters in this room closed and the door locked and it won't matter if she does come to before she gets her next dose. She can make as much noise as she likes. No one will hear her. You left the car in the yard? Good. You had better all turn up here to-morrow for further instructions."

"All right, Chief. But, I say—" Len had to swallow once or twice before he could go on. There was something so daunting in the aspect of that featureless white mask turned towards him.

"Couldn't Tommy drive her away late to-night and dump her on a common or somewhere fifty miles away?"

"He could, as far as I am concerned," said Brown, "she has not seen me. But she has seen him, and, just now, my dear boy, she saw you. I am afraid that where she is concerned your number would be up. It would not take the police long to find this house from the description she could give them. They would then proceed to comb the neighbourhood. I leave you to imagine the result of an identification parade. Think it over, and try to acquire a little more backbone. Good night."

CHAPTER V
THE BROTHERS

"THEY are late," said Stephen Drury.

His brother looked at his wrist watch for about the tenth time. He had wondered when Stephen would notice their guests' unpunctuality. "We must make allowances for their very antiquated bus. About the oldest car I've seen on the road. I hope the lunch won't be burnt to a cinder. I'd better go and soothe Mrs. Clapp."

He strolled out to the kitchen where he found the housekeeper hot and bothered.

"You told them one sharp, Mr. Martin, and it's twenty past, and you mustn't blame me if the lunch is spoiled. Such a nice young lady, too, and seemed considerate."

"I'll just go down to the gate," said Martin. He walked a little way up the lane and smoked a couple of cigarettes. He looked at his watch again. If they had been on the telephone the girl might have rung up from an A.A. box if they had had a breakdown. He went slowly back to the house. He found that Stephen had moved from the library into the dining-room in the wheeled chair he used to get about the ground floor and into the garden on the days when he felt well enough to exert himself.

"No sign of them?"

"No."

"It's past two. We'd better have our lunch, Martin. No use waiting."

Martin rang the bell. It was an unusually silent meal. Stephen seemed worried, but he made no further reference to the Borlases until they had finished and were sitting out on the terrace by the open window of the library. The house and garden, buried in the woods, lay very still, very peaceful in the golden light of the autumn afternoon.

"She'd have let us know if they weren't coming," said Martin abruptly.

"We may get a letter to-morrow morning," Stephen agreed.

He glanced at his young brother's candid face and seemed to make an effort to speak, "I daresay you've been wondering what it's all about?"

"I have rather," Martin confessed. "Of course, up to a point, I understand. The letter she brought you was from a—a great friend."

"Yes. That's her picture in the silver frame on my bureau. There's another on the table by my bed. We were in love with each other when I was attaché at the Embassy, but she was very young—Juliet's age—fifteen. Her father had a high place at the Court, and she was a friend of the Tsar's daughters. Her family meant her to make a brilliant marriage. Wires were pulled and I was sent back to England. That was in the June of 1914. I never saw her again, or heard of her until last Tuesday. She died—that girl told us how. She and her mother and father shot down in the ball-room of their great house on the Nevski Prospect. I remember that room. Wonderful crystal chandeliers and walls panelled with green brocade. I remember dancing with her the last time. She was a marvellous dancer. Light as a snowflake. We made desperate plans to run away together. But she was too well guarded. We could never have got across the frontier. Madness. But, if we had succeeded, she might be alive to-day."

"Hard luck," murmured Martin.

"Her letter—I'll read you the part that refers to the Borlases."

Very carefully he took the folded sheet of thin foreign paper from his pocket-book.

"You remember my dear old English governess, who used to take me to and fro to my music lessons? She is still with us and wants to stay, but there is a chance that she may succeed in getting across the frontier through a friend of hers whose husband has some influence with the new revolutionary government. The last time I was allowed to visit the grand duchesses at the Tsarskoe Selo their mother talked to me about England. She will never leave Russia herself, but she hopes the girls may be allowed to go there later on. She seems to think that she may be able to strike some kind of bargain with the authorities regarding them if things get any worse. Meanwhile, that they might not arrive penniless, she had planned to send some jewels over. She said, 'Nadine, I thought of that young man who was at the British Embassy, Mr. Drury. I am sure he is trustworthy, and if you can think of a plan to get them to him I will give them to you.' Like most Royalties she is very vague and impractical, and I could see she didn't realise the difficulties, but she was crying, and I hadn't the heart to discourage her. They are watched and spied upon and I think several of the servants whom she imagined to be faithful are really in the pay of the Bolsheviki. Nearly all their more valuable possessions have been taken from them, but she had hidden these hoarded stones very cleverly in a pot of cold cream. When she raked them out with a little pair of nail scissors I gasped, recognising the huge square-cut emerald that I had seen her wear as a pendant at my first and only State Ball, just before the war. I enclose a list of all the stones, but the emerald is the loveliest and the most valuable. She smiled that faint sad smile of hers when she saw me looking at it. 'That belonged to the Empress Catherine,' she said. 'It is worth—I forget—a great many roubles. It would be fifty thousand pounds. Something like that. There are not many others so large as that and without a flaw. There is a legend that it is the emerald that Nero used to look through.' She held it up to the light and then dropped it quickly in her lap as a servant came in with the samovar. So I accepted that great responsibility, and Mary is going to try to reach England carrying them and this letter. You will know what to do with them. I suppose they would be safest in a Bank. And if, later on, the grand duchesses arrive, you can sell some of the stones and give them the money."

"Good Lord!" said Martin. "And Mary, as she calls her, actually got here, and then died before she could fulfil her mission. And this packet of precious stones may have been kicking about in the shop ever since. I know what these antique dealers are. There's always heaps of junk. It's past three, Stephen. I don't think they can be coming to-day."

The older man was lying back in his chair. He looked more worn than usual, exhausted by the effort he had made.

"I don't like it," he said anxiously.

"But no one is likely to bother after fourteen years," argued Martin.

"You forget what she told us about the woman who came into the place to ask for Russian embroideries, and asked her about her aunt. That incident led to her discovering the letter sewn in the lining of her aunt's dress. It suggests that someone is taking an interest."

"Who could it be?"

"Who knows? Possibly one of the spying servants at the Tsarskoe Selo might have been thrown into prison. On his release years later he might succeed in following up clues that would lead him over here. Borlase, unfortunately, is rather an uncommon name. Or—there are a hundred possibilities."

"I hope you're wrong," said Martin uneasily, "I hate to think of that little girl getting into any sort of mess. She seemed such a decent kid. Well"—he stood up—"I must go and see how my birds are getting on. Did I tell you I got a standing order for eggs from the people who've taken the Abbey? They're running the place as a guest house or something. It's advertised in all the papers. Garage room for a hundred cars, and a good dancing floor."

Stephen was not listening. "Martin, if we don't hear from this girl or her father to-morrow I'd like you to run up to Town and see them. You'd better tell them what I've just told you. It isn't fair to leave them in the dark. The old man may know more of the matter than she does."

"All right," said the young man, but he looked worried. He ran his little chicken farm single-handed. It was the only way to be sure of even a small margin of profit, but it tied him; and though he was careful not to let Stephen know it, he did not care to leave him for more than a couple of hours at a time. Stephen's attempts to do things for himself rather than call on Mrs. Clapp to help him were apt to lead to minor disasters. He consoled himself with the reflection that the morning post was almost sure to bring a letter from the girl explaining their non-arrival.

But the next morning when he carried in the invalid's breakfast on a tray he had to confess that the postman had brought nothing but a bill from the corn dealer.

"Then you must go, Martin." Stephen reached for a time-table lying open on his table. "I've been looking up the trains. You can get one from Pulborough about an hour from now. You can do it on your motor cycle?"

"All right. I must change though. Can't walk about London in a khaki shirt and shorts." He ran from his brother's room, shouting for Mrs. Clapp.

He caught the train with two minutes to spare and reached Victoria soon after noon. During the journey he had been haunted by the strange expression on his brother's face. It was so unlike Stephen to be afraid. And yet—perhaps not. He had never feared for himself, but he might for others.

"Elmer Passage."

The taxi driver looked doubtful. "I dunno know as I—would it be that sort of a blind alley down across river beyond Vauxhall bridge? Leads to a boat builder's yard, but there's nothing doing there nowadays."

"The place I want is an antique shop."

"Ar. There is one down there. But I've never had to take a fare there before. Get in, sir."

The driver stopped at the entrance to the passage. "P'raps you wouldn't mind getting out here, sir? 'Tisn't above a hundred yards to the end. It's narrow, you see, and there's no place to turn."

"That's all right." Martin paid him and walked down the alley between the high blank walls of warehouses. It was a dull day with a cold wind blowing up from the river. He saw the funnel of a tug passing up stream over the top of the high gate of the derelict boat builder's yard at the far end of the passage. The bleak little cul de sac seemed utterly lifeless and deserted. He reflected that the Borlases could not rely on chance customers. The shop was half way down on the right. The faded yellow blinds were drawn over the windows and the glazed upper half of the door. He tried the door and found it locked. He rattled the handle and waited without result. Then he tried the side door. He could hear the bell ringing inside but no other sound. Martin wondered. The place looked shabby and unprosperous. It certainly seemed as if father and daughter had flitted. But the girl—he could have sworn she was honest. She might have been compelled—but she had not looked like that either. He went back to the shop door and tried to peer in between the edge of the blind and the frame. As his eyes grew accustomed to the darkness within he saw something so startling that he cried out.

"Good God!"

He ran up the alley. In the dingy main street there were lorries and vans waiting outside the entrances of warehouses. A couple of swarthy, foreign-looking men were lounging outside the public-house at the corner. Martin did not notice them. He was calling a large policeman who was walking away along the opposite pavement. The policeman's back was turned and he did not hear Martin's shout. There was no one else in the street. Martin, hurrying in pursuit of the representative of the law, darted out from behind a stationary lorry. There was a grinding crash. He felt himself falling for miles and miles. And then—nothing.

Chapter VI
ASK A POLICEMAN

INSPECTOR Hugh Collier, of the C.I.D., was just going out to lunch. He paused at the door to turn up the collar of his rain coat and thrust his hands into the pockets. The few remaining leaves of the planes along the Embankment were dripping with moisture. Boadicea and her chariot loomed out of the mist. The melancholy crying of the gulls circling over the river mingled with the hooting of motor-horns. Collier, looking up at the clouds, cannoned against a young man coming in the opposite direction.

"Sorry!"

"It's all right. Is this Scotland Yard?"

"Yes. What do you want?"

"I want to see a man called Collier. My brother used to know him."

"You see him now. I'm Inspector Collier."

"That's a bit of luck. I'm Martin Drury."

Collier's professional impassivity relaxed. His lean brown face was attractive when he smiled. He held out his hand. "I remember Colonel Drury. The bravest man I ever met. One of the best. How is he?"

"About the same. You knew his spine was injured!"

Collier nodded. "Hard lines. And you're the kid brother? He used to talk about you. A little chap at a prep school. I was in his battalion for a few months. Were you coming to see me as a policeman? Is there anything I can do?"

"Yes. It's rather a long story."

"Then you'd better come with me if you don't mind. I was just going to get a spot of lunch at the Lyons round the corner." Martin accepted with reservations. "I won't have anything but a cup of tea myself. I got a knock on the head yesterday and it's aching still. I woke up this morning in the accident ward of St. Martha's. They discharged me with instructions to go straight home and keep quiet for a day or two. After effects of concussion, you know, and all that, but though my head's a bit muzzy still I remembered enough to know that I ought to see you first."

Collier led the way to a table in the corner and near the window and gave his order to the waitress.

"Now," he said, "shoot. Who knocked you on the head and why?" Looking at his companion more closely he realised that his pallor was not normal and noticed the blue mark of a bruise on his left temple.

"Oh, that was an accident. The driver backed his van just as I was going round behind it. Nobody actually saw it happen and he drove away. Then a woman looked out of a window of the pub at the corner and called the policeman who was passing. Anyhow that's what I've been told. The point is that I was running after that bobby at the time. There's a dealer in antique furniture and stuff living down Elmer Passage. His daughter motored down to Sussex to see us one day last week. Her aunt had been governess in a Russian family years ago, people who were friends of my brother's. He hadn't known what became of them during the revolution and she was able to tell him. He wanted further details so he asked her to bring her father down to lunch last Sunday. She said she would but they never turned up. Stephen was worried. I ought to explain that the aunt escaped from Russia and brought with her a letter for Stephen sewn into the lining of her dress. She died without telling anyone about it, and the letter was only found last week. According to the letter she had been entrusted with some jewellery—"

"Valuable?"

"Very. Stephen's friend was a maid of honour to the Empress. There's a priceless emerald, an historic stone that is said to have belonged to Nero. That's legend, but it really did get set as a pendant for Catherine the Great."

Collier glanced over his shoulder to make sure there was no one near enough to overhear their conversation.

"Where is it now?"

"Heaven knows!" said Martin.

"More likely to get news of it in Hell," said Collier grimly. "These famous stones leave a bloodstained trail."

"It's queer you should say that," said Martin. "That's why I came to you after sending my brother a wire to tell him I'm still alive. He must have been in a state, poor chap, not hearing from me before. I came up to Town yesterday. I found the antique shop in Elmer Passage shut. The blinds drawn and no one about. There was a gap of about half an inch between the side of one blind and the door frame. At first I couldn't see anything, and then I saw the legs of an overturned chair and a bit of the floor with a huge reddish-brown stain on it. I'll swear it was dried blood. It was—a bit of a shock. That girl. She told us she and her old father lived quite alone. She drives about to country sales in her ancient fliv-ver, picking up junk. A little thing. You could pick her up and break her. Her body, but not her spirit. If anything's happened to her—God! It makes me sick to think of it."

"And that's why you were running after a policeman?"

"Yes."

Collier stared at him for a moment in silence. Then he signalled to the waitress for his bill. "We'll go there now," he said, "in a taxi."

They did not talk on the way. Martin leaned back and shut his eyes, glad of a chance to rest. His head was still aching rather badly.

The taxi driver stopped at the entrance to the Passage.

"Can't turn down there. Am I to wait?"

Collier answered "Yes." The nearest cab rank was some distance off and he wanted to spare his companion as much as possible.

The detective glanced up at the towering walls of the ware-houses on either side. "Is there no way out at the other end?"

The taxi driver shook his head. "There's a boat builder's yard. Nothing doing there now. Nothing doing anywhere, worse luck."

"It's half way down," said Martin as they moved away. "I say, what will you do? Are you allowed to go in without a search warrant?"

"The shop is open," said Collier.

He was right. The blinds were up and the windows displayed the usual stock of antique dealers, a small worm-eaten Pembroke table, a couple of Victorian firescreens, a set of Spode dessert dishes, some bits of old lace and embroidery and some odds and ends of brass and copper work. He looked at Martin and grinned.

"All's well that ends well."

"You must think me every kind of ass," said Martin. "Could I have dreamed it? It's awfully queer."

"Perhaps Miss Borlase and her father will be able to explain the mystery," said Collier. "I'll come in with you if you don't mind."

"Please do."

The shop bell tinkled as they entered. A very spruce young man came forward. He wore a pearl pin in his black satin tie, and he had a very sleek head and eyes a shade too close together.

"What can I do for you, gentlemen?"

Martin, recovering from this second surprise, asked for Mr. Borlase. The young man looked blank.

"Mr.—oh, that would be the former proprietor. This business has changed hands, sir, and is under entirely new management. Did you wish to make a purchase?"

"Rather sudden, wasn't it?" said Collier.

"I can't say, I'm sure. I know nothing about that. I am merely an employee. Did you wish to price one of the articles in the window?"

"No. We want to see Mr. Borlase. Who are your principals?"

"I'm afraid I can't help you much," said the young man smoothly. "I'm here simply to deal with customers."

Slippery, thought Collier, and can't look you in the face, but he is within his rights in not answering.

"How long have you been here?"

"Since nine o'clock this morning."

"I see. The shop was closed yesterday?"

"I believe so. I can't be sure. At any rate I wasn't here."

After an instant's pause during which the slight cast in his eye became more noticeable he added, "I was given to understand that the former proprietor has gone abroad. And now, sir—I'm rather busy."

"We must not keep you," said Collier. He was looking about him, a deliberate measuring gaze. "Perhaps if I call again in a day or two you will be able to give me Mr. Borlase's present address. It's rather important. Good morning."

When they were outside and walking back to the waiting taxi he said nothing. It was Martin who broke the silence.

"Do you think they—the Borlases—have done a bunk with the jewels? It looks like it, I suppose. All the same, I don't believe it. That little girl was straight."

"When you peeped through that chink in the blind," said Collier abruptly, "what did you think you saw? Tell me again exactly."

"The legs of an overturned chair, and a big reddish brown stain on the floor."

"On the boards?"

Martin was frowning with the effort to visualise what he had seen. "No. No. It was linoleum."

"Can you recall the pattern?"

"Yes. It was black and white, an imitation of tiles. Shabby and worn, but fairly distinct. By Jove! There was no linoleum on the floor this morning, was there? Bare boards."

Collier nodded. "Clean bare boards. They had been scrubbed recently. We're a day late, Drury."

"Then you think—"

"I haven't had time to think yet," said the man from Scotland Yard dryly, "but I'm going to. And you're going back to Sussex by the next train. Take a couple of days in bed. You look as if you needed them. I'll go with you to Victoria now and see you off."

"Decent of you," said Martin rather faintly. "I must admit that I feel rotten."

He hardly spoke again until the train was on the point of starting. Then he leaned from the window.

"If you find out anything you won't leave us in the dark?" he said anxiously. "Stephen will be worrying and so shall I. He feels responsible. The stones were being sent to him for safe keeping. Damn the stones. But there's the girl—"

Collier nodded. "Rely on me for that." A porter shouted to him to stand back and the rest of the sentence went unheard by Martin. "Take care of yourself!"

Collier wondered if the young man would have realised that that might be more than a mere figure of speech. It was just after three and he had another hour at his disposal. He spent it sitting on a seat in the Embankment Gardens. When he returned to the Yard he made his way to the room of Chief-Inspector Cardew.

"Can you spare me ten minutes, sir?"

"No. All right. Fire away." The room was thick with tobacco smoke. The man seated at the desk flapped his hands helplessly. "This fug! I smoke too much, Inspector. But if I don't I get irritable, and you wouldn't like that."

Collier grinned. "No, sir."

"Well?" Cardew fired off the monosyllable like a pistol. "What is it?"

Collier told his story, beginning from his chance meeting with Martin Drury.

His superior listened with increasing gravity, making a note now and again on his blotting pad.

"Yes," he said, when the other had finished, "you're right, Collier. We'll have to look into this. Of course there may be nothing in it. There may be some perfectly good explanation of what this young man thinks he saw. Furniture shops use furniture stains. I can imagine a spilt bucket of mahogany or rosewood stain looking very nasty indeed. He jumped at the conclusion that a crime had been committed. I think it is far more likely that this dealer, Borlase, has disposed of his business in a violent hurry and gone off with these stones."

"Young Drury seems sure the girl wouldn't do anything crooked."

The Chief grunted. "They found the letter sewn in the lining of her aunt's dress and she went down to Sussex the next day to deliver it. Suppose that during her absence her father made a further intensive search and discovered the packet of jewels where his sister concealed them fourteen years ago? Business is slack. On the verge of bankruptcy. Most little shop-keepers are these days. Wouldn't he be dazzled? Wouldn't he be tempted? And—mark this—if that's what happened we can't butt in. Who's to prove the stones aren't his?"

"Yes," said Collier slowly. "I didn't care for the young chap who's in charge there now. He didn't meet my eye once, and he didn't give a direct answer to any question I asked. Still, as you say, sir, there's very little to go upon, but—may I have a shot at it, sir?"

Cardew smiled. He liked to see his subordinates keen.

"I certainly think a few enquiries made in the neighbourhood . . ."

"That was my idea," said Collier eagerly. He had sketched out a plan of campaign as he sat in the Embankment Gardens.

"There's a public-house just round the corner, the Five Bells."

The Chief-Inspector grinned. "Sample their beer, eh? Quite a good notion. Report to me in the morning."

"Very well, sir."

Chief-Inspector Cardew finished initialling a batch of reports and took them down to the Commissioner's room. Sir James was about to leave, but he was in no hurry.

"Anything fresh?"

"Well—" Cardew gave him a brief précis of Collier's story.

"It may be a mare's nest," he concluded, "but Collier's a good man. He's done very well since he left the uniformed branch. He's got imagination."

"A dangerous gift," commented the other. "Still, in this case it may help. But for God's sake don't let him make a gaffe, Cardew."

The Commissioner was going to dine at his club. The rain had ceased and he walked up Whitehall, past the Cenotaph, glimmering palely in the gathering dusk, into Pall Mall.

His favourite table in the window of the club dining-room was laid for three, and another member had just seated himself. He was accompanied by a younger man. He glanced round and smiled as the Commissioner came up and the latter recognised Israel Kafka, the famous dealer and collector.

"Sir James Mercer. How are you, Sir James? Busy keeping an eye on those naughty night clubs? No chocolates after eight."

The chuckle that shook his huge body was so genial and devoid of malice that it was impossible to take offence.

"Wait till you're burgled. You'll be glad of us then," said Sir James lightly.

"No fear of that. My house is too well guarded, and the thieves know it. They would risk more than their liberty."

Sir James looked at him curiously. He had heard rumours of the elaborate arrangements made for the reception of uninvited guests at Kafka's house.

"By the way, this is my boy, my son, young Maurice." Kafka, like most men of his race, was a devoted father, and his pride in the young man was unconcealed. "A fine boy, is he not?"

Young Kafka, who was slim, dark, and good looking, smiled at Sir James. "Very embarrassing for both of us," he remarked. Winchester and Oxford, thought the Commissioner, and a grandfather who dealt in rags and bones in a foreign ghetto.

"Left college a year ago," old Kafka was saying in his thick, soft, slurring voice, "and has been adopted as a candidate by the Jessop's Bridge division to stand at the next election. He's Lord Bember's secretary, and engaged to his daughter, Lady Jocelyn. It's just been announced. You'll see it in the social columns of all the principal papers to-morrow."

"I congratulate you," said Sir James civilly.

He wondered how the young man liked being trotted out. He bore it with apparent calm, making no attempt to check his parent's confidences and eating his dinner as if he enjoyed it. It occurred to the Commissioner that he might pick up a bit of information they would be glad of at the Yard.

"Do you know anything of a small dealer called Borlase, Mr. Kafka?"

Kafka, who had been studying the wine list, gave his order to the waiter before he answered. "Borlase? To be sure I do. A stubborn fellow, outside the ring. No doing anything with him, and, of course, he never got on. He is the father of the robin."

"I beg your pardon?" said Sir James, not sure that he had heard aright.

Kafka chuckled again good-naturedly. "His daughter. As big as my thumb, and hops here and hops there like a little brown bird. We call her the robin and we let her pick up a few crumbs. I see her often at country sales. Only last week I saw her and had a little chat with her. We are very good friends. She is not afraid of old Kafka. She chirps very prettily and perches on his finger. So."

"Would you say the father and daughter were honest?"

"Honest? Oh, perfectly. Why? I do not like this. What has the police to do with my little Anne?"

There was an instant's pause. Maurice Kafka was peeling a peach and seemed to be taking very little interest in the conversation. The Commissioner, with a vague feeling that it might have been better not to introduce this subject, rose from the table. He was going to the theatre and had already missed the first act.

"Nothing, I hope," he said. "Good night."

CHAPTER VII
JOCELYN BUTTS IN

STEPHEN Drury lay flat on his back on his couch by the library window. He had a book but was not reading. Mac, who had been chasing a young thrush across the lawn, had returned with his tail between his legs to be lectured on the enormity of his proceedings. Stephen was very tired. Martin's telegram, which had been delivered by the village postmistress' small niece earlier in the day, had been an enormous relief but the effects of a sleepless night remained. Martin's message was reassuring but it conveyed no information. He had had no intention of remaining the night in Town when he went up. Stephen sighed. This affair of the Tsarina's jewels sent to England through Nadine was his pigeon, his still, in spite of that gap of fourteen years. That poor little crumpled letter lying next his heart was his warrant. It was agony to lie there helpless and useless, leaving this task she had set him to others. He lifted his hands and stared at them moodily. They were strong as ever, but what was the good of that while he could only get about on crutches?

He turned his head, hearing voices in the hall, and Mac growled softly. Mrs. Clapp put her head in at the door.

"It's Lady Jocelyn, sir. She wants a pair of roasting fowls and a dozen eggs. Will I see about it as Mr. Martin isn't back?"

"Yes, I suppose you had better."

Mrs. Clapp hesitated. "Is she to wait in the dining-room?"

The reply came from the hall. "I'm darned if she is. I'm coming in to talk to the Colonel." The old housekeeper was thrust aside and a tall, slim girl in corduroy riding breeches and a raspberry red jumper came smilingly into the room.

"I've wanted to do this heaps of times," she said as she dropped into the easiest of the easy chairs, "but Martin is always so hush hush about you. I say, keep your hound in leash, won't you?"

The Aberdeen was still grumbling. Stephen laid his hand on the shaggy head. "Quiet, Mac. He's not used to visitors."

He concealed his own irritation. What was this pushing young woman staring at? He must be civil for Martin's sake.

"I hope you told Mrs. Clapp exactly what you wanted," he said. "She is in charge of the farm while my brother is away."

"Fancy Martin being away," she said conversationally; "I thought he was chained to the mat. I only came down to-day. I got sick of being called to the telephone by idiots who wanted to congratulate me or be my bridesmaid or something. I've just got engaged. A ghastly bore, but I'm twenty-three, getting on, and it will be nice to have pots of money for a change. Oh, I know father's supposed to have made a lot at the Bar, but he's fearfully extravagant, and since he married again there's less than ever for Bertie and me."

"You are marrying a rich man?" said Stephen. He was wondering what effect this would have on Martin. If his brother was not in love with this girl it was not for lack of encouragement on her part. "Little devil," he thought as he watched the vivid face.

"He will be," she said. "His father's old Kafka, who presented that newly-discovered Rembrandt to the nation last year. He's simply rolling, but he expects his son to earn his living, so Maurice has to exist somehow on the salary he gets from father."

"He is Lord Bember's secretary?"

"Yes. It's a soft job really now that the other side are in. Father isn't bothering. He's hardly been to the House this session. He and Beryl—that's my stepmother—are always flying over to le Touquet and places. I used to go with him, but he doesn't want me now. I say, what a jolly room this is."

"I'm glad you like it."

"We haven't got anything old," she explained. "I suppose all these books and the picture over the mantelpiece are family stuff?"

Stephen smiled. "Yes."

"You've been here for hundreds of years."

"Well—it feels like that sometimes."

"I mean your forefathers. They were at the Abbey, and they used to shove the superfluous grandmothers and aunts in here."

His smile broadened. She was really very refreshing. "The Dower House. You have defined its uses exactly."

"You know the people who have just bought the Abbey are making it into an hotel, a week-end place for motorists?"

"So I have heard," he said. "Martin has been round and induced them to have eggs and poultry from us."

She was lounging round the room now, with her hands in her breeches pockets and her dark curly head tilted back to look at the carved ceiling and the oak panelling of the walls over the book shelves. "Are there any priest's holes or secret cupboards?" she asked casually.

"I never heard of any."

"How dull. Only this rather modern safe built into the recess. Is there anything very romantic and thrilling in it?"

"I'm afraid not. Sorry to be so disappointing, Lady Jocelyn."

"Never mind," she said. She seemed abruptly to have lost interest. She was frankly bored. "What an age your housekeeper is."

"I think I hear her now," he said.

She nodded. "Then I'll be going. When will Martin be home?"

"I expect him this evening."

"Then you can tell him I shall probably blow in to-morrow. Good-bye, Colonel Drury."

"I suppose I might have asked her to stay to tea," he said to Mrs. Clapp when she came in a little later. "I hope she didn't think me very boorish. I am so unused to—"

The old woman's sniff was eloquent. "If she'd wanted to stay she'd have asked herself."

"Ah. I daresay you're right."

"Bold as brass," said Mrs. Clapp, "and that young brother of hers down at the Vicarage with the other young gentlemen that's backward at their books is as bad. A set of artful young monkeys as they are getting out of the Vicarage windows at nights. You wouldn't believe the carryings on. And the Vicar, poor dear gentleman, buried in his books."

"Dear me," Stephen waited patiently while his housekeeper poured out his tea and buttered his toast. "By the way, did Lady Jocelyn pay you for the fowls and the eggs?"

Mrs. Clapp cackled. "Not she. I said, 'that'll be ten and six, my lady, if you please.' And she says, 'Put it down.' You don't get ready money, not from Crossways. I heard the other day down the village that they owe Mr. Mills at the general shop over fifty pounds and he's talking of going to law about it."

"Is there a staff of servants?"

"Only when Lord Bember and her ladyship come down and bring a couple of maids from their London house with them. Other times it's shut up. When Lady Jocelyn or her brother are there Mrs. Green goes in to oblige. Takes her all her time, she says, sweeping up cigarette ends and carrying empty bottles along to the rubbish dump over by the old chalk quarry. That sounds like one of they motor cars, Mr. Stephen."

She hurried out. Stephen, listening, heard his brother's voice. He had raised himself painfully on his elbow. He sank back, satisfied. Martin came in a moment later.

"Here I am," he began with a factitious heartiness that did not deceive the older man for a moment.

"What have you been doing? You look ill."

"That was a bit of bad luck and a fool of a lorry driver." He poured himself a cup of tea and drank it. "I had to hire a car at Pulborough to bring me home. Couldn't trust myself on my motor cycle. My head's still very dicky. I'll tell you what happened—"

Stephen heard him out without interrupting. When he had done he said. "You were right to go to the Yard. I'm glad you thought of Collier. He's a good chap. But—if anything has happened to those two, Martin, I shall never forgive myself."

"It won't be your fault."

"I should have warned her. I didn't tell her anything. I—I'd had a shock and I wanted to be alone, but that's no excuse. I've been regretting it ever since."

There was a silence. Martin leaned his aching head on his hands.

"I'm sure it was blood I saw on the floor of the shop," he muttered. "Oh, my God! What are we up against, Stephen? Who could hurt a little thing like that? Are there such beasts in the world?"

"You are too young," said Stephen bitterly. "The War's just a bad dream. You didn't even have it yourself. Someone told it you at breakfast. They shot Nadine—" he stopped himself. "You're all in, old chap. You've done your best, and I haven't thanked you. We won't talk any more now. To-morrow, after a good night's rest."

CHAPTER VIII
LOVE IN THESE DAYS

IN THE matter of housekeeping bachelors are apt to run to extremes; they are too meticulous or incredibly slovenly; and the Reverend Stanley Henshawe belonged to the latter class. Jocelyn drove up a weed-grown drive overhung by unkempt laurels to the shabby entrance. The steps had not been cleaned or the brasses polished for some time and the maid who came to the door when she had rung three times had a dirty apron and a smear of lamp black on her chin.

"I am Lady Jocelyn Vaste. Is my brother in? Will you ask him to come out to me."

The girl stared at her, open mouthed. "He can't Miss, I mean m'lady. He 'asn't been well and he's keeping his room."

"What's the matter with him?"

"I dunno, Miss. The doctor's been to him."

"The doctor? Doctor Brewer?"

"No, Miss. The other, the young one. Doctor Clowes."

"I'll go up to him. Let me pass, please," said Jocelyn impatiently.

The girl did not move. "The doctor said he wasn't to see nobody."

"Rot!" said Jocelyn vigorously. "I'm his sister, and I'm going to see him. I never heard such drivel."

The girl looked frightened but obstinate. "The doctor said—" She glanced over her shoulder and said with evident relief, "He's coming down now. He'll tell you," and retreated.

The doctor, a personable young man with a well-knit, active figure, came forward with a smile and an outstretched hand.

"Lady Jocelyn, this is an unexpected pleasure."

She answered abruptly. "What's the matter with Bertie?"

His smile faded. He, too, had received a good deal of encouragement, and perhaps he had expected a warmer greeting. His manner became more professional.

"He's on the verge of a nervous breakdown. I shall pull him round all right. But he's got to be kept quiet. Absolutely."

"Have you let my father know?"

"Not yet. I don't want to alarm him unnecessarily. Your brother is most anxious that he should not be informed."

"I see. Have you engaged a nurse?"

"Oh dear no. He's not so bad as all that. It's simply a matter of dieting and—well—easing off cocktails."

"Can I see him?"

"I'd rather you didn't, Lady Jocelyn."

She stood for a moment, staring moodily at the dirty doorstep. "That's all very well," she said at last, "you may be right, but I feel more or less responsible for Bertie. Father doesn't bother. I don't understand this sudden collapse. He seemed all right when I was down a fortnight ago. He lunched with me at Crossways and brought two of the boys who are reading with Mr. Henshawe." She looked past him towards the door of the study. "Is the vicar in?"

Clowes shook his head. "He isn't. You needn't worry, Lady Jocelyn. To be quite frank Bertie's been drinking rather more than is wise in his case."

"Nothing else?"

"What else do you imagine?"

Jocelyn shrugged her shoulders. "I don't know. There's no harm in Bertie, but he's so easily led. Shall I be able to see him to-morrow?"

"I can't make any promises. I want to keep him absolutely quiet for a few days."

"Is a visit from an elder sister likely to be so exciting? Oh, all right," she conceded. She went back to her car and climbed into the driving seat with a liberal display of slim silk stockinged legs. "Can I give you a lift?"

"Thanks. I've got my bicycle. I'm going home now."

"You're doing research work, aren't you? What does that mean exactly?"

He smiled. "You wouldn't understand. I'm acting as *locum* for the local man just at present. Are you quite alone at Crossways, Lady Jocelyn?"

"Yes. I haven't had a moment's peace since my engagement to Maurice Kafka was announced. Friends ringing up to congratulate and dressmakers wanting to make my clothes. I've come down here to be quiet—but not too quiet," she added. "Come and dine with me this evening. I've just bought a pair of Martin's best birds and I can't possibly eat them by myself. I was going to ask the vicarage crowd but I don't want them without Bertie."

Clowes, who had changed colour when Jocelyn made her casual reference to her engagement, had recovered his self-control.

"I should love to. What time?"

"Eight."

Clowes was punctual. Mrs. Greene had cooked the dinner and gone home, leaving them to wait on themselves. Jocelyn produced tinned fruit for the second course, and made coffee. Later they put records on the gramophone and danced. Jocelyn knew perfectly well that she was playing with fire. Clowes was in love with her. Jocelyn, restless and easily bored, found it amusing to lead him on. "It doesn't matter," she told herself. "Maurice doesn't really care." Maurice was thoughtful, considerate—and dull.

"Darling," whispered Clowes. She smiled at him, a dazzling smile. The young doctor's spirits rose.

Apparently her engagement was not to be allowed to interfere with her casual affairs. Clowes did not leave Crossways until after midnight.

"You're marvellous, Jocelyn," he said huskily as he held her close, staring down hungrily at the pretty painted face.

"You're rather a lamb," she said gaily.

"Shall I see you to-morrow?"

"Probably."

But when he called the next morning he found only Mrs. Green, glumly disapproving, clearing away the remains of their feast.

Her ladyship had gone back to London. No, she hadn't left no message.

Jocelyn, meanwhile, having garaged her car, had run her fiancé to earth in Lord Bember's library, where he was at work on some notes for a speech his employer intended to make the following week.

He looked up at her, smiling, as she perched on the arm of his chair. "Where have you been, Jo?"

"Only down to Crossways to ask for Bertie's blessing on our union."

"Did he give it?"

"I didn't see him."

"How was that?"

"He wasn't well. The doctor said he was to be kept absolutely quiet and that he was on the verge of a nervous break-down."

"I say! Too bad. I'm sorry. Does Lord Bember know?"

"No. He's not to be told."

"I see," said Kafka slowly. "I wouldn't worry too much."

"That's all very well," she said. "Oh, damn! Give me a ciga-rette." He slipped an arm about her. She kissed the top of his sleek black head, mechanically, for she was thinking of something else. Bertie's health, so far, had been the one satisfactory thing about him. His father had had to remove him from his prep. school and, later, from Harrow, but since he had been cramming for Oxford with Mr. Henshawe he had been extraordinarily well behaved. He had not even exceeded his allowance. Jocelyn had begun to feel almost happy about him. She prided herself on being hard and she would have hated anyone to guess how much she cared for her young brother.

"The doctor said he's been drinking. The vicar told father he never had any drink in the house, but I suppose he can get hold of it somehow. I wish now I'd insisted on seeing him."

"The doctor ought to know best," said Kafka.

"I've half a mind to go back now," she said.

"If I were you I'd allow him a few days to recover."

"All right," she said reluctantly, trying not to feel disappointed. He might have offered to drive her down in the new Rolls his father had given him for a birthday present.

"Selfish beast," she thought, aggrieved by the obvious fact that he was only giving her half his attention. "I'm glad I let Clowes make love to me."

"I think you're wise," Maurice was saying. "And now, if you don't mind, I really ought to get on with my job. Lord Bember wants to hurl a lot of statistics at the Government to-night, and I've got to verify them."

"Where is he?"

"Your father? I don't know. Lady Bember is lunching out."

"I'm not interested in Beryl's movements. Why father couldn't leave her in the chorus—beastly little Jewess—I beg your pardon, Maurice."

"It's all right." His handsome dark face was a little flushed, but he answered her quietly. "There are Jews—and Jews—just as there are gentlemen and cads in every race. I really must get on with my work."

"All right."

She left the library as abruptly as she had entered it. It was silly to mind. She was marrying him for his money, and he wanted her, she supposed, because she had some publicity value. Of course she had plenty of sex appeal. If you like to call that love, she thought bitterly, he probably found her attractive.

The old butler, cleaning the silver in the pantry, heard the door slam and shook his head. "Lady Jo and her tantrums."

CHAPTER IX
INSUFFICIENT EVIDENCE

INSPECTOR Collier went down to Sussex the following day. His errand was not a pleasant one, for he had to tell the Drurys that his superiors at the Yard, after considering his report, did not feel justified in embarking on any enquiry regarding the Borlases.

"You see, people have a right to go away without notice. And as to the jewels, it's all hearsay, isn't it."

"We're not asking the Yard to look for the jewels," said Stephen. "But I'm not easy in my mind about the girl and her father."

"If Scotland Yard won't find them I will," said Martin.

"I'm sorry to be such a wet blanket," said Collier. He hesitated. "I have to obey orders. In this case I don't agree with my boss, and he knows it. To my mind there's something fishy about the business. If you can scrape together a little more proof I believe I shall be able to wangle leave to carry on. Ring me up at the Yard."

"We're not on the telephone," said Martin.

"My fault," Stephen's rare smile was disarming. "It enables bores to get at one more easily, and bad news to travel faster. I prefer my fool's paradise, without any noise-making machines."

"No wireless either, eh?" said Collier. He lay back in his chair smoking one of his host's cigarettes and glancing appreciatively about him at the book-lined walls and the picture set in the oak panelling over the fireplace.

"Is that an ancestor?"

"That chap in the blue coat? Yes. Rather a bad hat, I fear. I am glad to have met you again, Collier. You like your job at the Yard?"

"Yes. I've never regretted joining the Force after I was demobbed. There's a chance to get on if one's keen. My Chief-Inspector's not a bad sort, but he's afraid I'll get a swelled head. He doesn't believe in too rapid promotion. As regards this case you've got to remember, Colonel Drury, that enquiries cost money, the taxpayers' money."

"All right," said the other, "I know it's not your fault. We'll have to hire some private enquiry agent, I suppose."

Collier nodded. "You might do that. Though probably he'd only cover the ground I've been over. Their charwoman knows nothing. She arrived at the shop on the Friday morning and found it closed. She was there on the Wednesday. Miss Borlase was out. The old man seemed just as usual. She was paid by the day. The daughter did her shopping at the little shops round the corner and from the street stalls. They don't owe a penny. They were generally liked and respected, but they kept themselves to themselves and made no friends. So there you are. I hate to seem a quitter, but I can't help myself. There is one thing I wanted to ask you, Colonel Drury, and that is whether you have a complete list of the jewels entrusted to Mary Borlase to bring over to England?"

"I have. Nadine Sariatinskaya enclosed one in her letter. The main thing was the square-cut emerald, sometimes called the Eye of Nero, that was set as a pendant for Catherine the Great; then there was a sapphire and diamond ring given by the Tsar to his wife after the birth of their eldest daughter and four diamond necklaces with pearl and diamond clasps which were given to the grand duchesses by their father. The Tsar gave three thousand pounds for each of those and the ring cost seventeen hundred. He had taken special pains to get a very fine sapphire of a shade that matched the Tsarina's eyes. She was a very beautiful woman, Collier."

"Yes. Poor thing. That's a total of over seven thousand, without the emerald."

"The emerald is historic," said Drury. "The Tsarina was wearing it at the last Court ball I was at, a few days before I left Russia."

"That was before the War broke out?"

"Yes. In May, 1914. It was a fearful responsibility for one woman to be asked to undertake, but you must remember that the circumstances were desperate. When the Tsarina gave the jewels to her young lady in waiting, Nadine Sariatinskaya, for her to transmit to England the circumstances of the Imperial family were already desperate. They were prisoners in the Tsarskoe Selo. A few of their remaining servants were faithful but some, no doubt, were spies in the pay of the revolutionaries. I suppose we shall never know how Mary Borlase contrived to cross the frontier. From what her niece told us the other day I gathered that she was months on the road and that she died as a result of the hardships she had undergone. She was entirely trustworthy. I am convinced of that. I remember her well. She acted as a kind of maid companion to Nadine, who was an only child, taking her to music lessons and so forth, a little woman always dressed in black, a pleasant, cheerful little body. I used to see them laughing and talking together as they walked down the street. I thought of her when the niece was here. The likeness is striking."

"You vouch for the aunt's honesty, and your brother for the niece's," said Collier, "and I hear that Borlase was a man with a reputation for straight dealing. That's why, candidly, I don't like the look of things." He was silent for a moment, and then, after a glance at his watch, he rose briskly.

"I must be getting back. I've stayed longer than I intended." He looked from one to the other. "I rely on you to let me know if there are any further developments. Just a little more straw and we'll start making bricks. Once the machine gets started it's pretty efficient."

The man on the spinal couch looked up at him wistfully.

"Stout fellow," he said. "Well—come down and see us some other time, won't you? A friendly visit. Good-bye, old chap."

"Good-bye, Drury."

They shook hands. Martin went into the hall with the visitor.

"I expect the kettle's boiling. You'll have a cup of tea before you go, or a whisky and soda? I'm afraid we don't go in for cocktails."

"Neither do I. A peg of whisky would be welcome. I must not wait for tea. I have to report at the Yard by eight and I like to allow a margin."

"You're catching a train at Pulborough?"

"Yes. The car I hired is waiting for me in the lane."

He drank the whisky. "By the way, would you like the first edition of the *Evening News*? I don't suppose you often get it down here." He laid the paper on the hall table as they passed out. The youthful driver of the hired car grinned at Martin when he saw him. "I've brought your motor bike tied on at the back," he said. "There she is, none the worse."

"Good Heavens!" said Collier.

The driver's grin expanded. "That's nothing. I brought two calves and a pair of geese back from Steyning market yesterday. That's why all the paint's kicked off the inside of the door and some of the stuffing's out of the seat." Martin stood for a moment at the gate watching the old bone shaker rattling down the lane under the overarching trees before he went into the field to feed his chickens. He had some coops to clean out and he worked for an hour before returning to the house. Usually he hummed tune-lessly but happily to himself as he pottered about his little farm, but this evening he was silent. At eight he sat down to a solitary supper of bread and cheese and beer in the dining-room. When he had done he returned to the library where he found Stephen lying in the little circle of light thrown by the shaded lamp, reading a book. He laid it down as Martin came in.

"So the Yard has let us down," he remarked.

"Yes." A wood fire smouldered on the hearth in the library all the year round. Martin kicked the logs together and stood gazing moodily down at the leaping flame until it died down again. "One can't blame Inspector Collier. I talked big but I'm damned if I know what to do next."

"Advertise," said the older man quietly.

Martin brightened. "By Jove! That's an idea. The personal column. *Will Anne Borlase or her father please communicate with—*do I put our name and address, or the lawyers?"

"I think I should use an initial. D. The Dower House. She'd understand. We don't want to be too explicit. I don't know if it has occurred to you, Martin, that if your suspicions are justified and a crime has been committed the perpetrators may find your interest inconvenient and turn their attention to us."

Martin looked at his brother. Stephen lay placidly pulling his dog's ears. He met Martin's eyes with his half smile.

"You're joking," said the young man doubtfully.

"No. I mean it. Face the facts, my dear boy. If you're right we're up against a gang. A gang that has killed once is peculiarly dangerous. They'll be hanged if they're caught. They've nothing more to lose."

Martin was still incredulous. "You mean that we may be in actual physical danger?"

Some note in his voice caught the attention of the Aberdeen who growled in answer.

"It would be rather amusing," murmured Stephen. "I have my old service revolver here in a drawer of my writing table, and I used to be a fairly good shot."

"That's all very well," said Martin, "that sort of thing may amuse you, but I shall shiver in my shoes. Why didn't you say all this to Collier?"

"*Cui bono?* He had his orders."

"Well, I'm blowed," said Martin, "you old fire-eater, preparing to pot all comers. But—seriously, Stephen, you don't mean it?"

"I daresay if we stop now we shall be safe enough."

"If we—well, I'm not going to stop. You don't want me to?"

"I do not."

"Then let's get this advertisement off our chests. In all the papers—by the way, Collier left an *Evening News*. It's in the hall. I'll fetch it."

He went out and returned with the paper which he gave to his brother.

"I don't think Collier even looked at it himself. He told me he was busy all the way down writing his report on another case he has just concluded. Bother. My fountain pen's gone dry."

There was a pause while Martin filled his pen and his brother unfolded the paper and glanced down the columns.

"I say, Martin, listen to this."

"All right. Carry on."

"'A young woman was rescued from a perilous position twenty feet below the top of the cliffs to the west of Beachy Head this morning. A coastguard whose attention was attracted by the screaming of the gulls that build their nests in the cliff looked over the edge and saw her lying on a narrow ledge in an apparently unconscious condition and in imminent danger of slipping to fall on the rocks hundreds of feet below. He obtained assistance and with the aid of ropes she was brought up. She was suffering severely from shock and was unable to give any coherent account of herself and her identity has not yet been established. She has been removed temporarily to a nursing home at Eastbourne where it is hoped that her relatives will come forward and take charge of her. She is described as being about twenty years of age, of slight build and rather below the average height, with brown eyes and brown bobbed hair."

Stephen laid down the paper. "That sounds like Anne Borlase, Martin."

"It does. But how on earth—" Martin's hands were shaking as he took a cigarette from his case. "It's pretty ghastly. What would she be doing there? Beachy Head's a favourite jumping off place for people who are tired of life. It—it needn't be her."

"Of course not. But I think we ought to make sure. You haven't really got over that knock on the head, Martin. It's aching still isn't it?"

"Not enough to prevent me from doing anything necessary. You think I ought to run over to Eastbourne? So do I. Fortunately Jim Pratt brought my motor cycle back from Pulborough. I'll start early in the morning."

Stephen was silent for a moment. Then he said, "You haven't yet grasped the implications. If this girl is Anne Borlase we can rule out accident or attempted suicide. We don't know what has happened to her since the day she came here, but I think we'll be safe in assuming that her continued existence would be inconvenient to the people who've taken possession of the antique shop in Elmer Passage. If she had fallen to the foot of the cliffs her body would have been carried out to sea by the receding tide. That ledge will have upset their calculations."

"You mean that she's still in danger?"

"I'm afraid she is."

Martin stood up. "I'll go now," he said.

CHAPTER X
MARTIN DOES HIS BEST

MARTIN found the nursing home, a large house, screened from the road by a high laurel hedge. It had been pointed out to him by a policeman on the beat. It was late and the windows, all but one, were dark. After some delay the door was opened by a sleepy night nurse.

"I'm frightfully sorry," said Martin, "but I think one of your patients may be a friend of mine."

"You can't see anybody at this time of night. You'd better call again in the morning. Not too early."

She was about to shut the door.

"Just a moment," he pleaded. "I've come miles. It's urgent. At least, it may be. That girl who fell over the cliff. If I might just have a peep at her—"

Before the nurse could answer a sharp authoritative voice intervened from the back of the hall. "That will do, nurse. We cannot be disturbed like this. Tell him I'll ring up the police if he does not go away."

The nurse answered, "Yes, Matron." Then, lowering her voice, and with a scared glance over her shoulder, she whispered. "It's no use. Come in the morning."

The door was shut.

Martin went back to his motor cycle and remounted. For this he had ridden at a breakneck speed through the sleeping villages of the Weald when he might have been getting some much-needed rest. Collier, no doubt, would have insisted on having his questions answered at any hour of the day or night, but he had the authority of the law at his back. "I ought to have bluffed," thought Martin, wishing that he had more self-confidence, but it was too late for that. He found a small commercial hotel, and spent the remainder of the night tossing and turning on a lumpy bed. Stephen was worried. "I'm a bit of an ass," thought the young man humbly, "but old Steve isn't. He's seen a lot, and thought a lot, and suffered more than enough, poor chap, and God help him. That Russian girl. I've often wondered about that photograph in the silver frame, but he never said a word. He keeps things to himself, does Stephen."

He left the hotel after an early breakfast, and at nine was back on the doorstep of the nursing home.

The house, seen in the grey light of a wet and stormy October morning, did not inspire him with confidence. Its stucco front and white curtained windows looked aloof and unfriendly. The waiting-room into which he was shown by a cross-looking maid struck cold and had the atmosphere inevitable in places where people are continually undergoing the agony of suspense. He remained standing until the matron came in with a rustling of starched skirts. She was a stout, middle-aged woman with hard eyes and an ill-tempered mouth. Her manner was defensive.

"I don't know your name," she began.

"My name is Drury. Martin Drury. I have come to see one of your patients. The lady who met with an accident on the cliffs. I think she may be a friend of mine."

"Indeed." She did not ask him to sit down and remained herself standing near the door. "What is your friend's name?"

"Borlase. Miss Anne Borlase."

"That settles it," she said briskly. "You will have to look elsewhere. Good morning."

She opened the door and waited for him to pass out, but he did not move.

"Has she been identified?"

"She has."

"Who is she?"

She answered stiffly, "I am not at liberty to say. Naturally her friends want to avoid unpleasant publicity."

"Her friends," he repeated. Perhaps it was all right, but he was not satisfied. "I suppose she is still here?"

"As a matter of fact she is not. Her friends came for her last night and took her away."

"I see," he said rather blankly. He moved towards the door under the moral compulsion of those steely eyes.

"It seems rather a hush-hush business. I wonder if you were wise to lend yourself to it."

That may or may not have found a joint in her armour. She made no reply. The interview was at an end. He found himself back on the step with the door closed behind him.

Coming into the road he regarded his battered motor cycle with distaste. There was a garage in the town dealing in second hand cars. He had noticed it on his way from the hotel. He rode back to it. The elegant youth in the showroom, after hearing his requirements, handed him over to an older man in stained overalls who eyed Martin's machine with amused contempt.

"You want us to take that in part payment of one of our used four-seater saloons? I'm afraid—"

An hour later Martin left the garage the proud possessor of a fourth hand car, certainly not a looker, but warranted willing and without vices, which had cost him exactly twelve pounds. It was Stephen who had suggested his bringing his cheque book. If he had found Anne he would have had to pay the nursing home fees before he could bring her away. As it was—he drove slowly along the sea front and drew up at a parking place. He wanted to think. A parking attendant came up and gave him a ticket. Martin, rousing himself, looked at his watch. Stephen would be wondering what had become of him. Was there anything else he could do before he went home? A few enquiries at the police station? He left his car and found his way there on foot.

A burly sergeant just coming out stopped to ask what he wanted.

"It was just that I thought the lady who fell over the cliff might be a friend of mine. When I called at the nursing home I was told that her people had come and fetched her away last night."

The sergeant hitched his belt. "Well," he said, "what's your trouble?"

"Well"—it occurred to Martin that a little re-arrangement of the truth might be advisable—"the matron was very busy and she referred me to you for details."

"I see," the sergeant seemed satisfied by this explanation. "As a matter of fact she rang us up rather late last night, about ten o'clock, and told me the young woman's brother had come and removed her. He explained how it happened. They were having a picnic up there, having come in two cars. His sister must have strayed too near the edge and slipped over. No one noticed at the time and when they left, the people in the first car thought she was in the second. He seems to have settled up with the matron and he sent us a ten pound note for the police orphanage and I daresay the coastguards got something too. So that's that. About your friend—has she been missing long, sir?"

"No. What was this young lady's name?"

For a moment he feared that the sergeant was not going to tell him, but apparently he saw no need for secrecy.

"A common name," he said. "Brown. Plenty of them about."

"Did the brother leave an address?"

The sergeant removed his helmet to scratch his head. He was a fat, slow, heavy man whose seniority was obviously due to long service rather than to any display of acumen.

"He might have done with the matron, not with us."

There was nothing more to be said. Martin thanked him and left the station. He would get something to eat and leave the town. He entered a confectioner's shop in the main shopping street and ordered a cup of coffee and a ham sandwich. He had finished and was thinking of asking for his bill when a young woman in nurse's uniform came in, sat down at a table next to his, and ordered a strawberry ice. Martin, recognising her, wished her good morning. She smiled and seemed glad to see him.

"Did you call again?"

"Yes. Why didn't you tell me last night that they'd taken that patient away?"

"I couldn't before Matron. You know she was listening from the back of the hall. The old cat. Thank goodness I'm leaving next month."

The night nurse, off duty, was a young person of an oncoming disposition and very willing to be seen engaged in earnest conversation with a good-looking young man. He moved from his table to a seat facing hers.

"Rather funny, taking her away like that, wasn't it?" he suggested.

"I thought so. Fishy, I thought, getting the poor thing out of bed, only half conscious, and bustling her off. Of course there were heaps of rugs, and it was a lovely car so she wouldn't get cold. But I'm telling it all wrong. They came about nine o'clock and the matron was in the hall, as it happened, so she opened the door to them and took them straight into her sitting-room. After a bit she came up to me and told me to stay with Mrs. Nesbit, that's one of the other patients. 'Mr. Brown's come for his sister,' she said, 'he'll help me down with her.' I said without thinking, 'Is she fit to be moved?' and she glared at me and said, 'If she wasn't I shouldn't let her go.' So of course I said no more. And I don't say she wasn't. There were no bones broken nor internal injuries. Just scratches and bruises, and, of course, shock. And, between you and me, she's a dope addict. I saw the needle pricks on her arm when I was washing her. Well, I heard them shuffling downstairs with her. I went to the window and peeped out and saw them taking her down the path, sort of half-leading, half-carrying her. I could see the roof of the car over the hedge and the chauffeur waiting, but I drew back, then I was afraid matron might look up and see me watching. She's a terror, you know, really."

"A wrong 'un?"

"Oh, I wouldn't say that. I shouldn't have stayed as long as I have. Of course, she's on the make. The charges are something shocking. Twelve guineas a week for a bit of rice pudding and a few doses of senna tea."

At his suggestion she had another ice and volunteered the information that she was going to spend her afternoon at the Pictures. She had told him all she knew, and there was nothing to be gained by further delay. He thanked her and took his leave. Only one thing remained to be done before he started on his homeward way and that was to write out the advertisement that was to appear in the personal columns of the principal newspapers and get the necessary number of postal orders to be enclosed with them at the general post office. When that was off his mind he fetched the car from the parking place and took her over the hill by Ocklynge. She needed fresh paint, but she climbed well. A bit of luck, he reflected, finding a car of that make. If he could have forgotten Anne, Martin would have felt quite happy. But—his face clouded—he could not forget her. Queer how people could vanish like that, utterly, like stones dropped into a pool. And his imagination presented him with a picture of a girl's white face sinking down, down through dark water.

The horrid fancy acted like the prick of a spur. He accelerated. The aged car responded nobly. The needle of the speedometer crept up.

CHAPTER XI
THE BREAKING POINT

MARTIN, on his return, found his brother in a state of ill suppressed irritation very unusual with him.

"That young fellow who is acting as *locum* for old Brewer called this morning," he complained. "He insisted on seeing me, and Mrs. Clapp was weak enough to let him in. He said Brewer had told him to keep an eye on me during his absence. I told him I was not having any treatment, and that he must have meant somebody else, but he merely smiled and carried on. Mrs. Clapp had to take Mac away and shut him up in the next room. Mac simply loathed him."

Mac wriggled a little nearer and licked his master's hand.

"Darned cheek," said Martin indignantly. "I can see you're tired out. What did he do to you?"

"Oh, a pretty thorough overhauling. If it wasn't so unlikely I'd say it was sheer curiosity. They say he's clever, don't they? I fancy they are right. He's a quite uncanny knack of finding out the places where it hurts most to be prodded. He told me he had been a ship's doctor, but he always wanted to do research work, and when he came into a bit of money he settled down here to conduct some experiment or other."

"I believe he's one of Jocelyn Vaste's victims," said Martin. "I saw him one Sunday afternoon playing tennis with her on the hard court at Crossways. I've met him about. He's one of those chaps with abrupt manners. I daresay he improves on acquaintance."

"I daresay," said Stephen, "but I hope he doesn't come here again. How did you get on at Eastbourne?"

Mrs. Clapp had wheeled in the tea wagon. Martin filled their cups and helped himself largely to bread and butter. "It was like this," he began. When he had done the elder man's face was very grave.

"It sounds uncommonly fishy to me," he said. "Why should she be moved at such an hour and before she had even recovered consciousness? It is what I feared might happen if the girl was

Anne Borlase. I'm glad you sent up the advertisement. It should appear in all the papers to-morrow. Of course there's nothing definite, but it's suspicious." He sighed.

"Mrs. Clapp tells me you had your lamp burning all night," said Martin reproachfully.

"I can't rest until I know what has become of those two, Martin. I feel responsible. And now we can only wait for an answer to the advertisement. By the way, you mentioned Lady Jocelyn just now. She called the other day. She wanted a couple of chickens and some eggs. Mrs. Clapp saw to it. Have you been paid?"

"Rather not. The Vastes never pay until they're obliged. You didn't see her?"

Stephen smiled. "Yes, I did. She walked in. A highly-coloured young woman, but not without attractions. She told me she had just become engaged to her father's secretary."

"Yes. It was in the papers." Martin sounded heart free, and his brother was inwardly relieved. "Stout fellow. She'll need a bit of managing. Mind you, Stephen, I know she's not the style you'd approve of, but there's a lot of good in Jocelyn. She's got all the grit that was left out of her young brother. Jocelyn—I know she sounds hard—but she'd never let you down."

Martin swallowed his second cup of tea. He had arrears of work to get through. There were eggs to be left at the vicarage and with several of his regular customers in and about the village, and he meant to call at the Abbey, recently opened as an hotel, and remind them that they were giving him a weekly order.

He attracted more attention than usual in the village and had to stop several times to receive congratulations on his new car. The postmistress, who sold sweets and tobacco and reels of cotton as well as stamps, came into the road to look at it.

"The eggs won't rattle about so much as they did in the sidecar, Mr. Drury. One of those I had from you last week was cracked."

"I'll give you another instead. And I'll have a packet of Player's."

"I'll get it for you. It's closing time really, but the doctor is telephoning. It's such slow work getting a trunk call."

Clowes came out of the shop as she went in to fetch the cigarettes and, seeing Martin, stopped to speak to him.

"I say, I wish you'd apologise to your brother for me," he began. "I looked again at the memorandum old Brewer left for me when I got home. I was to insist on a thorough examination of one of his patients. I thought it was Colonel Drury. Too late I discovered that it was Drew. I'm most awfully sorry. I'm afraid he must have thought it a very high-handed proceeding."

"I'm afraid he did," said Martin. He had been angry on Stephen's account, but his anger melted at the other's frankly-expressed regret. Clowes was not such a bad chap, after all, he thought. He knew that Stephen, like most invalids, was apt to take fancies to some people and be unreasonably prejudiced against others.

"I'll tell him," he said. "I'm afraid there's nothing to be done for him. He was nearly two years in hospital before he came home."

Clowes nodded. "I haven't seen this car before. I thought you used a motor cycle and side car on your rounds."

"I bought her this morning in Eastbourne. She's not much to look at but she runs surprisingly well. By the way, I've never called at your place. Can I supply you with eggs, guaranteed new laid?"

"I daren't," said Clowes. "I have a Mrs. Meggotty to clean up twice a week and she supplies me with eggs laid by her hens. A kind of super egg, according to her, though they are often inclined to be stale. She's a terror, and I'm absolutely under her thumb."

They both laughed. "Isn't it rather a bore getting your own meals?" enquired Martin.

Clowes shrugged his shoulders. "Oh, I subsist chiefly on biscuits and whisky and soda. Regular meals are totally unnecessary and a shocking waste of time."

"Really?" Martin, who was the possessor of a healthy appetite, looked at him doubtfully. It seemed to him that the young doctor was rather sallow and fine drawn and that his brown eyes were feverishly bright. He had heard it said that Clowes had come to live in the country for the sake of his health as well as to do some unspecified research work. There had been rumours of a break-down cutting short a promising career in a West End practice. Presumably he had tried sea air first. He was known to have put in a couple of years as a ship's doctor. "Well, I'm glad we met like this," he said heartily. "Good-bye." He held out his hand and Clowes, his thin face lighting up, gripped it hard.

"We might see a bit more of each other," he suggested.

The little postmistress had come out with the cigarettes. Martin paid for them and drove on. He still had a dozen eggs in the car to be left at the vicarage, which was past the church and on the outskirts of the village, at the beginning of the lane that led past Clumber Place through the woods to Bury.

He left the car in the lane and went up the neglected drive and up the path through the overgrown laurels to the back door. He knocked and waited for some time but nobody came. He knew that the vicarage servants, left very much to their own devices, were notoriously lazy and unreliable. Probably they were both out. He had set down the basket of eggs and was turning away when he heard what sounded unpleasantly like a stifled moan. Martin hesitated, recalling certain very disagreeable rumours concerning Mr. Henshawe's pupils. Everyone in the village knew that the vicar, though a fine Greek scholar, was hopeless as a disciplinarian. The sound was repeated. Martin hesitated no longer but walked round the corner of the house. A ray of light from an open window on the ground floor shone on to the path.

The blind had been drawn down, but so crookedly that Martin could see into the room. Its sole occupant, a young man, was sitting at the table with his back to the window, in a huddled position, with his touzled head resting on his arms. He jumped up, hearing some sound outside.

"Who's that?" His voice was shrill with terror.

Martin recognised Lady Jocelyn Vaste's young brother Bertie. "It's only me," he said quickly. "Drury. I've brought some eggs. I couldn't make anybody hear. I say—is anything the matter?" Bertie Vaste smeared his wet cheeks with the back of a trembling hand. "Everybody's out but me," he said dully. "I—I haven't been well. That's—that's all." He came up to the window, drew up the blind, and stood playing nervously with the tassel and gazing with tear-dimmed eyes at Martin's good-humoured face.

Martin was shocked, and he was also embarrassed. He had not cried himself since he left his prep. school. "There must be something," he insisted. "You've had bad news? Your sister—Lord Bember—"

"No, no. It's all right."

"Rot. Is it toothache? I know that can be pretty ghastly. Much better have it out."

"No," The weak young face, pathetically blotched and discoloured, was quivering.

Martin was soft-hearted. He could not leave a rabbit in a snare, or a wild bird in a cage. "Look here," he said, "there's something wrong. Let me help. Do the other chaps bully you?"

"It isn't them so much. It's—I can't tell you."

"Does your sister know?"

"Jo? No. You—you'd better go, Drury, and leave me to it."

"Think again, Vaste."

"It's no use, I tell you. If they find you talking to me you'll be for it."

"Why?"

Young Vaste pushed his tumbled hair back from his forehead. "If I give the show away they'll kill me." He glanced over his shoulder. "I've half a mind though—just wait a sec while I make sure there's nobody in the house." He hurried out of the room and Martin heard him running up the stairs and opening and shutting doors. When he came back he was breathless. "Old Henshawe's gone to Chichester to some clerical beano. He won't be back for a couple of days. The other chaps are off somewhere." He came nearer and lowered his voice to a husky whisper.

"It's the girl."

Martin started violently. "What?"

"The girl. She brought your brother a letter last week."

"Good Heavens! Are you mixed up in that business?"

Vaste flinched. "Don't look at me like that. It wasn't my fault. They—he makes me do things. He forces me. I—I haven't minded before. The Council of Ten we call it. It was good fun and it paid, and why shouldn't people have drugs if they want them—"

"Drugs?"

"Yes. But if you tell you'll be sorry. It isn't that. It's the girl." He shuddered. "It's been horrible ever since I saw the blood on the floor of the shop, though that was nothing to do with us. She was on our hands after that. He made me—the—the Chief—said 'You little worm, you've got to be in it up to the neck, and then you won't peach.' I thought it was finished, but it isn't, and I can't stick it."

Martin's lips had gone dry. Anne in the hands of this degenerate and his companions. It would not bear thinking of.

"You'd better come along with me and make a statement to the police."

"No, I won't. I can't do that."

"Where is she?"

"I don't know."

His voice sounded sullen. Was he already repenting having said so much? Martin made an effort to restrain his fierce impatience.

"You must tell me a bit more if I'm to be of any use."

"He fixed up an accident, but it didn't come off. He's going to try again. He plans it, but he makes me do it. Oh God!" His voice cracked. "I wake up in the night, sweating with fear. I can't. I can't."

"Let me take you up to Town now, Vaste. You can tell your story to a chap I know at Scotland Yard. They'll keep your name out of it and give you protection."

"You don't understand. I can't. It's impossible. Oh, I don't know which way to turn."

"It's the girl," said Martin. "Did you push her over the cliff?"

"Yes. He made me. We took her in the car. She was drugged. She didn't feel anything. How did you know? She only fell a few feet on to a ledge. I was glad when I heard, but he said—"

"Who is he?"

"I can't tell you that."

"Can't you stand up to the brute?"

"No. But if she could be got away he couldn't do anything. I shall hear where they've put her to-morrow, I expect. Let me think."

Martin waited, and after a minute the boy went on eagerly. "I'll write it down and put it somewhere. I never go far without them, but I practise the organ in the church sometimes. There's a new grave with some wreaths on it close to the path that leads from the vicarage garden gate to the vestry door. I'll slip a note under one of them. That's the best I can do. I don't care what steps you take after, but they mustn't know I've blabbed. And for Heaven's sake go away now. I want to be in bed when they come in."

"Are all the other fellows here members of this gang of yours?" asked Martin curiously.

"No. No. Of course not. Don't ask questions. I mustn't answer you. I've told you too much already."

"Vaste, will you swear that she's in no immediate danger?"

"Yes. Whatever plan he makes I shall have to carry out. He knows I'm sick with fright, and he gets a kick out of that. He hates me. I'll do what I said. No more and no less. I trust you, Drury, not to give me away. You're decent, I know. Remember, I trust you."

He shut the window and pulled down the blind. Martin went back to his car and drove home.

He found Stephen playing Patience.

"You've been a long time."

"I've found out something. Young Vaste is in this business."

"What?"

"The disappearance of Anne Borlase. He pushed her over the cliff."

Stephen raised himself on his pillows to get a better view of his brother's face. "He told you that?" he said incredulously.

"It is amazing, isn't it, but I believe he was speaking the truth. He's in a blue funk now. I didn't get any coherent story. He's terrified of his associates, and especially of one who makes him do things. The whole thing would be grotesque if it wasn't so sinister. The vicar's not fit to have boys of that type in his charge. They're all rotters, and they'd be at Borstal if their parents weren't rich. They've been playing at gangsters and have got themselves into a real mess."

"You're sure it wasn't an elaborate leg pull?" said Stephen.

"Certain. He'd been crying. Poor devil, he was simply dithering."

"How old is he?"

"About nineteen. Jocelyn's fond of him, but I fancy he's always been a trial."

"We'd better get hold of Collier again," said Stephen. "This is beyond me, It wants expert handling. The jewels don't matter so much now—though I suppose it's the jewels they are after. It's the fate of this girl and her father."

"Yes." Martin was walking restlessly up and down. "I wonder how they heard of them? These boys at the vicarage can only be a part of the show, Stephen. If only Vaste comes up to the scratch. He really does want to save her, but he's weak and he's terrified of the others."

"I wish we could get at Collier now."

"It's a pity we're not on the 'phone," said Martin.

"They are useful in emergencies," his brother admitted. "You could ring up from the village post office, but the wrong people might get to hear about it. It's past ten o'clock. You called at the Abbey to-night, didn't you? Did you see the manager?"

"Yes. I wasn't struck with him. Some kind of foreigner. One of those fellows who are apt to be insolent when they aren't being oily. He was very short with me but I've got my weekly order for eggs—damn!"

"What's the matter?"

"I've just remembered that I left my basket of eggs on the kitchen doorstep at the vicarage."

"No harm in that. The cook will find them and assume that you knocked and couldn't make anyone hear."

"Yes, but Vaste was so anxious no one should know he'd been talking to me. Those eggs may give the show away."

"I wouldn't worry about that. You were doing a routine job. You're tired, Martin, and no wonder. We can't do anything to-night. Go to bed now. You can run over to Pulborough as early as you like and ring up Collier from there."

Martin was still walking about the room, picking things up and putting them down again. Stephen watched him anxiously. It was obvious that the strain of the last few days was telling on him. He was looking thin and worn.

"I can't stand this waiting about and doing nothing," he complained. "If Collier had read the *Evening News* coming down in the train, if we had seen that bit about the accident a little sooner I might have got to Eastbourne in time to call that fellow's bluff at the nursing home. That matron ought to have smelt a rat. She'd no business to let the girl be carried off like that, only half conscious. Do you realise, Stephen, that they've probably got her hidden somewhere in this neighbourhood?"

Stephen, who had resumed his Patience, took up the knave of spades and placed him on another pile.

"Yes. But wearing out the carpet won't help her, old chap. We'll do our best to-morrow. I'll call you at six."

Martin moved irresolutely towards the door. "Aren't you going to bed?"

"Not yet. I shouldn't sleep. Good night."

Chapter XII
THE HIKER

Inspector Collier had not arrived when Martin rang up Scotland Yard the following morning from the post office at Pulborough.

"One moment," said the voice over the wires. "Is it the case we shelved for the time being? Further developments? Very good. The Inspector will come down again."

A train was mentioned and Martin undertook to meet it. Collier would be arriving in time to lunch at the Dower House. Martin drove home, ate a poor breakfast, and, setting his teeth, got to work in the outhouse he used as a carpenter's shop, on a new pen. He was on the platform at Pulborough when the London train came in. He looked eagerly at the few passengers who got out, but Collier was not among them. His heart sank. A bearded hiker wearing sun spectacles came up to him with outstretched hand. "So good of you to put me up."

"Good Lord—" he began as it dawned on him that this rather slovenly figure was identical with that of the spruce young plain clothes officer he had expected to see. He checked himself, warned by a quick pressure of the lean sunburned hand that gripped his.

Collier talked on in a loud, hearty voice as they crossed the bridge about the rubbings of church brasses he hoped to get in

Sussex, and it was not until the car had swung round the difficult steep corner on to the road to Petworth that he resumed his natural manner.

"If anything more has happened here in the last forty-eight hours, Drury, we can't be too careful. As a hiker, with the usual hiking hobbies for taking snapshots and so forth, I can have a look round without attracting attention. Did you know any of the people on the platform?"

"No. As it happened there was no one from Ladebrook."

"You are sure of that?"

"Practically. I know all the villagers. Of course there are a few newcomers in those bungalows they've built on the common, and I believe the people who are running the Abbey as an hotel have imported their staff."

"Well, if you can drive at the same time you might tell me what has happened since I left you two days ago."

Martin told. When he had done Collier, who had listened with increasing gravity, said "If only I had looked at that *Evening News* instead of writing up my report on another case. I'll have to see this young Vaste, Drury, and persuade him to come clean."

"I've been through the churchyard once this morning," said Martin. "It's a short cut into the village from Bury lane, fortunately. I looked under the wreaths, but he was to leave a note when he went to play the organ. Fancy a chap like that playing the organ."

Collier smiled. "Nothing in that. Criminals, even hardened criminals, are almost exactly like other people. That's what makes a policeman's life such a hard one. You say he made some reference to blood on the floor of the shop. That corroborates your story, Martin—may I call you Martin?"

"Of course."

"The charwoman was working there on the Wednesday morning," said Collier. "Borlase paid her as usual. There is no record of his being seen after that. These boys may have murdered him. In fact, it is almost a certainty. Vaste said they didn't, but we can discount that. He's Lord Bember's only son, isn't he? Lord Bember has been a good deal in the limelight one way and another. Made a lot of money at the Bar and forced his way to the

Front Bench in Parliament. A bit too brilliant to be trusted by his party, but a good man in a scrap. I've read some of his speeches. He flays his opponents. I wouldn't care to get on the wrong side of a man like that."

"Here we are," said Martin. He opened the Dower House gate and ran the car in instead of leaving it in the lane.

It was Collier's suggestion. "It will be safer," he said.

Martin laughed. "There are no car thieves here."

"Don't be too sure of that," said Collier drily.

Stephen greeted the bearded hiker with lifted eyebrows. "Did Martin penetrate your disguise? Is it necessary?"

"He did not. I thought it advisable to camouflage though I detest false hair. It's hot and it tickles."

By common consent they avoided any discussion of their problem until lunch was over and Mrs. Clapp had taken the coffee into the library where Stephen, who had not gone into the dining-room, awaited them. But they had hardly sat down when the housekeeper came back with a note.

"For you, Mr. Martin. It didn't come by post. I found it in the letter box."

Martin opened it. "I say—it's from young Vaste, quite jaunty in tone, asking me to supper at the vicarage to-night. Can you beat it?"

Collier held out his hand. "May I see it?" He read it through. "Sounds all right. Has he ever asked you before?"

"Never."

"You'd better go," said Collier. "I'll have a look round meanwhile. Do you know his fellow pupils?"

"I've seen them slouching about the village in jazz pull-overs and trailing scarves, with gaspers stuck to their underlips."

"How many are there?"

"I couldn't say. Five or six perhaps."

"I suppose they are rotters or they wouldn't be there?"

"I wouldn't go so far as that—but—well, they are either so backward as to be in need of special coaching, or they have been expelled from school. Henshawe lets them run wild."

Collier nodded. "Promising material for an experienced criminal to handle. That's what's happened probably. Just a game at first, and then they are too far in to get out again. Lots of working-class lads get caught like that by some older man who talks big and throws his money about and dazzles the poor fools. You say young Vaste let out that they had been smuggling dope?"

"He said something about it."

"There's a lot of that going on," said the detective. "If that's the case these boys are probably only an unimportant part of a gang whose headquarters may be in London or on the Continent, or possibly in some town like Portsmouth or Southampton. Some of the men who go in for it wouldn't stick at murder, but it does not often come to that over here. The packet of white powder that is slipped into the hand of some wretched addict in a Soho night club may have cost a couple of lives, but the victims are more likely to be found in the slums of Alexandria or Marseilles than here."

"Quite," said Stephen. "The shattering effect of recent events on young Vaste goes to prove that this is the first time he and his companions have resorted to physical violence. Poor devil. He doesn't mind dishonesty but can't stick the rough stuff. The leader is a bully and apparently has a special down on him. You ought to be able to extract a full confession from the miserable little worm, Collier."

"I think so too. But I daren't rush things," said Collier. "If they suspect him of betraying them before we can give him adequate protection he'll be for it."

"It's queer that they should be trying to get hold of the jewels that were sent to you after all these years just when Anne Borlase found the letter sewn in her aunt's dress," said Martin.

"Not so queer really. The starting point was the woman who came into the shop and asked for Russian embroideries and said she had known her aunt. It was she who prompted the girl to go over her aunt's belongings and so find the letter. The woman was almost certainly a member of the gang, sent to make sure they were on the right track."

"You've joined the flats," said Collier. "It was not so clear in my mind. There's one thing—I heard it just before I came down. The shop was not re-opened for long. It's closed again now. Think that over, Drury."

"I have all the time there is," said Stephen, "I lie here and think."

"I wonder," said Collier slowly, "I wonder what lies behind this invitation to supper. Is it Vaste's idea, or has he been put up to it?" He turned to Martin. "It looks as if they wanted to get you out of the way, immobilized, for an hour or two."

"Out of the way of what? I shall be in their way, if anything. It's just what I wanted, an opportunity to size up those young blighters."

Collier lit another cigarette. "Yes. But it works both ways. They'll be sizing you up. And during the process your brother will be alone here."

Martin started. "Do you mean that they would dare—I won't go."

"Rot!" said Stephen forcibly. "My dear Collier, I do hope you are right, and that some of Lord Bertie's friends will pay me a visit. I confess it hadn't occurred to me, but I see that if they have not found the jewels they may be imagining that I have them. And, that reminds me, Lady Jocelyn Vaste was here the other day, and she noticed that safe built into the wall."

"She can't be in this!" cried Martin.

Collier got up and went over to the windows. "If we leave you to-night, Drury, we must make adequate arrangements. Are there shutters like these at all the other windows?"

"On the ground floor. Yes."

"They must be closed before your brother leaves the house. If I could remain with you we'd leave everything open and see what happened, but I must pick up the note Vaste promised to plant in the churchyard, and act on that." He made a sound indicating impatience. "If I had a couple of men with me we might round up the gang to-night. I've a feeling that they're going to make a move that will put them in our power; but my superiors at the Yard haven't yet begun to take this seriously."

"There's the village policeman," said Martin doubtfully, "but Vaste seemed so sure that our only chance of saving the girl was to keep the police out of it."

"Yes," said Collier, "but if we don't find her in the next twenty-four hours we shall have to come into the open, broadcast an S.O.S. and make an intensive search of the countryside. We daren't risk further delay. We must face the facts," he said, and something in his tone struck a chill to Martin's heart; "whether they killed the old man or not their lives depend on her silence, and they'll stick at nothing to ensure it."

CHAPTER XIII
THE EMPTY HOUSE

IT WAS past three when Collier left the Dower House and walked on down the lane that led through the woods to the village of Ladebrook. His appearance in the little main street evoked no surprise. The villagers were used to hikers of both sexes and expected them to stop and cry "Marvellous!" before the oldest and most insanitary cottages. Often they took photographs. In extreme cases they sat, precariously perched on folding stools, and painted pictures.

Collier, who believed in playing a part thoroughly, used up one roll of films in the street before he went on to the church. He took three snapshots of the church from the churchyard, which was screened from the road by a row of old yew trees, and noted that a path led from the vestry door to a gate in the wall dividing the churchyard from the garden of the vicarage, but he did not linger as he had no wish to attract the attention of anyone who might be looking from the upper windows of the vicarage. The interior of the church was dark and smelt mouldy. Collier wandered up the aisle, his footsteps echoing loudly in the silence, and saw the hour glass by the pulpit, and the Tudor brass in memory of one Stephen Drury, Knight, of Ladebrook Abbey, in the chancel. The organ was a new one, evidently quite lately installed. There was a pile of music on the organ seat. It struck Collier, turning it over, that some of it was rather beyond the range of the average village organist. He tried the door leading into the vestry and found it locked. The bells were in the tower at the east end.

It was time for a cup of tea. He found his way to a cottage displaying a notice: Teas and Minerals. An old woman answered the door and showed him into a tiny sitting-room whose bulging walls were covered with gaily-coloured oleographs and framed mourning cards, and returned after a short interval with a loaded tray.

"I've boiled you two eggs," she announced, "you've come a good few miles, I daresay."

Collier had his ordnance map spread out on one end of the table. She joined him as he bent over it.

"And you can find your way by that? I bain't no scholard myself. Never had no schooling. I'm eighty though you mightn't think it. I mind the time when the old Squires, the Drurys, was at the Abbey. Blankets and beef and port wine at Christmas in those days. Now I gets the old age pension."

"That's better, isn't it?"

"Well, I'm glad of it coming in reg'lar," she admitted, "but old Mrs. Drury was a good, kind lady. The old squire he was a spender though, and they come down in the world and the big house was sold. Their grandsons be living in the neighbourhood yet, up to the Dower House."

"And who has the Abbey now?"

The old woman sniffed her contempt. "One of they cinderlicks."

Collier, after a moment of confusion, realised that she meant a syndicate. "They've turned it into an hotel. My great niece went up there and got took on as an under chamber-maid, but I don't know as her mother'll let her stay. There's a deal of coming and going in they moty cars, and dancing to all hours."

Collier was still studying his map. "There's another big estate marked here. Clumber Place. Who lives there?"

"It used to be the Leesons, but the family died out. Then a doctor had it for what they calls a private asylum, meaning a mad house, and he had the walls made higher and blocked up one of the entrances to the park. There was some kind of trouble. I don't rightly know what for, I was away at the time in India along of my husband who was a soldier, and when I come home, after he died out there, the place was empty and shut up as it is to-day. Could you manage another egg, sir?"

"Thank you, I think not. I'll try a slice of this cake. I've just been having a look at the church. A picturesque old building, but it looks neglected."

"Ah," she shook her head. "I've nothing against Mr. Henshawe, but he hasn't got a wife to look after him, and he's always up in the clouds like. Very learned, they say he is, and has young gentlemen at the vicarage teaching 'em all sorts—but not manners—for taking 'em by and large they're a set of young monkeys and a regular nuisance in the village, and one or two in the past up to mischief that would ha' landed them at the Sessions if they hadn't had fathers to pay for the damage they'd done."

Collier paid for his tea, shouldered his pack, and wandered away along a lane that led away from the village in a westerly direction. He had taken the opportunity while he was in the churchyard to examine the wreaths on the new grave to the left of the lych gate, but without finding any note, and he thought it best to wait until after nightfall before he tried again. Meanwhile he meant to have a look at Crossways, Lord Bember's week-end cottage. He came upon it half a mile beyond the village, a rather garish affair of white rough cast, red tiles and green paint, with a large garage attached, and a hard tennis court. It stood in about an acre of ground which had been left in the rough.

Collier unlatched the gate and walked up the drive. He was approaching the door when it opened and a woman came out.

She eyed him distrustfully. "What did you want?"

"Is there anyone at home?"

"No, there isn't. I come up every day for an hour to open the windows and keep the place aired. They come down any time. Lady Jocelyn was here on Monday and stayed the night. Are you a friend of the family?"

"We have mutual friends. I thought, being in the neighbourhood—"

He turned and walked back to the road with her. "The garage is empty, I suppose," he said casually.

"I couldn't say, I'm sure. There's room in it for three cars, but I don't have to meddle with it. The house is my job and quite enough too with the mess the young ones make. I'd larn them if they were mine."

"I shouldn't have thought it was necessary to go in every day when they're not there. It's a long trudge for you from the village."

"You're right there. As a matter of fact I sometimes miss a couple of times when I know the place is straight."

"Quite right," said Collier heartily. "If I follow the lane past the house where will it lead me?"

"It don't lead nowhere. At least, only to the old chalk quarry that's used now for a rubbish dump. His lordship has been making a fuss about that. He says it breeds rats and that they're beginning to over-run his place, and it's a fact that I've seen them on the tennis court in broad day-light."

"Ah," said Collier, "rats are troublesome things. Well, I must be getting along. I've got to go back to the village. I've lost the view-taker from my camera. Good afternoon."

He walked on briskly and had soon left her far behind.

His afternoon had not been wasted. He had received corroboration of the story he had heard from the Drurys and had envisaged certain possibilities. It seemed certain that Anne Borlase had been held somewhere in the district since the previous Wednesday, and that when the attempt to dispose of her by means of a faked accident had failed, she had been brought back to her original hiding place. Collier, while studying the map, had sketched out a plan of campaign. First, he meant to go back to the churchyard as soon as the gathering dusk made it possible for him to do so unobserved. It was still too light. He climbed a stile and sat for a while under a hedge smoking cigarettes and worrying as he was apt to do in the early stages of a difficult and complex case. He could not blame the authorities for leaving him to make his preliminary investigations alone. Quite recently a considerable amount of public money had been wasted and a number of officers had been employed for days in searching for a woman whose disappearance had proved to be voluntary and in the nature of a practical joke. Naturally the result had been to make the police afraid to commit themselves too far with what might turn out to be a similar case. Collier wondered, rather grimly, if the appeal to Anne Borlase that had appeared in the personal columns of all the principal newspapers that morning would attract the attention of any enterprising journalist in search of a story. A mystery involving Lord Bember's son would have many repercussions. On the other hand powerful influences would be at work to hush up any scandal that concerned, however indirectly, a political party. Collier sighed impatiently. His beard, attached with spirit gum, was making his chin itch, and he found the khaki shorts of a hiker inadequate as a protection against the rigours of an English October. The rain that had been threatening all the afternoon was beginning to fall. He unstrapped his waterproof from his pack and put it on. The weather was vile but it had its advantages from his point of view. It would keep people indoors. It was dark, too, much earlier than usual.

He walked briskly down the lane and through the village, meeting no one on the way. It was now past the hour at which Martin Drury was due to arrive at the vicarage. If young Vaste had carried out his promise to leave a note for him in the churchyard it must be there now. Collier passed through the lych gate and went directly to the new grave on the left of the path. The three wreaths that had been placed there after the funeral still lay on the mound. He switched on his electric torch and lifted each of them in turn. Each had a card wired on. He read the inscriptions. To my dearest Husband. From his sorrowing sister Alice. From Doris and Bert. There was no other writing. Intent on his search he fumbled over the wired sprays of fading flowers.

"May I ask what you are doing?"

Collier turned rather quickly to the tall shadowy figure that faced him across two intervening headstones. He had been prepared for a possible interruption and was ready with his explanation.

"I've lost the view-taker from my camera. I was taking some snaps of the church this afternoon and it occurred to me that it might have dropped hereabouts in the long grass." He let the white ray of his torch play over the figure of his interlocutor.

The other jerked up his hand. "Don't dazzle me with that thing. You'd better come back in the morning to look for anything you've lost. There's a right of way through the churchyard or I shouldn't be passing through. It's a short cut to one of the farms. You're a stranger here, aren't you?"

"Yes," said Collier pleasantly. "On a walking tour. A charming village. I had intended to walk on to Midhurst but I couldn't tear myself away. I want to take a rubbing of the brass in the chancel to-morrow.

"You're putting up at the inn?"

"Probably. Can you recommend it?"

"Certainly." The other seemed to hesitate for a moment before he wished Collier good night and passed on.

Collier lingered, flashing his torch over the adjacent graves to give colour to his story of the lost view-taker. He could see a light in one of the lower windows of the vicarage gleaming through the overgrown laurel hedge that screened the house from the church-yard. His colloquy with a chance passerby had not disturbed him since he had been able to give a good account of himself, but he was troubled by the absence of the promised message from Vaste. Did it mean that his courage, a flash in the pan at the best, the piti-ful despairing courage of the coward driven to bay, had failed him; or had his partial betrayal of his associates become known to the other members of the gang and steps been taken to prevent him from carrying out his plan? Collier wondered uneasily whether it might not have been better if he had called at the vicarage during the afternoon and made an attempt to see Vaste. Too late now. The young men must be at supper now with their guest, prob-ably in the room whose lighted window he had noticed. He left the churchyard and turned to the right, leaving the village behind him and swinging along through the misty darkness at a good rate.

When he had covered about a mile he stopped, switched on his torch, and looked about him. He was deep in the woods, and trees on either side over-arched the road which had not been tarred, and was evidently little used. On his right there were chestnut palings, on the left an unusually high stone wall surmounted by rusty iron spikes. There was a gate in the wall a hundred yards further on. He walked up to it and examined it in detail with the help of his torch. It was fastened with a rusty padlock and chain and his first impression was that it had not been opened for years, but, looking more closely, he saw that both the hinges of the gate and the keyhole of the padlock had been recently oiled.

Collier's spirits rose. He felt sure now that he was on the right track. He produced a wire contrivance and spent five minutes on the padlock. At the end of that time the hasp clicked. He pushed the gate open. As he had expected it swung back on its oiled hinges without a sound. He shut the gate after him and carefully replaced the padlock and chain before he walked up the long avenue of trees that led, as he knew, from his study of the ordnance map, to the house called Clumber Place.

Soon he saw it looming up before him, black and silent. He went up the steps and tried the door. It was locked. He walked round the paved terrace, moving without a sound in his rubber-soled shoes, and tested each window as he came to it, noting that the inside shutters were closed. He went down the flight of steps at the end of the terrace, and was making his way through a tangle of overgrown shrubberies to the servants' quarters at the back when he heard the sound of a powerful motor engine coming apparently from the front of the house. Turning, he retraced his steps, but though he had run along the terrace he was too late. The car had been driven all out. He had listened as he ran and had noted the momentary check while the gate was being opened. It was well away now, and there was no means of telling if it had turned to the left, towards the village, or to the right, making for the main London to Portsmouth road.

The house, then, had not been so empty as it seemed. Had its secret occupants become aware of his arrival? He thought not. Unless, of course, he had been followed from the village. That was a possibility, and a very unpleasant one, but he did not allow it to deflect him from the course he had mapped out. He went quickly round from the main entrance to the stable yard. There was no garage. Clumber Place had no modern improvements. But, switching on his light for the first time since he reached the house, he saw, on a patch of stone pavement that had been sheltered from the rain by projecting eaves, distinct traces of motor tyres. Evidently the car had been kept in the coach-house. He made another deduction. The tyres were wet when the car was brought out and could, therefore, have been under cover for only a very short time. Collier set his teeth. He had a feeling that hitherto he had only known in nightmares, the feeling that something terribly urgent depended on him, while he stood there in helpless ignorance of what to do next. Was he wasting precious time here? He crossed the yard to the house and, after making a perfunctory trial of the back door, broke a pane of the scullery window and climbed in.

Something scuttered away in the darkness. Switching on his light he saw rat holes in the wainscot. The house was a solid Georgian mansion with three stories, a basement and cellars. The agents, who had had it on their books for many years, could have told him that there were five reception and eighteen bedrooms, but that would not have saved him the trouble of a methodical and thorough search of the premises. And all the while, as he passed from one empty dusty room to the next he had the sensation of being followed. The black passages, the huge cold black pit into which the stairs descended, seemed to lie in wait for an intruder. Auto-suggestion, he told himself. If he had not known that the place had been a private mad house with a doubtful reputation that had stood empty for many years he would not have noticed its oppressive atmosphere. He found, what was more to the point, some evidence of recent occupation in one of the large ground-floor rooms. A heap of mouldy straw that might have been used as a bed, a broken Thermos flask, scattered cigarette and match ends. He faced the fact that if he had arrived a few minutes earlier he might have made a discovery of far greater importance. He felt morally certain that Anne Borlase had been there, and that she had only just been removed.

Had young Vaste tricked them, or had he been prevented from leaving the promised message in the place appointed?

Was there any hope of saving the girl now?

As he crossed the hall the white ray of his electric torch passed over the dusty plaster group of Niobe and her doomed children crouching in the niche at the foot of the stairs.

"Nice cheerful subject, I don't think," said the young man from the C.I.D. irritably, and was startled by the sound of his own voice breaking that heavy silence. The light of his torch was growing dim. "I'll come back in the day time," he told himself, "and go through the darned place with a tooth comb." He left the house as he had entered it through the scullery window.

CHAPTER XIV
THE BELL

MARTIN stopped at the vicarage gate, leaving his newly-acquired car in the road. As he walked up the drive to the door he could hear a gramophone blaring out a one-step. It ceased abruptly as he rang the bell. He waited, wishing himself elsewhere. The prospect of sitting down to a meal with young Vaste and his fellow pupils was definitely unpleasant. He had not realised until now what an effort he would have to make to be tolerably civil. The slatternly maid opened the door.

"Will you step this way, sir?"

He hung his hat and coat on the hall stand and followed her into the shabby dining-room.

The lamp was lit and the curtains drawn, and the table laid for supper. A sallow youth wearing horn-rimmed spectacles advanced with outstretched hand.

"Pleased to meet you," he said in a high affected voice, "I'm Outram. Let me introduce you. Williams and Thompson." He indicated a stout young man in a striped pullover, and a bony lad with sandy hair and light lashes, who were sitting together on the broken-springed settee and sniggering over a French comic paper. "And these other two chaps are Loftus and Bright. Bright's a new boy," he added with a sneer, "and we haven't yet decided whether he's as bright as he looks."

Everybody except Martin laughed at this jest, including the victim, but Martin noticed that he flushed too.

"Where's Vaste?" asked Martin bluntly.

"He's most frightfully sorry and all that, but he's got one of his bad heads. He's not been a bit well lately, poor chap. He's had to go back to bed, but he's asked us to entertain you, and of course we're only too pleased, aren't we, you chaps? Sit here, won't you? The eats are ghastly, but we've got plenty of drink. See to the cocktails, Tubby," the fat youth scowled and Outram corrected himself rather hurriedly. "Thompson, sorry. Stick on another record, Loftus."

Loftus obeyed and the savage rhythm of a Tango played with a fortissimo needle drowned the scraping of chairs as they drew up to the table. The food was, as Outram had warned the guest, unappetising, cold mutton with mint sauce and potato salad, followed by stewed prunes and custard, but they began with cocktails and went on with champagne.

"We can't run to this every night," Outram explained. "This fizz is a present from a friend of poor old Bertie's. Too bad that he isn't here to help us drink it"—he refilled his own glass—"and yet perhaps it's just as well. His head, you know," he tapped his own solemnly.

Martin thought they had all been drinking before he arrived. The blaring of the gramophone made general conversation impossible. Thompson was the only one of the party who ate heartily. Williams, whose light lashes flickered incessantly, leaned his elbows on the table, smoked one cigarette after another, and talked exclusively in undertones to Loftus, who betrayed a mixture of elation and alarm at being the object of so much attention. After a while Martin, who had been watching them, leaned towards him across the table.

"You and Bright are the only ones I haven't seen about the village. You haven't been here long, have you?"

Before he could answer Williams intervened. "He hasn't. I've been telling him we're very democratic here. He'll probably be meeting the errand boy from the general shop in the village next. After the poulterer, the grocer, what?"

There was an odd breathless little pause, during which Martin, seething with fury, reminded himself that they were all more or less drunk. Outram's effusive garrulity had not concealed the fact that they were all inimical, with the possible exception of poor young Bright, who was merely bewildered and unhappy.

Martin's eyes travelled round the table, noting Thompson's thick red paws—he was still stolidly engaged with his prunes—Williams' raw boned freckled wrists, and the spatulate fingertips of Outram, stained with nicotine. He thought of Anne in these hands and for a moment he saw red. The moment passed and he was aware of an uprush of power that seemed to carry him along on the crest of a wave.

He laughed. "Why not? If the errand boy doesn't mind. Let's hope he's not too particular."

Williams looked angry but Outram laughed, and his amusement was obviously unfeigned. "Serve him right," he said, showing his white teeth in his rather too expansive smile. "I've been wanting to meet you, Drury. There aren't many kindred spirits in this hole. I've heard of your brother. A big noise in the War, wasn't he? The bravest of the brave, like that other chap, one of Napoleon's marshals?"

"He's brave," said Martin shortly.

"A helpless invalid as the result of war wounds, isn't he?"

"Not quite helpless."

"Oh!" Outram drained his glass and refilled it, spilling some wine on the already stained tablecloth. "Stick on another record somebody, or we shall get dull. What do you mean by not quite?"

"I mean—not quite," said Martin, "do you keep that gramophone going when the vicar's at home?"

"Rather. He doesn't have his meals with us. He sits in his study and chews with Horace, or some other beastly classical blighter, propped up by the cruet. We go in to read with him. He's a darned good crammer, I'll say that for him. If Williams and I don't scrape through next time it won't be his fault. And personally I'm jolly glad he's not strong on personal supervision."

Bright had put on a record from *Showboat*. Thompson began to bellow the refrain.

"You and I, we sweat and strain—"

Williams threw his napkin ring at him. "Shut up, you bull of Bashan. You're out of tune. You're grating on the sus—susceptibilities of the chicken farmer. Too much noise. Silence in the ranks."

Bright, nervously anxious to please, lifted the needle from the record, and switched off.

Martin was trying to decide what he should do next. Why had Vaste asked him to supper and then shirked meeting him? Was the leader of the gang, the man whom Vaste feared, whom he called the Chief, Outram, or Williams? Each in his way was a type of the degenerate. Or were they only subordinates and told off to hold him there inactive while something was happening elsewhere? Outram was offering his cigarette case. Martin shook his head.

"Thanks. If you don't mind I'd rather have one of my own. I'm sorry Vaste isn't well. I think I'll run up to his room for a minute before I go. I won't disturb him if he's asleep." He got up as he spoke and was out of the room before anyone could object. He heard a chair hastily pushed back and a babel of excited voices as he ran up the stairs. Evidently they had been taken by surprise.

He knew the vicarage of old. He had played there as a small boy with the children of a former vicar and knew that there were six bedrooms on the first floor, the servants sleeping in the attics. He went quickly down the passage, opening doors as he passed them.

"Vaste. I say, Vaste!"

There was no answer.

As he returned to the landing Outram was coming up the stairs, followed by Thompson.

"Make yourself at home, won't you—" he began.

Martin interrupted. "Which is Vaste's room?"

"The first on the right. He's asleep, I expect. He's got some stuff the doctor's given him. Wait here with Thompson, and I'll see." Outram went in, shutting the door after him, and Thompson slouched forward and stood in front of it. Martin eyed him meditatively. If it came to a scrap he was hopelessly outnumbered. The landing was lit by a gas jet turned low. He glanced over the bannisters and saw the other three grouped together in the hall. There was no sound from the servants' quarters.

Apparently the maids were both out again.

Outram came out of Vaste's room. "He's not there," he said.

"He said he was going to lie down, but perhaps he changed his mind and thought he'd like a breath of fresh air. I—What's that!"

The night had been still but for the steady drip drip of rain from the eaves, but now the silence was shattered by the loud metallic clang of a church bell.

They stood staring at one another while the echoes died away.

"That's queer," said Martin. "Isn't the church locked up at night?"

Outram and Thompson looked at each other, avoiding his eyes. Loftus came half way up the stairs.

"I say, you fellows, did you hear that? What do you make of it?"

Outram licked his dry lips. "Nothing. It's no business of ours."

"Suppose it's somebody shut in and trying to attract attention?"

"They'd go on ringing. Not just once. Parminter, the sexton, has got a key. It's his job."

"He might not hear if he's at the White Hart. It's the other end of the village," said Martin, struck by Outram's evident desire not to move in the matter.

"The vicar's key is hanging in his study," said Loftus, emboldened by Martin's presence to assert himself. "I really think we ought to make sure there's nothing wrong."

Thompson glowered at him. "Wrong? Don't be such an utter ass."

Loftus' fair girlish face was flushed, but he persisted.

"I don't mean seriously wrong, of course. But Vaste often goes to practice the organ, doesn't he? Perhaps his head got better and he thought he'd play a bit, and then he may have fainted or something, and only just come to."

"Rot!" said Outram, but Martin nodded. "There may be something in it. I'll go with you, Loftus."

"Will you?" said Loftus eagerly. "Splendid. I'll get the key."

Martin, ignoring the others, who stood about uncertainly, went down to the hall and put on his raincoat. The ringing of the bell, though it had startled him for the moment, had not disturbed him so much as the fact, just discovered, that Vaste was not in the house. Had his expressed desire that Anne should be saved and the plan to leave a note on the new grave in the churchyard been tricks intended to deceive and gain the time required by the gang to cover their traces? It began to seem only too likely. But he had no time for reflection. Loftus had returned with the key. They went out together by the front door and down the path to the side gate that opened into the churchyard and so, by a faintly marked track among the graves, to the vestry door. Martin produced his torch and directed its light on the lock while Loftus fumbled with the key. The boy's hands were shaking. "I can't help feeling there's something wrong," he repeated. "Everybody's been a bit on edge to-day somehow. I mean—they've baited Bright more than usual. I don't know about Vaste, of course."

"When did you see him last?"

"Me? I haven't seen him at all. He's been in bed practically ever since I came. The other chaps, who are pals of his, go up and sit with him, but I've only been here a week." He lowered his voice. "Are they coming after us?"

Martin glanced behind him and saw three shadowy figures grouped a little distance away.

"Yes. Waiting to see us make fools of ourselves. Never mind. We'll carry on. I agree with you that we ought to make sure that nobody has been shut in the church by accident. Has the key stuck?"

"No."

The ancient nail-studded door swung inwards and admitted them to the vestry, which in pre-Reformation days had been the Lady Chapel. A cheap deal cupboard filled one corner and there was a row of hooks for the cassocks and surplices of the choir. An old-fashioned lanthorn with a half-burnt candle in it stood on a table by a pile of hymn books with some charred matches surrounding it. Martin touched it and found it warm. He lit the candle without commenting on a fact that proved conclusively that somebody must have extinguished it only a few minutes previously. His young face had lost its boyish look.

Loftus, glancing at him, was startled. "I say," he whispered, "what is it?"

Martin gave him the lanthorn. "You carry that. Come along." They left the vestry by the swing door behind the organ and, skirting the brass lectern, came into the middle aisle of the nave. Martin stood, switching the light of his torch over the time-worn pavement with its threadbare strip of matting, the Norman arches, the lancet windows. There was no sound but his breathing and that of his companion. He spoke suddenly, so suddenly that Loftus jumped.

"Is there anybody here?"

There was no answer.

Loftus touched his sleeve timidly. "It was the bell," he murmured.

"I know." He walked steadily if rather slowly down the aisle to the back of the church. The lower part of the tower in which the bells hung was screened from the nave by faded curtains of dark red baize. Martin, parting them, entered the enclosed space in which, on one evening during the week and twice on Sundays, the village ringers pealed the five bells. He heard a thin cry from Loftus and the lanthorn crashed on the stone pavement. He steadied his own hand with an effort and kept the light from his torch on the grotesque puppet-like figure that swung from one of the ropes, its dangling feet nearly touching an overturned chair.

CHAPTER XV
WHERE IS ANNE?

"I'D LIKE to know what it all means, Mr. Stephen," said Mrs. Clapp. "Mr. Martin was round the house before he started fastening the shutters over all the windows, which hasn't been done in all the years I've been in your service. Anyone would think we was going to stand a siege. What with him going off late at night on his old motor bike and coming home in a car, and strangers in and out I'm all of a fluster."

"I don't wonder," said Stephen. "Would you like to go down to the village and spend the night with your married niece? It might be a good plan."

The old housekeeper shook her head. "And leave you? No, Mr. Stephen. I'm not afraid. You needn't think that. But I would like to understand what all the fuss is about. It began ten days ago when that nice young lady came. She was nice, but she brought trouble along with her."

"I will tell you," he said, "if you stay with us you have a right to know. Sit down, won't you? It may take some time."

Mrs. Clapp, who had old-fashioned ideas of what was fitting, sat on the edge of a chair near the door.

Stephen, who knew her to be trustworthy, told her the story as he had heard it from Anne Borlase. "You know we expected her and her father to lunch on the following Sunday. Martin went up to Town to find out why they hadn't come. The shop was closed. We have made other discoveries since and we've reason to believe that there is a gang after the jewels and that they may imagine I have them in my possession."

"Oughtn't you to go to the police, sir?"

"We have, Mrs. Clapp. Would it surprise you to hear that the hiking gentleman who lunched with us to-day is a detective sent down from Scotland Yard? Not a word of all this to anyone. You understand that."

"Of course, sir. Thank you, sir. I'll be bringing in your supper now."

His supper—a cup of broth and a slice of dry toast—was brought in and the tray removed in due course. Mrs. Clapp, now that her curiosity was satisfied, seemed quite unperturbed. Stephen heard her going up to her room as usual soon after ten. Mac had been let out, for a run in the garden and had returned. Evidently there were no strangers about or he would have barked. He jumped up on his master's couch and curled himself up to sleep within reach of his hand.

Stephen had been reading, or trying to read. He put his book down and lay, every sense alert, waiting, his eyes on the clock. A few minutes before eleven he heard the front door opened. He turned towards the library door. His brother's step and another's. Martin and Collier came in together.

"Well?" he said eagerly.

"Wait a minute, old chap," Martin's voice sounded strained. "We both need a drink. We met at the gate. I don't know how Collier got on, but I've had a shock. Whisky, Collier?"

"And how," said Collier.

Martin turned to the side table where the house-keeper had left a decanter and a syphon of soda water with glasses.

"How about you, Stephen?"

"Peace, perfect peace here."

Martin drank and set down his glass with a hand that was still unsteady. "Young Vaste has committed suicide."

"What!"

"He wasn't there when I went to the vicarage. Gone to bed with a headache. I had supper with the others. I wasn't at all happy. You never saw such a set of unlicked cubs. I was thinking of coming away when one of the church bells rang. It was just clanged once and—somehow—it startled us all. I forgot to say I'd gone upstairs to see Vaste, and he wasn't in his room. I thought we ought to see what it was, and one of the others agreed with me, so we took the vicar's key and went over—and we found Vaste's body hanging in the tower. He'd knotted a cord to a hook in the wooden platform and tied it to one of the ropes that come through for the ringers. He'd stood on a chair and knocked it over." He shuddered. "I touched his hand. It was ice cold. Poor devil."

"What did you do then?" asked Collier.

"Well, we cut him down and—and covered his face. The chap who had come with me felt sick and had to go outside. The others had followed."

"How did they take it?"

"I was too upset myself to notice much, but my impression is that they were scared stiff. One of them said he'd go for the doctor. I offered to get the policeman. I found him just about to start on his last round. I went back with him. When we got to the church we found the others had pulled themselves together and carried the body back to the vicarage. There didn't seem to be anything more I could do so I came home. What about you, Collier? Had he left a note on that grave?"

"No. Or, if he had, someone had taken it. I went on to Clumber Place. It's isolated, and it's been empty for years." Collier paused. "As a matter of fact I believe the girl was there until this evening."

"What makes you say that?"

"Someone's been in and out lately. The hinges of the gate are oiled. And when I was on the farther side of the house I heard a high-powered car go down the avenue. I ran, but I wasn't in time to see it. I got in then through a window and searched the house thoroughly. I found traces of occupation in one room on the ground floor where there were several old packing cases half filled with straw. I think she was in that car. If I'd got there a little sooner—"

For a moment he had forgotten the effect of his attitude on his hearers. He sat huddled in his chair before the fire, holding his cold hands to the blaze. He looked sick and weary.

The Drurys watched him anxiously.

"You—you think we've lost any—any chance we had of finding her?" said Martin huskily.

He roused himself. "No. I don't say that. But I was relying on Vaste to come clean—"

"Vaste," said Martin. "He said the Chief would force him to do whatever they planned to do to her. That's what he was dreading. That's why he hanged himself. My God!"

"I think now that I may have been followed from the village to Clumber Place. If so she was taken away at a moment's notice. She'd give no trouble. You may be sure she's been kept under the influence of drugs. But there can't be many places to which one can take anyone in that state without answering inconvenient questions. This Chief may be a one-piece super criminal, but I'll bet he's getting all hot and bothered over this. I'm inclined to believe that Vaste was telling you the truth, that there were other people after the jewels, and that his gang is not responsible for the murder of the old man—if he was murdered. If so it follows that they haven't yet committed a capital crime, and so are far less likely to proceed to extreme lengths with the girl. You see my point. If you've done one killing you may as well do another. You can't be hanged twice over."

"But they did push her over the cliff. There was a ledge, but they didn't know that."

"The question is where has she been taken." Collier unfolded his ordnance map and spread it over the table by Stephen Drury's couch. "Another empty house in the neighbourhood?"

Stephen, raising himself a little on his pillows, studied the intricate network of by-roads, farm tracks and footpaths.

"Not that I know of," he said. "But why should it be an empty house? The ringleader, the unknown quantity, our friend Mr. X, may be living hereabouts. Find him first, Collier. But you can't do anything more to-night. Better get a few hours' rest. The spare room is ready."

Collier glanced at his wrist watch. "Twenty to twelve. I suppose you are right. Can you let me have an alarum clock? I'd like to be down by five at the latest. And I shall want to borrow your car, Martin. I shall have to report this evening's work to the Yard, and get help, and that will be better done from the nearest A.A. call box than from the village post office. Where is the nearest one?"

Martin thought a moment. "The nearest? I'm not sure. I've never had occasion to use one. But there is one about four miles from here. Must we wait for the morning? I can run you there now."

Collier looked worried. "I can't get hold of the people I want at this hour. The Higher Command at the Yard are human beings, you know. They've got homes and families and they go back to them now and then. But it's urgent, and it's not as if I didn't know what I want. All right. It may save an hour or two."

Martin stood up. "Come on then. I haven't garaged her. We shan't be gone long, Stephen."

"One moment. Can you let me have a large piece of brown paper and some string first. I brought something along with me from Clumber Place and I want to make a parcel of it."

"Can't it wait until we get back?" said Martin impatiently.

"Do what I tell you," snapped Collier.

Five minutes later they were out of the house again. Mac, puzzled by these excursions and alarms, jumped down from his master's couch and went pattering round the room, stopping to sniff long and earnestly at the untidy brown paper package that Collier had left on the floor.

Stephen watched him. "We'd like to be in this, wouldn't we, Mac? Who knows? There may be a chance for us yet."

CHAPTER XVI
THE QUARRY

A FEW hours later an aged touring car drew up at the gate of the Crossways. The driver, a tall, soldierly-looking man with a lean, sunburnt face and a close-cropped grey moustache, got out and was joined by his daughter, a slim young girl, wearing the white linen overall of a kennel maid, who had been sitting at the back with two bloodhounds on leashes. Two men who had been waiting in the lane came forward to meet them and the leader introduced himself.

"I am Detective-Inspector Collier and this is Mr. Martin Drury. Good of you to come out at this unearthly hour."

"Not at all, Inspector. It's nuts to us to get the chance to try out our dogs, isn't it, Elsie? By the way, I'm Major Curtis, and this is my little girl. We tumbled out at five when the Yard rang us up and we'd have been here sooner, but it would have been suicidal to drive fast in this mist. It'll clear off when the sun gets a bit higher."

Elsie Curtis had turned to Martin. "Aren't they sweet? Castor and Pollux. Castor has the best points. He's won prizes at all the shows. What's it all about?"

"We're trying to trace a girl who has disappeared. The Inspector thinks she was carried off in a car last night. He's got a blanket she may have been sleeping on."

Collier and Major Curtis were walking up the drive. The raw new house, with its walls of rough cast, its staring red tiles and green paint, loomed up before them out of the thick white mist that made it impossible to see more than a hundred yards in any direction. The others followed and they all stopped before the garage, a separate building on the left.

"I haven't got the hang of this yet," said Major Curtis. "What are you after?"

Collier, who was no longer wearing his hiking disguise, had assumed his more official manner. It was necessary to impress on this ex-officer the fact that he was a person with authority to take a certain course, and no one knew better than he did that the ice was thin.

"We are looking for a girl who disappeared over a week ago. We have reason to believe that she was moved from her former hiding place last night in a car, and if we can trace that car we shall be a step nearer the solution of our problem."

"You expect to find the car in this garage?"

"Well—it may be." Collier was manipulating the lock as he spoke. He did not want to give the major time to draw back. Curtis looked on with a frown. "Haven't you got the key?"

"I've got one that will fit."

"Have you the permission of the owner of this place to enter his garage?"

"I haven't had time to communicate with him, but he'd give it right enough."

"It seems a high-handed proceeding," said Curtis. "I think you should have obtained leave. You're practically forcing this garage door. Elsie, I'm not sure that we should associate ourselves with this."

"Don't be silly, darling," said his daughter. "Scotland Yard asked us to help and they're responsible."

Collier flashed her a grateful smile before he turned to Martin.

"Take the blanket out of the brown paper wrapping now. Let the dogs have it."

He went back to the lock and this time his efforts were crowned with success. One half of the big double doors swung back on its hinges. There was space within for several cars, but there were no cars there.

Collier's face fell for a moment. Then he moved forward eagerly, stooping to examine wet marks of big tyres on the concrete floor.

"A car was backed in here not many hours ago. Back to the gate, Martin. Thank goodness the lane has never been tarred." He hurried down the drive, followed by the others.

"Here we are!" he said exultantly. "The car came in from the village—the only way it could come as this lane ends in a disused quarry. Coming out it turned in the other direction. There's a double set of tracks. The car was driven towards the quarry and back again. We'll have a look at the place, Martin. I should be glad if you'd follow in your car, Major Curtis."

The lane, a chalk track leading up to a shoulder of the Downs, was bordered by high ragged hedges of hazel and hawthorn. As they proceeded they all became increasingly conscious of a sickly smell of decay.

Presently Martin signalled to the following car to stop. They had reached the entrance to the old chalk quarry.

The pit from which the chalk had been carted away was partially filled with mounds of vegetable matter and household refuse, for the quarry had been used for some years as a rubbish dump for the village. The farther side was hidden by the mist. Some of the older hillocks were partly covered with coarse grass and weeds.

"Plenty of scent here," said the Major, who was helping his daughter to hold the dogs. "Pah!"

"What are those things moving about?" asked Elsie. "Rabbits or rats?"

"Rats, and out-size ones. One could get some sport here with a couple of terriers if one could stand the smell," said her father. "I should think it would carry as far as that house we were at just now when the wind's in that direction."

"I believe it does," said Martin. "I heard Lord Bember has been complaining."

Major Curtis started. "Lord Bember? Do you mean that that place belongs to Lord Bember?"

Martin, realising that he had dropped a brick, glanced guiltily at Collier, but the detective was not listening. He was studying the ground. He had already asked them to remain on the grass at the side of the lane to avoid superimposing their foot-prints on any marks that had been made previously.

Curtis shrugged his shoulders. "Well, I suppose the police know what they're about. I shouldn't care to antagonise Lord Bember myself, and I hope it will be made clear that I'm not responsible for breaking into his garage."

"You're such a law-abiding old thing, darling," said his daughter tolerantly. "You can all put the blame on me if you like." She was smiling, but her smile faded as Collier came over to them and she saw the look on his face.

"I want you to see if the dogs can pick up a scent down there, Major Curtis—or one of them if you can't manage both. I won't ask Miss Curtis to undertake it because I don't know what they may find."

"Rubbish," said the girl vigorously, "I'm not early Victorian. I shan't swoon or anything. I'll take Pollux, Daddie. Where's that blanket? Oh, you've brought it, Mr. Drury. Here you are, Pollux. Take your time, old boy."

"That's right," said Collier. "Now bring them over here where the car stopped. You can see footprints and a slurred mark where something rather heavy was dragged along."

They all waited breathlessly while the two bloodhounds shouldered each other, snuffling at the trodden grass smeared with chalk to which they had been led. Martin, who had never seen bloodhounds at work before had expected them to bay, but their silence as they strained on their leashes was more impressive than any sound they could have made.

"They're on to it," gasped Elsie Curtis. "I'll have to—"

Pollux was away over the edge of the pit, slithering down the steep slope and dragging his young mistress after him: Castor followed with the Major, with Collier and Martin bringing up the rear. But at the foot of the slope it became clear that the dogs were at fault and that the scent was lost.

The pit was partially and unevenly filled with accumulated rubbish which had been carted in formerly from that side and latterly from the farther end of the quarry.

"Lord Bember objected to the carts coming up this lane so they've been using another way up by Simmonds' Farm," explained Martin.

The dumps among which they stood were partly covered with weeds and riddled with rat holes. The broken tins that formed the bones of those amorphous bodies of junk were red with rust.

"It won't be here," said Collier. "We must try the other side."

They made their way across, circling two mounds and crossing the open space in the middle. The mist was still very thick and the acrid odour of decay was in their nostrils.

"What a horrible place," said Elsie. She had lost some of her cheerful self-confidence and kept close to her father. The Major looked puzzled and unhappy. Collier's face was grimly determined, his eyes, red-rimmed with fatigue and lack of sleep, glancing from left to right. Martin was white to the lips. Collier had not told him what he expected to find, but he could guess.

They reached the place where rubbish had been shot recently and stood looking up at the mass that shelved up to the brink of the quarry.

"How often do they bring the stuff? Do you know, Martin?"

"Yes. There was rather a fuss about it a few months ago and we were asked to sign a petition. It's not only Ladebrook. Clumber and Malling Common dump their rubbish here. The carts collect once a week. There'll be a fresh lot thrown in to-day."

"I see. Just try the dogs all along here, Major Curtis. We've got to look out for any spot where the stuff seems to have been shifted."

"What are we looking for, Inspector?"

"Something in a sack." Collier's tone did not encourage further questions.

Pollux, after some preliminary snuffling and scratching in the loose mass of rotting cabbage stalks, waste paper and rags and cinders, had lunged off to the left with Elsie clinging gamely to his leash. Her father shouted after her, "there's broken glass in this junk. Mind he doesn't cut himself."

Pollux was already routing excitedly in the heap fifty feet away. Elsie called out. "Inspector, come here quickly. It's here—what you said." Her voice cracked.

They all three hurried towards her, and Collier, steady as a rock now, took command. "Hold in the dogs. Lift the other end, Martin. Now lay it down."

The mouth of the sack which had been lying partially covered with scattered ash and litter, was tied with string. Collier cut the string with his pocket knife and gently turned back the rough jute material.

"My God!" stammered Curtis, "it's a woman."

They all stood for an instant, motionless, gazing down at that muffled figure. Then Collier, stooping, drew away the woollen cardigan coat that covered the head. There was no blood and no marks of rough usage beyond the fact that a handkerchief had been used as a gag. The eyes were closed. Collier removed the gag. The lips were swollen and discoloured.

"Is she—dead?"

Collier did not answer at once. He felt her heart and her pulse.

"Hardly perceptible. You haven't a flask of brandy, Major? I was a fool not to think of bringing one."

"I have," said Curtis.

Collier took it from him and moistened the bruised lips.

"That will do for now. We must get her out of this. I am most grateful to you, Major Curtis. I needn't tell you that this is a case of attempted homicide. You may be called on to give evidence of this morning's work, but until then I must ask you and Miss Curtis not to say a single word about it to anyone. You understand? I want the devil who did this to think he's got away with it. Come along now, Martin, you and I can carry her between us. Carefully. There may be internal injuries."

The Major clicked his tongue. "Shocking. A terrible business. That such a thing should happen in a place like this."

"Poor thing," said Elsie shakily. "She looks awful. Would you like me to run down to the village and bring back Doctor Clowes? He's doing locum while the old one is away and they say he's clever. He might be able to bring her round."

Collier hesitated, his eyes on that pitiful, unconscious face.

"You couldn't do that in a village like Ladebrook without attracting attention. I'd rather not."

"Nonsense, man!" cried the Major, with the irritability of badly shaken nerves, "the poor girl's life may depend on receiving skilled attention. If she dies you'll be held responsible."

Collier's face hardened. His mind was not made up, but he resented dictation. "We'll see when we've got her out of the quarry. Now, Martin."

CHAPTER XVII
THE VERDICT

THE inquest on Lord Herbert Vaste was opened on Saturday morning in the village schoolroom. In spite of the shortness of the notice given and the early hour a number of sensation-mongers had found their way to Ladebrook and there was a long line of motors down the village street. The back of the room was uncomfortably crowded but there was plenty of room on the front benches where the father and the sister of the dead boy sat together. Lord Bember's granite-hewn face revealed nothing of his feelings. Lady Jocelyn in a daring black and white frock cut with the new shoulder-cape was twice observed to be touching up her lips with the aid of the mirror in her hand bag, but her eyelids, under their load of bistre, were swollen with crying.

The coroner opened with a brief account of the tragedy.

"There is no mystery about this case, gentlemen of the jury. It is an extremely sad and most regrettable affair, but perfectly clear and straightforward. The deceased, having been delicate as a boy, was backward with his studies and came here some months ago to be coached by the Reverend Mr. Henshawe. Unhappily, in his laudable anxiety to catch up with his contemporaries, Lord Herbert overworked, and a nervous breakdown ensued. You will hear the evidence of Doctor Clowes, who was in charge of his case in the absence of Doctor Brewer, who has been in practice here for many years. The facts are not in dispute. He went to bed on Thursday afternoon, complaining of a headache and asking that he might be left undisturbed. That evening, while his fellow pupils were at supper in the room below, he slipped out of the house. He had been playing the organ in the church for an hour before lunch and he had a key of the west door in his possession. He went into the church and"—the coroner's glance rested for a moment on the bowed head of Lady Jocelyn—"and committed the rash act. There was no motive. The only son of a devoted father, with every prospect of a brilliant career if he followed in that father's footsteps. I do not wish to add to the distress of his bereaved family by dwelling on this point." He consulted his notes. "I will call Harold Loftus."

The statement of young Loftus, whose air of youthful candour made an excellent impression, corroborated the coroner's story.

Doctor Clowes was the next witness. He had been out visiting a patient when one of the young men from the vicarage came to fetch him, but a message had been left for him and he had hurried over to the church as soon as he came home.

"I could not have done anything if I'd got there sooner. The others had cut him down and tried various methods of resuscitation, but life was extinct."

One of the jurymen leaned forward.

"Beg pardon, sir. I heard the bell clang myself. The wife and I wondered whatever it could be. I take it that's when the poor young chap kicked over the chair. How long would you say elapsed between that sound, the knell, as you might say, of his departing soul, and the discovery of the body by the other young gentlemen from the vicarage?"

"You should have asked the previous witness that question," said the coroner.

Loftus, crimson with embarrassment, stood up. "It's difficult to say. We talked a bit before we started. About ten minutes."

"I see. Thank you. I suppose, Doctor Clowes, you had no reason to anticipate any attempt at suicide?"

"Good Heavens, no! It was a fearful shock to me. He was run down and his nerves wanted toning up. Nothing definite. He seemed better. I've worried over it a lot since, but I can't see what I could have done. It must have been a sudden impulse."

"Quite. As far as I can see no blame attaches to anyone. That will do. Doctor Clowes." Once again the coroner consulted his notes. "I will now call Mr. Maurice Kafka."

Kafka, who had been sitting behind the bench reserved for the press, rose and came forward. He was dressed in mourning and his manner was subdued.

"You are Lord Bember's secretary and a personal friend of the deceased?"

"That is so."

"When did you see him last?"

"I'm not sure of the date, but it was several weeks ago."

"You were coming down from Town to see him on Thursday?"

"I was. Unfortunately I started rather later than I intended. Then I had engine trouble. I put that right, but it was too late when I reached the village to call at the vicarage. I put up for the night at the Ladebrook Abbey Hotel, and I didn't hear of the tragedy until the following morning."

"Had the deceased any worries? Was he in debt, for instance? Young men sometimes exceed their allowances."

"If he had he didn't tell me. He was—shall I say young for his age. But—really I think nervous breakdown is the only possible explanation."

At this point the juryman who had intervened before asked another question. He was a lay preacher at the local chapel and fond of the sound of his own voice. Lord Bember who, as a politician, was familiar with the type, glowered at him resentfully but Maurice Kafka answered with his usual grave courtesy.

"No, I was not the bearer of any message from the father of the deceased. He had no reason whatever to dread my coming, and, in point of fact, he was not expecting me. His sister was worried about his health and I thought I would run down and see how he was getting on." He turned again to the coroner who made him a little bow.

"That will be all, Mr. Kafka."

Maurice was going back to his seat when Jocelyn beckoned to him to sit by her.

"Isn't this hellish!" she whispered. "I'm dying to smoke but father says I mustn't. How many hours are we to be stuck in this hole?"

He could hear the scratching of many pencils from the press bench just behind than. The coroner was summing up.

"Hush," he whispered. "It will soon be over now."

Jocelyn looked at him and was vaguely comforted. He had been very good to her in his silent, unobtrusive fashion during these two terrible days. "I shan't be marrying for money after all," she thought "Or because he's really rather beautiful to look at. He's strong. Why are people so beastly to the Jews? I like them."

The coroner's summing up was little more than a repetition of his opening gambit. He hurried over it, anxious to spare the relatives of the dead boy a prolongation of their ordeal. The jury, having been told what they were to say, proved amenable. "Suicide during temporary insanity caused by over-study."

The court rose.

The local police inspector who had been in charge came over to Lord Bember, who was being helped into his overcoat by his secretary.

"If you will come out by the back door, my lord, you will avoid the crowd in the street. I have told your chauffeur to bring your car into the lane."

The Inspector was a big man, but Lord Bember towered over him. The granite-hewn face had an unaccustomed pallor and the thick, sensual lips were set in lines of weariness and pain. His suffering was evident, but no one would have dared to condole. He nodded absently. "Very well. Thank you, Inspector. Come, Jocelyn."

He took his daughter's arm as he moved away. Maurice Kafka lingered for a moment to speak to the Inspector.

"About the removal of—a motor hearse was to be in readiness to take Lord Herbert's body back to London."

"That's right, sir. I saw the undertaker's men before the enquiry opened and told them to stand by until we got the verdict. A matter of form. They'll have started by now. I sent my sergeant round at once. I understand that the family are in favour of cremation?"

"That is so. Thank you, Inspector, I must not keep Lord Bember waiting."

Collier, who had been present at the back of the room, had slipped out just before the crowd, entered the police car that was waiting for him, and been driven away. He reached Scotland Yard at one o'clock. His superiors were away having lunch and he had time for a hurried meal himself before they returned. He was summoned eventually to the room of the Assistant Commissioner, Sir James Mercer. Sir James was seated at his desk and Chief-Inspector Cardew stood with his back to the fire. Sir James was chewing an unlit cigarette. Cardew looked worried.

"Sit down, Collier."

"Thank you, sir."

"This is an extraordinary case, Inspector."

"Yes, sir."

Sir James cleared his throat. "I admit I didn't take it too seriously at first, but the more recent developments are very disquieting. Will you just run over the main points, Inspector? I'd like to refresh my memory."

"Very good. Sir James." Collier leaned forward, with his hands clasped between his knees, and fixed his eyes on the carpet while he made the required effort. "I was just going out to lunch on Tuesday week when Mr. Martin Drury called at the Yard. I met him at the door. He was asking for me. I had known his elder brother, Colonel Drury, in France, but had lost sight of him since. We had lunch together and he told me that on the previous Tuesday a girl named Anne Borlase had come to their house in Sussex and had brought a letter addressed to his brother which had been brought over from Russia fourteen years ago by her aunt. The writer was a lady-in-waiting to the Tsarina and had been entrusted by her with some jewels of great value which were to be taken to England for safe keeping. These jewels included a famous emerald, known as the Eye of Nero, a historic stone that had belonged to the Empress Catherine."

"Has this story any corroboration?"

"In what way, sir? The Drurys are reliable witnesses. I've had enquiries made about the emerald. It was a part of the crown jewels of the Romanoffs. Nobody knows what became of it."

"Very well. Carry on."

"Anne Borlase and her father ran an antique shop, one of those very old-established businesses that go on when the whole character of a neighbourhood has changed. They knew nothing, or, at any rate, the girl knew nothing about the jewels, and the aunt had been dead for years. Colonel Drury asked them to come down to lunch the following Sunday. They didn't turn up, and the younger brother, Martin, came up on the Monday to see what had happened. He found the shop closed, and looking through the blinds he fancied he saw bloodstains on the floor. He was going to fetch a policeman when he was knocked down by a lorry and he spent the next twenty-four hours in hospital with slight concussion. When they let him go he came straight to the Yard. It had to be looked into so I went back to the shop in Elmer Passage with him. We found it open and a young man in charge. He said the place had changed hands, and that was that. It sounded all right and we had very little to go upon. There was just one point. Drury said he had got the impression that the floor was covered with a shabby black and white linoleum. The dark red stains had shown up on that. When we went in there was no linoleum, just bare boards. Well, I reported the matter to Chief-Inspector Cardew and he allowed me to make some further investigation. I tried the nearest public-house and got on to the husband of the charwoman who had worked there two mornings a week. She was sore because she'd been given no notice. She had arrived and found the shop closed. So unlike Miss Anne who was always so friendly-like and kind, and they hadn't said a word to her about leaving. That in itself was interesting, but she also confirmed young Drury's impression about the linoleum. An imitation of black and white tiles. She couldn't be mistaken. She'd scrubbed it often enough. There's another point, sir. Elmer Passage is ideal from the point of view of a criminal. It's isolated. The Borlases' is the only dwelling-house and it's surrounded by high blank walls of warehouses. It's a cul de sac, blocked at the end by a derelict boat builder's yard on the river side. The yard gate is locked, but an active man could climb over it."

Sir James nodded. "You agree with Shakespeare that the means to do ill deeds makes ill deeds done. But a murder case rather needs a body as a starting point, young man. However, don't think I'm out to discourage you. Go on with your story. I want to know how you link up the mystery of the disappearance of an antique dealer and his daughter with young Vaste."

"Well, Chief-Inspector Cardew decided to shelve the case for the moment. We could always take it up again if any fresh evidence turned up, and meanwhile there were plenty of jobs on hand. As the Drurys were personal friends of mine he very kindly allowed me to go down to Sussex and inform them personally. I explained to them that if any further evidence of criminal activities turned up the investigation would be resumed. I had a copy of the *Evening News* with me in the train. Unfortunately I scarcely looked at it as I was busy over some notes on the Balham forgery case. I left the paper with them and after I had gone they noticed an account of a girl's fall over the cliffs between Eastbourne and Seaford. It's a favourite place for suicides, but the girl had fallen on a ledge and was not, apparently, very seriously injured. It might have been an accident. She had not regained consciousness and had not been identified. Martin Drury thought it sounded like this girl who disappeared."

Sir James was turning over the notes he had made. "Anne Borlase?"

"Yes, Sir James. Young Martin went to Eastbourne and called at the nursing home to which she had been taken, only to find that she had been claimed by a person giving the name of Brown, who said he was her brother, and removed the night before. Martin saw a nurse afterwards who mentioned that the girl was a drug addict. There were fresh needle punctures on her arm."

"Was Anne Borlase that?"

"I should say not, sir. But if she has been kept a prisoner she has probably been drugged."

"Of course. Go on, Inspector."

"Martin Drury went home. The following evening he was calling at the vicarage and happened to see young Vaste alone. The boy was in a state of collapse, crying and incoherent, but Drury gathered that he, with some others, had been engaged in some profitable form of law-breaking, smuggling dope, in fact. From what he did say it appears that they had got on the track of the Romanoff jewels and inveigled the girl away from the shop. Whether it was they who ransacked the place and disposed of the old man is not clear. Vaste said not, but it isn't likely they would admit it. Anyhow the girl was on their hands. As you know, sir, the Drurys rang up the Yard again and I went down."

Collier went on to describe the results of his investigation.

"Clumber Place has been their headquarters and they kept the girl there. If we can prevent the gang from finding out that we know that much we may catch them."

Sir James nodded. "I see. You want to avoid any display of activity. I agree. If the newspapers get hold of this it will be a first-class sensation, and Heaven only knows where it would end."

"I realise that, sir."

The others were silent. After a moment Collier resumed. His initial nervousness as to the effect of his narrative on his superior officers had passed. It was growing clearer in his own mind as he went on.

"Young Vaste's suicide was a blow. I'd been depending on him to turn King's evidence. He was sick of the whole business, poor devil. But the main thing was to find the girl. That was fear-fully urgent if I was to find her alive. I assumed that she would be drugged and more or less unconscious. I've never tried carting a young woman in that state about the country, but in a densely populated island like ours it can't be easy. When I got back to the Drurys' house about midnight I had another go at the ordnance map. There was only one other unoccupied house in the neigh-bourhood, and that was Crossways, Lord Bember's week-end cottage. A woman goes in most days to air the place, but there's nobody there at night. I reckoned with the possibility that young Vaste supplied his associates with a key of the house. I rang up the Yard and secured the assistance of Major Curtis, who lives in that part of Sussex and is a well known breeder of bloodhounds. I had half expected to find the car in which she was removed in the garage, but the garage was empty. I thought it unlikely that the criminals would take the fearful risk of leaving the girl in the house after daybreak. The lane past the house led to the old quarry now used as a rubbish dump. We found her there tied up in a sack. A couple of hours later her body would have been buried under several tons of refuse."

Sir James moved uneasily. "What a ghastly end. The people who did this thing must be brought to justice. When she recovers consciousness—what does the doctor say, Cardew?"

The Chief-Inspector shook his head. "She's very ill. We can't rely on getting any evidence from her for some time to come. When she speaks we can get on with it, but meanwhile we've really very little we can depend on. We might have persuaded young Vaste to talk, but he's dead. He was under somebody's thumb. The question is, whose? And if his little lot didn't kill old Borlase, who did? We induced the coroner to rush through the inquest on that wretched boy. He thought it was to spare Lord Bember's feelings"—he turned to the Assistant Commissioner.

"Are you satisfied with Inspector Collier's conduct of this case, sir?"

Collier's heart seemed to miss a beat. There had been no word of commendation so far, only comments on the nature of the evidence. Surely, though he was conscious of having made mistakes, they would give him credit for having found the girl in time? His suspense was not prolonged. Sir James was known to expect a great deal from his subordinates. He was hard to please, but he was quick to recognise and encourage keenness.

"I consider," he said, "that he has done remarkably well with the means at his disposal. I certainly think that the case may be left in his hands for the present. Henceforth, Collier, you will be given every assistance. It's your pigeon. But"—he paused a moment, and in that moment betrayed his underlying anxiety—"don't do anything drastic without consulting us. We can't have this turned into a newspaper stunt. Lord Bember has been a figure of national importance. His party is out of office, but he was once a member of the Government, and he may be again. He's well known on the Continent as an English politician. Hardly a statesman perhaps, but a man with a touch of genius and a good deal of driving force. A scandal involving him might have very unfortunate repercussions. The newspaper reports of the inquest on his son were just what we wanted. A tragedy of neurasthenia. Effect of overwork. What's your own opinion, Collier?"

"I think he was driven to it, sir. Somebody's morally responsible for his death."

Sir James nodded. "Quite; and there's more to it than that. Look at this report from the police surgeon. We rang up the local police and asked him to make a very careful examination, and this is the result. That village doctor who saw him first and gave evidence at the enquiry must be a fool. It suited us, of course." He gave the young detective-inspector a sheet of typescript.

Collier glanced over it. "My God!" he muttered. "Does Lord Bember know?"

"Not yet."

"May I tell him? I'd like to get his reaction."

Sir James looked at Cardew. "What do you think?"

"He's a hard nut to crack," said Cardew, "but I think he should be told."

Collier stood up. "May I have Sergeant Duffield?"

"Yes. Use tact, and remember it's a hush-hush job."

CHAPTER XVIII
COLLIER CARRIES ON

LORD Bember's butler eyed the two detectives coldly. "I don't think his lordship can see anyone. Have you an appointment?"

"No. But my business is urgent. Will you take him my card?"

The man's manner changed slightly as he glanced at the bit of pasteboard on his salver. He left them to wait in the hall but, returning in a moment, showed them into a room on the left of the front door.

"His lordship will be with you directly."

Collier noted the shelves well stocked with works of reference, the big mahogany writing table and the roll-top desk, and the Remington in its case. A large photograph of a young girl in a jewelled frame stood on the writing table. It was inscribed in a scrawling hand, "To Darling Twums, from his Birdie."

Duffield, who was a married man, grunted disapprovingly. Collier smiled. "That's the second wife. She was on the stage."

There was no time for more before Lord Bember entered, his white shirt-front gleaming in the shaded lamp-light, the inevitable cigar between his lips, his eyes like points of steel under the heavy brows.

"Well?" The weary, husky, curiously attractive voice was curt and impatient. "You've been sent from the Yard, I gather, Inspector. I've had a tiring day, but I can spare you three minutes." He looked at the clock and compared it with his wrist watch.

"I am sorry, my lord, but we thought it probable that you would be leaving Town."

"Quite right. I am. I shall motor from Golder's Green to Croydon to catch the air-liner to Paris to-morrow morning. What's the trouble? Has my chauffeur run over somebody and funked telling me about it?"

He leaned negligently against the writing table, his hands in pockets, facing the two plain clothes policemen as he had in his time faced so many interviewers, and with the same hardly-veiled contempt.

Collier, irritated by his manner, found it easier than he had expected to go on. "It's about your son, sir. We have reason to believe that he did not commit suicide."

"What?"

"The evidence at the coroner's inquest was straightforward enough, but actually it left a lot of things unexplained. That was all to the good. It doesn't help the ends of justice to have all the information available pawed about in public before an arrest has been made. It gives the guilty parties a chance to cook up their alibis and mess about generally."

Collier knew he was on safe ground here. Lord Bember had been one of the peers who had complained in the House of the zeal of coroners.

"Quite." His heavy face relaxed a trifle and he shifted his cigar to the other corner of his mouth. "But what are you suggesting? If ever there was a clear case of felo de se—" He glanced over his shoulder as the door opened. "Is that you, Jocelyn?"

"Yes. I didn't know you were engaged."

"This is my daughter. Inspector. No objection to her hearing any theory of the police, I suppose?"

"None."

Lady Jocelyn's black evening frock with its exiguous bodice held up by a string of pearls over one shoulder hardly suggested mourning, but Collier saw that she had been crying.

"We are not satisfied," he said, "but what I have to say will give you pain. Wouldn't it be better—" He glanced at her father, who indicated the door with a sideways jerk of his head.

"He's right. Get out, Jocelyn."

"I shan't. I'm the only person in this house who cares a damn what happened to Bertie. You were all for letting him alone so long as he didn't bother you for money. Why did he kill himself? That's what I want to know. There's something behind it. Yes, father, I know you want it hushed up. The less said the sooner forgotten. Heaven knows I don't want any rotten publicity stunt over Bertie's grave. He isn't even going to have a grave, anyway. But if he was driven to it I won't stand for shielding anyone who's responsible."

"Driven to it. Rubbish," said Lord Bember.

Collier intervened. "Driven to it by whom, Lady Jocelyn? Were you aware of any undesirable influence? We are depending on you to assist us."

"I've no idea," she said. "Perhaps I'm wrong. He's been on the verge of a nervous breakdown. He was highly strung always. I can't help it, Father. It's the truth."

Lord Bember threw the end of his cigar into the fire.

"All right," he said indifferently. "Please yourself. Get a move on for God's sake, Inspector. I dine at eight."

"Very good." Collier had retreated into his official shell. It was evident that his sympathy would be regarded as an impertinence. He produced his notebook and turned over the leaves. "Lord Herbert's body was discovered hanging in the church tower by two young men who had come over from the vicarage to find out why the bell had tolled. It was not deemed necessary to call them both at the inquest, but the village constable who was on the scene first took down statements from both. For reasons into which I need not enter now these statements were forwarded to the Yard and my superiors there were struck by a detail which does not seem to have been noticed by the local police. Martin Drury said he touched the dead boy's hand and it was cold. Loftus also said his hand was cold. Yet, if we take the brief but violent clanging of the bell as the moment when the chair was kicked over, he cannot have been dead more than a few minutes. The doctor's evidence does not help as nearly an hour elapsed before he arrived on the scene. It was a curious point, but not enough alone to arouse suspicion. The two young men were naturally very agitated and might have been mistaken. There are degrees of coldness, though, as a matter of fact, Loftus said, cold as a stone. The body had been removed to the police mortuary. Doctor Clowes and the police surgeon were agreed that the cause of death was strangulation by hanging. In a sense that was true—but the medical expert sent down from the Yard made a more thorough examination and he discovered that three vertebrae of the neck had been fractured, a fact that suggested that the deceased had fallen from a far greater height than was indicated by the overturned chair."

"I don't understand," said Lady Jocelyn.

"Neither do we, my lady, as yet. But the indications are that a crime has been committed and I am going down to Ladebrook to make some enquiries on the spot." He turned to Lord Bember. "Might I have a key of your week-end cottage there?"

"Certainly." He took a key from a bunch in his writing table drawer. "Here you are, and much good may it do you. The whole thing is fantastic, Inspector. My son was a fool and a waster, but he hadn't an enemy in the world. He had all the virtues of the weakling, gentleness, amiability, the wish to please at all costs. You've got to be a man to make people hate you." There was a silence in the room when he had done. Lady Jocelyn was standing apparently looking down at the fire, but actually fighting back her tears. Poor Bertie.

Poor Bertie. The two policemen standing stiffly by the door— they had not been asked to sit down—saw only her dark head and were unaware of her emotion until she whirled round on them with a sudden violence that startled the stolid sergeant. Tears were running down her cheeks. She brushed them away with the back of her hand, impatiently, with a gesture that would have recalled her brother to Martin, if he had been there.

"There may be something in it. Bertie's been strange lately. He wouldn't tell me anything, but I believe he was being bullied again. It happened before, when he was quite little, at his prep school. He couldn't stand up to it. He knew you despised him, Father. He had no one to turn to." She looked at Collier. "I'll help you if I can."

"Thank you, my lady."

"You're a fool, Jocelyn," said Lord Bember. "Can't you see that they can only make bad worse? But there's nothing in it. I see no reason to put off joining my wife in Paris after the cremation to-morrow. If I am wanted you can apply to my secretary, Mr. Kafka, Inspector. Good evening."

Collier met his cold gaze steadily. It was only natural that Lord Bember should be irritated by the police theory. Like most self-made men he had welcomed publicity in the past, but this was the wrong kind. He agreed very readily to Collier's request that their interview should be regarded as confidential.

"Of course. You hear, Jocelyn. Not a word of this. And now, really, Inspector, though I must applaud your zeal, you have taken up a lot of my time. Good evening."

When they were out in the Square with the cold night air blowing in their faces Collier turned to his companion.

"How's that for a bereaved father?"

"Don't seem 'ardly 'uman," was the sergeant's verdict. He had children of his own and he had been profoundly shocked by Lord Bember's cynicism.

"Oh, he's human enough," said Collier. "Stiff-necked, that's all. He can't forgive the boy for not doing him credit. Hard as nails, I admit, but his pose of indifference is rather overdone."

"He wasn't over-pleased with his daughter for saying what she did," remarked the sergeant.

"She may be useful if she really means it," said Collier thoughtfully. "She's engaged to her father's secretary, Maurice Kafka, the only son of the famous dealer, the man who gave a Rembrandt to the nation last year."

"That's funny," said Duffield.

"Why?"

"Because Borlase, the missing man, was an art dealer too in a small way."

Collier had parked the car along the railings of the Square garden. "We'll have a spot of dinner now," he said as he pressed the self-starter.

"Where are we going?"

"I'm not sure yet," said Collier, slowing down as he turned into Park Lane. "I'll have to interview that secretary fellow, but whether it's better to do it now, or to run down to Ladebrook first—anyway we'll have to go back to the Yard. I've given the river police a job of work and one of their men will be coming in to report about nine."

They discussed the case over their meal at the Corner House. Sergeant Duffield was slow and cautious: where his more brilliant companion leapt at a conclusion he followed laboriously, testing every step. Their different temperaments and methods made for harmony. Duffield was a poor starter, and Collier gave him the required impetus. Collier was apt to be carried away by his vivid imagination, and his sergeant's stolid common sense supplied the brake.

"I've told you what I was doing on Wednesday night, Duffield. Young Vaste's gang had removed Anne Borlase from the nursing home at Eastbourne and were going to make a second attempt to get rid of her, using him as they had used him before when she was drugged and pushed over the cliff. My job was to find where the girl was hidden. Once we knew that she was in the neighbourhood it was fairly obvious. Clumber Place had been empty for years. It stood in the middle of a park, well away from the road. Anything might happen there. I went there and was going round one side of the house when I heard a car driven away down the avenue. If only I'd had the sense to fasten the gates, Duffield, I might have caught a Tartar that night! I was nearer our friend the First Murderer at that moment than I've been before or since—to my knowledge, that is. That must have been a busy evening for him. It makes me quite tired only to think of it. The chap deserves a medal for his industry."

"I don't know about that," said Duffield. "He only took the girl up the lane to the old quarry, shoved her into a sack and left her where the carts would tip their rubbish the next morning. Simple and effective. I wonder it hasn't been done before. But it beats me how you guessed."

"Oh, I looked at the ordnance map and tried to think what I should do if I had a body on my hands. But that wasn't all, Duffield. What's the evidence regarding young Vaste? His fellow pupils at the vicarage say that he was practising the organ in the church for a couple of hours before lunch. Coming in he complained of a headache and went to his room to lie down. He asked to be left alone, and, in fact, he was not seen again alive. Or was he? At the inquest it was assumed that he lay on his bed throughout the afternoon and evening, and then, while the others were at supper in the dining-room, got up, went across to the church and hanged himself with a cord attached to one of the bell-ropes. Add to that the fact that, though there was practically no drop, three vertebrae of his neck were broken, and that when he was cut down after an interval of ten minutes at the outside he was so completely dead that his body was cold. Does that satisfy you?"

Duffield was chewing his steak with the patient thoroughness that was his principal characteristic. He answered after a moment. "I suppose you think the leader of the gang had learned that Vaste meant to blab, and that he planned another murder that would look like a suicide?"

"Exactly. Coffee, please, Miss. And he's been so damned clever that he may get away with it yet. You know as well as I do how many murders there have been where the police have been morally certain of their man, but have lacked the necessary evidence. But"—Collier's lean brown face hardened—"I'll catch him if I can. That business of the rubbish dump. Simple and ingenious, as you say. The simplicity and ingenuity of a devil. I'd like to send him back where he belongs."

CHAPTER XIX
FATHER AND SON

An hour later Collier was back at the Yard.

The heap of sodden junk lying on a sheet of tarpaulin on the floor of Chief-Inspector Cardew's room at the Yard smelt horribly of Thames mud.

Cardew wrinkled his nose in disgust. "Be quick about the job, Collier, for Heaven's sake. This stuff has been waiting for you for ten minutes. I'll have to have the place fumigated."

Collier nodded to the constable of the river police who stood by the door.

"You brought it? Thanks. I'll just give it the once over before we hear your report." Regardless of the mephitic odour of his treasure trove he bent over it eagerly, turning over formless objects with his penknife and scraping delicately at mud-encrusted surfaces with the blade.

"Good," he murmured. "Good. See this? It looks like a black pudding. It isn't. It's a man's woollen sock, original colour probably grey, filled with sand. You could crack a skull with that. And these—these are strips of linoleum with a pattern of black and white tiles. There should be traces of blood on them still though they've been lying for over two weeks now in the mud of the river bed. Where exactly did you find this stuff, Jackson?"

"We carried out your instructions, Inspector, and dredged round the boat builder's yard at the end of Elmer Passage. There was a timber ship anchored there lately. She left three days ago."

"A timber ship? Are you sure?"

"Of course I'm sure. It's our business to know. A Russian, she was, from the port of Odessa. Russian captain and crew, but all O.K. Papers in order and all."

Collier looked at Chief-Inspector Cardew. "With the Eye of Nero on board?"

Cardew shrugged his shoulders. "Perhaps. But the jewels are not a part of our job. What light does this throw on our enquiry?"

"Vaste swore the shop in Elmer Passage was wrecked when he and his companion arrived. Maybe these Russians were before him."

"It begins to look like it. But they must have had accomplices over here. Who re-opened the shop and put in fresh stock, and then shut it again? I suppose you think that when the criminals who killed old Borlase cleaned up the mess they carried all the stuff that couldn't be put right again into the yard and threw it into the river with the body, and that the body was swept away by the tide?"

"That's right," said Jackson. "If there was a body it wouldn't stay there long. There's a strong current along that bit. It may fetch up along by Greenwich way if it isn't taken right out to sea. We don't get them all, not by a long chalk."

"Just so. Well, we'll have these bits and bats analysed for bloodstains. Anything else, Collier?"

"I'd like a call put through to the nursing-home at Horsham. If his daughter has recovered consciousness she'll be able to help us. They didn't seem too hopeful about her. The poor kid's been through a lot. If she could only tell us—she must have seen some if not all of the gang."

"Evidently," said Cardew. "if it's true that they've made two attempts to do her in—and we can prove one at any rate. They may be trying again. What have you done about it?"

"I've got two men watching the house where she is, and I've warned the matron that she's to admit no visitors save those authorised by me. She's to have no food from outside either. No fruit or chocolates by post. I've tried to think of everything, but she's on my mind rather."

"Well, you can use my telephone."

Jackson, of the river police, had gone, and the mass of rubbish raked out of the river bed had been removed for analysis. Chief-Inspector Cardew was preparing to go home. He began to clear his desk for the night while Collier waited with the receiver at his ear.

"Hallo . . . hallo . . . yes . . . Inspector Collier speaking. How is your patient to-night? About the same? I see. Remember what I said. You can't be too careful. Good-bye."

He rang off and turned to the older man.

"No chance of getting anything from her yet. It's unfortunate. With her help we could probably round up the gang within twenty-four hours I think perhaps I ought to see Lord Bember's secretary to-night."

His voice sounded weary and Cardew, who had just locked his desk, looked round at him. "I wouldn't," he said.

"Why not?"

"What have you done to-day?"

"I attended the inquest on young Vaste this morning. Then motored back to Town and reported to you here. Then I saw Lord Bember, had some food, and returned here."

"And worried," said Cardew, not unkindly. "I know you, my lad. You take things too hard. Go home and get a good night's rest but don't oversleep yourself. You'd better catch the secretary as early as possible. It's young Kafka, isn't it, the son of old Kafka, the art dealer? He was the most brilliant man of his year at Oxford, president of the Union and all that. He'll be a hard nut to crack if he isn't out to help, and I suppose he'll take his cue from his employer. You won't do much good with him if you go now, feeling like a chewed rag. And that brings us back to one of the puzzling features of this case. Why did Lord Bember treat you as you say he did?"

"That's easy," said Collier, "he foresaw the wrong kind of advertisement. A good press. That's all that matters nowadays. Good night, sir."

He took the Chief-Inspector's advice, and went straight home to his flat in Battersea. Fortunately he was a good sleeper and he woke refreshed at seven. At nine he was ringing the doorbell of the famous art dealer's house in Regent's Park. He had had to ring once already at the gate in the ten foot wall surrounding the grounds and had been admitted, after passing his card through a grating, by a man servant whose broken nose and prognathous jaw suggested a pugilistic past. Collier smiled to himself at these precautions. He had heard that old Kafka was fond of boasting that his house was burglar proof, and that he employed several devices of his own invention to trap the uninvited guest, but all the arrangements he had noticed so far were commonplace enough and very reasonable considering the value of the furniture and bric-à-brac, the books and pictures gathered together under that roof. For Kafka was not merely a dealer of international reputation: he was an ardent collector on his own account.

But though the rest of the house was like a museum the small room on the right of the door into which Collier was shown was very bare. It was, in fact, one of Kafka's own inventions, the apartment in which strangers underwent a trying out process. Collier had only time to observe that the three chairs and the table were clamped to the floor before young Kafka entered. He was dressed as on the previous day, in mourning, and, again as on the previous day, when Collier had watched him giving his evidence before the coroner, his dark, good-looking face was inexpressive as a mask. But he had a charming voice and charming manners.

"Inspector Collier from Scotland Yard? Do sit down. Will you smoke?" He proffered a platinum case with his initials in diamonds.

Collier accepted a cigarette. Apparently it was to be easier going here than in Berkeley Square.

"May I know what you've come about?"

"Certainly. We are investigating the circumstances under which Lord Herbert Vaste met his end."

"I thought that was settled yesterday."

"Not altogether. You knew Lord Herbert well, Mr. Kafka?"

"As he was the son of my employer, naturally I saw a good deal of him when he was at home. We got on very well together, but I can't say we were intimate. He was several years younger than I am. At Lady Jocelyn's request I tried to influence him, but I fear without much success."

"Did you get him out of any scrapes?"

"Once or twice."

"What sort of scrapes?"

"Well—he was very extravagant."

"You lent him money?"

"Yes."

"Did he pay you back?"

Maurice looked for a moment at the ash on his cigarette before he answered, "No. I didn't really expect him to. I didn't dun him. Please don't think that."

"You are—please forgive these apparently impertinent questions, Mr. Kafka—you are very well off?"

Maurice smiled for the first time. "I'm afraid not. My father is, but I have to live on my salary, plus a rather small allowance. Please go on, Inspector. Ask any questions that occur to you. I have nothing to hide."

"Of course not," said Collier, with a suavity that almost equalled that of his interlocutor. "Lord Herbert was extravagant. I suppose he mixed with a fast set? Could you give me the names of some of his friends?"

"That's not as easy as it sounds. People are so casual nowadays. They barge about calling each other Bunny and Baby, and falling in and out of love when they hardly know one another by sight. He's been down at Ladebrook for nearly a year. His father hoped he'd pull himself together. He wanted him to go to Oxford eventually."

"You often went down to see him?"

"Fairly often. Yes."

"Where did you stay?"

"Sometimes at Lord Bember's week-end cottage, Crossways, and sometimes with my married sister. She has a cottage at Bury."

"Did it ever strike you that he had got into some kind of trouble which he was afraid to confess?"

"He was very nervy. I thought he was drinking more than was good for him."

"Had he any special friend among his fellow pupils at the vicarage?"

"Not that I know of."

"Has he borrowed money from you since he went to live at the vicarage?"

"No. He hadn't asked his father for money either. Lord Bember was pleased about that. He had not run up any bills either. They'd have come in by now. Lord Bember had made him promise not to get into debt again."

"He was afraid of his father?"

"I should say so. Lord Bember can be rather formidable. I shouldn't care to get on the wrong side of him myself."

Collier reflected. "So—Lord Herbert had been extravagant, but had turned over a new leaf?"

"Apparently."

"Did it ever occur to you that he might be getting money from another source?"

"You mean," said Kafka easily, "from the Jews? No. He wouldn't have got it, Inspector. No security. Lord Bember lives up to the last penny of his income. This is quite between ourselves of course. In the matter of extravagance there wasn't much to choose between him and poor Bertie."

"I see." Collier left that. "You thought he was drinking too much. Has it ever struck you that he took drugs?"

"Drugs? No."

"Has he, to your knowledge, any drug addicts among his associates?"

"Not to my knowledge."

Collier was reminded of Humpty Dumpty. He resisted an impulse to quote "Impenetrability. That's what I say," and beamed at Kafka, who gazed blankly back at him.

"You run a car, Mr. Kafka?"

"Yes."

"Might I see it?"

"Certainly. Do you want to buy one? I've got it at Kent's garage round the corner. They'll show it you. Tell them I sent you. It's a dark blue saloon, very roomy and comfortable. A Bentley."

"Have you had it long?"

"Ten days. My father gave me a Rolls for my birthday, but I couldn't live up to it and I wanted the money. I sold it and bought a Buick second hand. A fellow I know took a fancy to that and I made fifty on that deal. I'm rather great at selling cars. It's a hobby of mine. Profitable, Inspector. I'm a Jew, you know. We're supposed to be rather good at business."

"That's very interesting," said Collier, and he meant it.

"This car you've got now. Very kind of you, but I don't want it. It broke down when you went down to Sussex the day of Lord Herbert's death?"

"How did you know? Oh, of course, it came out at the inquest. It was a nuisance because I was so late that I turned in at once instead of going round to the vicarage."

"Did you call at Crossways before you went to the Abbey?"

"Yes, I did. It had crossed my mind that Lady Jocelyn might be there. I hadn't seen her for a couple of days. She'd been staying with friends in Hampshire and might be going to Ladebrook on her way back to Town. I knew she was worrying about her brother. But the house was shut up so I went along to the hotel, and only heard what had happened when I came down to breakfast. I hate to seem inquisitive, but what is all this about?"

Collier snapped the elastic band of his notebook and stood up. "We're just making a few enquiries," he said vaguely, "and there's another matter. I wonder if your father would be so kind as to spare me a few minutes of his time? He could probably assist us, being an authority and an expert and all that. It's another case. I'm afraid I'm rather out of my depth."

"I'm sure he would be delighted," said Maurice Kafka. "Just wait here a moment. I'll tell him. You'll excuse me. The cremation at Golder's Green is at eleven and the time is getting on."

The Inspector, left to himself, looked about him curiously. The only window was set high in the wall and filled with frosted glass. No doubt it was protected on the outside with an ornamental grating of Florentine iron work like all the other windows on the ground floor. The walls were bare but for one picture which appeared to Collier's uninstructed eye to be an Old Master of the Flemish school. If there were any man traps here they were carefully concealed. There was a telephone on the writing table and a strip of dark red Turkey carpet under it. The three chairs had seats upholstered in wine coloured leather, high upright backs and arms of some dark highly polished wood, and were very comfortable. But why were they clamped to the floor? Several possible answers occurred to Collier. He got up and walked about until the door opened and Mr. Kafka came in.

Old Kafka had never had his son's good looks. With the passage of time he had grown so stout and unwieldy that in his black frock coat he reminded Collier of a barrel of tar. But the expression of his swarthy face was good-humoured and there was no doubt about his intelligence. He spoke with a strong foreign accent.

"Sit down, Inspector. My boy tells me you need some help of me, no? You have picked up something cheap, eh, a book or a picture, and think it may be valuable, like that Rubens which I bought at a sale in a house in Cornwall for fifteen shillings and could sell to-morrow for fifty thousand. Oh, it is safe there. If you came within a foot of it a bell would ring. If you touched it other things would happen." The old man beamed. He seemed to be filled with a rather child-like pride in his own ingenuity.

"A man who has beautiful things and does not take care of them deserves to lose them. And now—what can I do for you?"

"It's just this, Mr. Kafka. You know most of your fellow art dealers, I daresay, even the little ones?"

"Not all, but many."

"Do you know a dealer who has a small shop in a cul de sac called Elmer Passage on the south side of the river, in Lambeth, to be exact. It's a poor location for a luxury trade but the house and adjoining yard and outbuildings and the land are his own free-hold. He's old-established and his father was there before him. Lately I fancy he's hardly been making ends meet."

"I know of him," said Kafka slowly. "I have not seen him for a long time."

"A fortnight ago the woman who went twice a week to his house to scrub found the place shut up. It was closed. It remained closed apparently for five days. I called the morning of the sixth day and found the shop open again with a young man in charge who professed a complete ignorance of its former owner's where-abouts. The next day it was closed again, and it has remained closed."

"Well," said Kafka, "what of it? Can't a man leave his own shop without telling the police? It pleased him to go away. So. It seems to me that it is his affair."

"Certainly, if that were all," said Collier, "but we have reason to believe that a crime has been committed."

He was watching Kafka closely. The old man did not move but his heavy-lidded eyes, which he usually kept half closed, seemed to film over and, from being bright, to become dull beads of jet.

"A crime?" he said. "What crime?"

"Murder."

"Of whom?"

"Borlase has disappeared. We think it probable that he has been murdered."

"That is foolishness," said Kafka decidedly. For some reason he seemed relieved. It was indubitable that for a moment he had been anxious. That moment had passed. "I cannot help you," he said almost jauntily, "because I know nothing, but I will hazard a guess if you like. He has gone to live abroad with his little girl, with his little robin who used to hop so prettily about our feet picking up the crumbs. He may have had his reasons, good and lawful reasons that do not concern the police, for not leaving his address."

"And why was the shop re-opened for one day only, Mr. Kafka? As a business man you might be able to suggest some explanation that has not occurred to me."

"I can suggest certainly. Mind you, I know nothing. Borlase may have sold his stock to another dealer who sent one of his assistants along to carry on the business. The assistant, after one day, reported to his employer that there had been no customers and that the neighbourhood was unsavoury and its inhabitants unlikely to spend their earnings on beaded footstools and second-hand books. The stock would then be removed to other premises. Is that too simple and obvious to please you, Inspector?"

"Not at all," said Collier, "you can't be as sick of mysteries as I am, Mr. Kafka. Thank you very much."

He stood up. Kafka rang a bell on the table and the man servant who had admitted him appeared and escorted him out of the house and down the covered path to the gate in the high wall.

Kafka meanwhile drew a large silk handkerchief from his coat pocket and wiped his forehead. Presently he rang again.

"Ask Mr. Maurice to come to me."

"Mr. Maurice has gone out, sir."

"Ah, to be sure. Golder's Green. I had almost—I must think," he muttered to himself as he shuffled heavily in his fur-lined slippers across the magnificent hall. "I am old. I am old."

CHAPTER XX
THE QUESTION

THE house in Berkeley Square seemed unnaturally quiet that night. There was not a sound from the servants' quarters, and Jocelyn, who had dined alone, had switched off the wireless in the drawing-room where she sat trying to read a novel. After the cremation at Golder's Green she had declined Maurice Kafka's offer to drive her back to Town and had gone instead with Lord Bember to Croydon Aerodrome. There was a question she had to ask her father before he left and she brought it out just as they reached the gates.

"Father—between ourselves—do you think there was anything in what that policeman said about poor Bertie's death?"

Lord Bember's manner with a pretty woman varied between good humoured toleration and curt impatience. The inference was that they had their uses, but not as conversationalists.

He shifted his cigar before he answered.

"Not a thing. Absolute balderdash. Forget it."

Was he really as stony-hearted as he chose to appear? Was it a pose? If it was, how dared he keep it up with her? For an instant she was too angry to remember that she was afraid of him. "Father—didn't you care for Bertie at all?"

He glared at her. "How dare you ask me that?"

"And I was just thinking how dare you pretend to me!" she flashed back. "Suppose he was murdered as that policeman suggested? Don't you want the murderer brought to justice?"

He made no answer. The car had stopped and the chauffeur was opening the door.

Jocelyn saw the air liner leave. Lord Bember, about to go on board, had nodded a casual farewell to his only remaining child.

"If you care to join me and your stepmother in Paris we shall be very pleased," he said perfunctorily.

Jocelyn had gone home and had spent the rest of the day lying down after taking aspirin with a cup of tea. She did not sleep. She lay and thought, or tried to think. She put on a new frock for dinner, a grey and silver. She was sick of black. She had worn nothing but black for nearly a week. One couldn't go on mourning for ever.

She had no appetite but she forced herself to eat. She had a liqueur with her coffee. Then, having switched off the loudspeaker, she rang up Kafka's house in Regent's Park.

"Hallo. Can I speak to Mr. Maurice? Lady Jocelyn Vaste speaking, Yes. Oh, is that you, Maurice? Will you come round and talk to me? I—I want cheering up. You will? Right. Good-bye."

He arrived twenty minutes later. During the interval her mood had changed and she received him coolly.

"Too bad to drag you here to be bored stiff."

"I'm never bored with you, Jocelyn."

"Sweet of you to say so."

He smiled at her. "Irritated, exasperated. Not bored. At least, not so far."

"If you cared for me you'd have come to-night without waiting for me to ring you up. You must have known I should be miserable."

He said nothing to that but he sat down on the settee beside her and drew her into his arms. He was so seldom demonstrative. She had sometimes wondered why. It was odd that the man you were engaged to was the only one who did not try to kiss you at every opportunity. The fierce pressure of his lips on hers enlightened her. There was a rather prolonged silence before she released herself and leaned back, white and shaken.

"Oh, Maurice—"

"Are you angry?" he asked.

"Darling, of course not."

"I didn't come because my father seemed a bit off colour and I didn't like to leave him. I shan't be able to stay long now, Jocelyn,

I'm afraid, though I hate the idea of leaving you alone here. You ought to have gone to Paris with your father."

"And help my stepmother buy more hats than she could wear if she was a she-hydra? Anyway, I wouldn't leave England now. I want to help the police. They think there's some mystery about Bertie's death. Two detectives from New Scotland Yard called here last night and saw father. He wouldn't believe there could be anything in it, but I'm not so sure."

She glanced up at the dark impassive face, mask-like now that he had recovered his self-control.

"I've been thinking that there may be something I can find out on the spot that didn't come out at the inquest. I want to go down to the village tomorrow and stay at Crossways. You can drive me down if you like."

"I'm sorry, Jocelyn. I can't to-morrow. I told you my father was unwell. There's some important business. I may have to deputise for him. Can you wait a day?"

"No. All right, Maurice. Don't bother. I'm quite equal to driving my own car. I just thought—" for an instant her lip quivered. She was telling herself bitterly that men were all alike. They took what they wanted, and when you asked for something they had some excuse. She got up and lit a cigarette. "Hadn't you better buzz off? I don't want Mr. Kafka to imagine I'm keeping you from him. He might hate me more than he does already."

"He doesn't hate you, Jocelyn."

"You can't tell me he approves of your engagement. He was frightfully polite the only time I've seen him, but I'm not a complete fool."

Maurice shrugged his shoulders. "He's old-fashioned. He would rather I married a girl of my own race, but—"

"I expect he's right." Blindly she sought relief from the intolerable nervous strain of the last few days. "We're not a bit suited to one another. You'd better take this."

She dragged the diamond ring from her shaking finger and held it out to him.

"Jocelyn—"

She stamped her foot. "If you don't take it I'll throw it at you."

"Very well," he said very quietly. He left the room and a minute later she heard the house door closed.

She sank into the nearest chair. Her heart was thudding, her knees knocking together. It had all happened so quickly that her main sensation was one of stunned surprise. She certainly had not meant to break off her engagement when she rang up Maurice. He had been so sweet at first. For a few minutes she had been so happy, so sure that it was all right and that she was really in love with him, after all. And then—he had shown her, hadn't he, that she was really of very little importance to him. He had the oriental view of women. That was it.

"He wants a doormat," she told herself, "I'm glad I broke it off." She tried, not very successfully, not to imagine her young stepmother's acid comments and her father's icy irritation. She got up and walked restlessly about the room. She picked up the telephone receiver. Should she? For an instant she hesitated, "Give me—New Scotland Yard, please . . . yes, Lady Jocelyn Vaste speaking. Can I speak to Inspector"—she searched her memory and found the name she wanted—"Inspector Collier."

An official voice replied asking her to wait a minute. Then another voice intervened.

"I am Inspector Collier."

"Oh, I just wanted to know if you've made any progress? Is there anything I can do?"

"Are you speaking from Berkeley Square?"

"Yes. I'm alone. My father has gone to Paris."

"Quite," said the voice dryly. There was a tiny pause. Jocelyn guessed that the speaker covered the receiver with his hand while he turned to someone else. "May I come round now?"

"Of course. Yes, please do."

Jocelyn rang the bell. "I'm expecting a Mr. Collier, Lambert. Show him up here when he comes."

She occupied the interval in making up her face. When Collier arrived all traces of emotion had vanished and it wore the air of faintly impertinent surprise which had puzzled him until he realised that the craze for plucked eyebrows was responsible.

"Do sit down. You'll have a cocktail? Do you like dry Martinis? Lambert, two dry Martinis, and if anybody else comes I can't see them."

"If you'd waited another five minutes you wouldn't have found me at the Yard, Lady Jocelyn. I was just leaving. I'm on my way home now."

She liked his lean brown face and steady eyes. His voice, too, was pleasant. Unconsciously she sighed.

"Did you really mean what you said last night about my brother?"

"I certainly did. It would have been unpardonable to intrude at such a time otherwise."

Her eyes widened. "You really think he was—murdered?"

"Yes."

"Oh!" She broke off as the butler brought in the cocktails. She drank hers. Collier set his down on a table within reach. He did not really want it, but he had thought it better to accept. He was watching her more closely than she realised. He disliked the hard, glittering type of girl, restless, feverishly clutching at a good time at any price, but he did not allow his feelings to appear.

She turned to him abruptly when the butler had gone out again.

"You must know something about Bertie that I don't. Do you mind telling me what it is?"

He was wondering uneasily whether she was to be trusted. You couldn't put tabs on people of this class. Moral standards were out of date, and they didn't know the meaning of fear. No jobs to lose, no financial worries. At least, he supposed not.

"All right," he said. "It's not going to be pleasant."

She nodded. "Go on."

"Your brother was weak, wasn't he? Easily led?"

"Yes."

"He got into bad hands. I can't say when it began, whether before or after he was sent to Ladebrook vicarage. He became a member of a gang with one or two of the other young men at the crammer's. I think their job was peddling dope, smuggled cocaine and heroin. One of them, a young fellow named Outram, has a brother, a pilot at a civil aerodrome, who may or may not be in it. It's a paying game until you're found out, and an inexperienced boy like your brother wouldn't realise what a dirty business it is until he was too deeply involved to get out of it easily. Then, somehow, the more responsible members of the organisation got on the track of some jewels, a part of the Russian Crown jewels, that were taken out of the country in 1917." He told her briefly what he had heard from the Drurys. When he had done she sat for a minute gazing at him before she spoke. "You really believe this—this gang kidnapped this Borlase girl while they ransacked the shop for the jewels and killed her father? It's absurd. Bertie turned sick if he so much as saw a scratched finger. He wouldn't go out shooting. That was one of the things that annoyed father."

"That's just it, Lady Jocelyn. Your brother was forced into an intolerable position. The man whom he called the Chief was determined that he should take part when they embarked on a business far more hazardous than smuggling dope, and when he saw that he had pushed the lad too far he silenced him."

"You mean that he was murdered by one of the gang? By the Chief?"

"I think so."

"But—when? how? who is this man?"

'That is what I have to find out, Lady Jocelyn."

"Do you suspect anyone?"

"We know a certain number of facts about him. That's all I can say at present."

"What facts?" He noticed that her voice was not quite steady.

"Well, he's obviously no stranger to Ladebrook. He owns, or at any rate has the use of a motor car and he has considerable muscular strength. Unless he had assistance, and that, of course, is a possibility."

"What do you mean?"

"When Martin Drury went to the vicarage that night he found five of the vicar's pupils in the dining-room. The sixth—your brother—was ostensibly up in his room, in bed with a headache. The theory accepted at the inquest was that while the others were at supper he left the house, went into the church and hanged himself with a piece of cord attached to one of the bell ropes, causing the bell to ring. One bit of evidence that we deliberately allowed to pass unnoticed because, alone, it wasn't enough, makes that untenable. Ten minutes later the body was cold. You see"—at this point in his reconstruction Collier could never quite control his professional enthusiasm—"we haven't a shadow of real proof that Lord Herbert was in his room at eight. He may—in my opinion he almost certainly did leave the vicarage at some time during the afternoon. He was to have heard what the gang had planned. I think he may have been driven to open rebellion. The desperate courage of the coward. Luckier people with nerves less highly strung don't know what that can be. The real hero is the man who is afraid—and still goes on."

"Poor Bertie!" she murmured. She held out her hand impulsively.

"Thank you, Inspector. I—I like to think he wasn't altogether despicable." He saw the tears in her eyes. "I told you last night that I wanted to help," she went on. "I thought of going down to Crossways. There may be talk in the village. I might hear something."

He thought a moment before he nodded. "Quite a good idea. People will talk more freely to you than they would do a stranger. You can get at me through the Drurys, or ring up the Yard, but I rely on your discretion. You'd be no use if it got about that you were in touch with the police."

"I'll do my best," she said.

He got up. "Then I'll be going. Good night, Lady Jocelyn."

He had nearly reached the door when she spoke again, and this time with an evident effort. "Inspector. One moment—" He waited.

"You—you are sure that the verdict at the inquest was wrong?"

"I'm afraid I am. I am sorry to distress you."

She had taken a cigarette from a box on the mantelpiece and was tapping it on the back of her hand. "Never mind that," she said. "Never mind me. You have no proof as yet—but have you any idea in your own mind of—of the person responsible?"

"I would rather not answer that question, Lady Jocelyn."

"I see. Thank you. Good night."

Collier shut the door and went downstairs. The butler was waiting in the hall to let him out. Collier glanced at him absently. His thoughts were elsewhere. He had noticed that Lady Jocelyn was not wearing her engagement ring.

"Was Mr. Kafka here this evening?"

The butler answered stiffly. "Yes, sir. He left not long before you came."

Collier crossed the pavement and hailed a passing taxi. The rain had ceased, but he was tired and wanted to get home quickly. Too tired to put two and two together, or to surmise why one and one had come apart. His brain would be fresher, he hoped, in the morning.

CHAPTER XXI
JOCELYN AND OTHERS

JOCELYN had just put on her brakes to avoid a dog as Doctor Clowes came out of the village shop. He stood for an instant, staring, before he crossed the road to her.

"Hallo," he said casually, "engine stalled? Can I do anything?"

"No. Why can't they teach their darned mongrels to keep out of the way? Fancy meeting you at this hour of the day. I thought you swotted in your lab. grafting germs on rabbits or something in the mornings."

He laughed. "That's what the village surmises. It's not quite so obvious as that. And just now I'm doing most of old Brewer's work for him."

"Yes, of course." Jocelyn was reminded that if Doctor Brewer's *locum* had not been away this young man would not have been called upon to make those vain efforts to restore her brother to life. She had seen him only the day before yesterday giving his evidence at the inquest in the village schoolroom. He, at any rate, seemed to have no doubts as to the cause of death. Or had he kept them to himself? It occurred to her that she might get more out of him than the police had done. He was looking at her eagerly.

"Have you come down to stay? May I come to see you?"

She nodded. "Yes. Come to tea. About four."

"Thanks. I will."

He looked after her as she drove down the village street, passing the church to stop at the vicarage gate.

Jocelyn rang the bell and asked to see the vicar. The cook, who seemed sulky and scared, showed her into the study, a mouldy-smelling room with book-lined walls, and greatly in need of dusting. Mr. Henshawe rose from his desk to receive her. He was an elderly man, looking pathetically shabby and uncared-for, with vague pale blue eyes and a cold and distant manner.

"Please be seated, Lady Jocelyn. I—I am rather busy. Next Sunday's sermon—"

"I won't keep you long," she said bluntly. "I've come to take away Bertie's things. May I go up to his room?"

"Oh—certainly. It has been visited on several occasions by the—ah—the police. All this has been very unpleasant for me, very unpleasant. It has done me harm," said the vicar complainingly. "Two of my pupils left me yesterday."

"Which were those?"

"The most recent arrivals. Loftus and young Bright. And my servants have both given notice. Most upsetting and annoying. Just as I had gathered enough material to start on my chapter dealing with the Diet of Worms. How can one concentrate—"

Jocelyn had not come with the intention of giving the vicar what is vulgarly called a piece of her mind. She had expected him to be humble, apologetic, but apparently he considered himself ill-used. All right, she thought. Let him have it.

"If you mean my brother's death, it wouldn't have happened if you'd looked after him properly. You deserve to lose all your pups. You've let them run wild. If you want to know what I think of your behaviour, Mr. Henshawe, I'll tell you. Absolutely rotten. So there!" she concluded, slightly out of breath.

The vicar was unused to criticism. If the parish murmured he had remained sublimely unaware of the fact. He had been for many years completely self-absorbed and self-satisfied. His book, a treatise on the Reformation, had been his only interest, and his pupils a disagreeable necessity. He considered that he had done his duty to them when he had given them two hours of coaching daily in his study. It was outrageous that this painted young woman should address him in such terms.

"I think you forget yourself." His pale eyes were bright with anger. "Abuse will not mend matters, but I will ignore it."

He rang the bell.

The cook answered it so promptly that she might almost have been listening at the door.

"Take this lady up to Lord Herbert's room. By all means take away anything that belonged to him, Lady Jocelyn. Good morning."

"Good morning," said Jocelyn. In the hall she turned to the cook. "You needn't take me up. I know the way. The vicar tells me you're leaving."

"Yes, m'lady, and not waiting to the end of my month neither. Me and Gladys are both going and Mr. Henshawe must manage the best he can. This house fair gives me the creeps since that happened. There was too many goings on before, what with the young gentlemen getting out at nights on the sly, and some of them tormenting the others what couldn't stand up to them, but we stuck it because there wasn't no missus to order us about or stop a girl from getting a breath of fresh air when her work's done. Thank you, my lady, I'm sure," she added, as half a crown changed hands. "Can I help you pack the poor young gentleman's clothes?"

"No, thanks."

Jocelyn met no one on the stairs or the landing. Once in the room that had been her brother's she locked herself in. It had been searched by the police and the contents of the drawers and the wardrobes had been piled on the bed, but his books were still on the shelves, and his photographs as he had arranged them on the mantelpiece.

Jocelyn looked about her. Was the key to the mystery of her brother's fearful end to be found within these four walls? The photographs included one of herself in a silver frame. The others were of young women highly decorative and entirely unknown to her. Two had sprawling signatures. Yours to a cinder, Dot and Ever Thine, Babs, but somehow she did not think that they had meant much to Bertie. She turned rather hopelessly to the folded suits, grey flannel, blue serge, brown tweed, evening suits, tennis flannels, silk underwear, socks and ties, rows of shoes. How could she get all those into the two suit-cases under the bed? There were the books, too, a small heap of battered textbooks and a larger heap of the cheap thrillers that had been poor Bertie's favourite reading. Jocelyn realised that she would have to leave them to be packed by someone else after all. That room with its closed windows and stripped bed appalled her. It was so commonplace with its fumed oak suite and flowered wall-paper; but the boy she had loved had suffered there the last extremity of fear, and the traces of his agony lingered and were impressed on her troubled mind.

Her cheeks were white under their rouge and her forehead was wet when she went out on to the landing. The house was still very silent, but she had heard the scraping of a chair and an occasional murmur of voices from the young men's sitting-room downstairs. Mr. Henshawe's three remaining pupils were there, Outram lounging on the window seat, Williams, who was sucking sweets, on the broken-springed sofa, and Thompson, who was trying to work, at the table. All three stood up as Jocelyn appeared in the doorway. They seemed more abashed than the occasion warranted. Outram reddened, Thompson's jaw dropped, and Williams' light lashes flickered. There was a moment of tense silence before Outram found his voice.

"I say—do come in, Lady Jocelyn. Won't you sit down? Williams, you lazy hound, shove that chair along."

"Thanks," she said, "but I can't stay. I just wanted to ask if you'd pack my brother's things and send them up to Berkeley Square for me. I was going to do it, but there's more than I expected. You'll need a packing case for some of the stuff. And I couldn't stand that room somehow." She sank into the chair they had brought forward for her and shut her eyes for a moment.

They stood staring at her small, vivid face, her sleek black curls and slender vibrant body in the emerald green skirt and jumper. It was like Jocelyn, with her defiance of all conventions, to wear green the day after her brother's funeral. The absence of mourning had shocked the vicar, but he was no judge of character. Thompson, with a queer abrupt gesture, had lumbered away to the window where he stood looking out at the overgrown shrubberies and the church tower beyond. Outram, standing his ground, met those reckless dark eyes when they opened suddenly and blazed at him.

"What happened to Bertie? I believe you all know."

Outram licked his lips. "Nothing more than came out at the inquest, Lady Jocelyn. We were all terribly sorry, weren't we, Thompson?"

"Terribly," Thompson agreed, without turning round.

Somehow their protestations rang false. Jocelyn pushed her hair back from her forehead in the tired fashion that was becoming habitual with her. These boys. They had been up to Crossways more than once with Bertie when she had brought a couple of girl friends down for week-ends. She had danced with all three. Her attitude had been one of good humoured contempt. They were slackers, wasters, or they would not have been at the vicarage trying to make up for lost time, and they were years younger than she was. She had dealt easily with their timid, clumsy attempts to make love to her. Now, somehow, the position was different. It was she who wanted something and they who refused. She felt their resistance under their apparent sympathy, like some solid obstruction, like a stone wall against which she might beat in vain.

"His room. It's overhead, isn't it? Over this one, I mean?"

"Partly over this and partly over the dining-room, I think."

"You heard me moving about just now?"

"Yes, but we thought it was one of the servants."

"You would have heard him that last night if he had been there?"

Outram glanced at Williams before he replied.

"We had the gramophone on. There was a lot of row. We'll pack his stuff for you, Lady Jocelyn."

Jocelyn, passionate, undisciplined, forgot discretion. "He wasn't there. I know more than you think and I'm going to know it all before I've done. I mean to make some people wish they'd never been born."

"That's O.K. with us, Lady Jocelyn," said Outram. "He was your brother, and he was our friend." His voice was as glib as ever but there was a queer patchy colour in his sallow face.

Jocelyn got up and left the room, slamming the door after her. She saw the cook lingering at the far end of the passage but she did not stop to speak to her. Two minutes later she was in her car again and driving up the lane to Crossways. She had the keys of the house and the garage. Mrs. Green had been up to the house before lunch and had opened the windows for an hour and lit the fire in the lounge. There were plenty of tinned provisions in the pantry. Jocelyn had nothing to do but put a kettle on the gas stove to boil for tea.

She was pouring out her second cup when Clowes walked in.

"Sorry I'm late," he said as he sat down by her on the settee which she had drawn close up to the fire. "I hadn't finished my round. Chilly, eh? That's not like you. Let me feel your pulse." Jocelyn glanced down at the strong fingers, stained yellow with nicotine, that held her wrist, and bit her lip hard. This man attracted her physically. She had let him make love to her before when she was engaged to Maurice. Why should she hesitate now that she was free? He could make her forget for an hour or two at least. But afterwards? Jocelyn was not in the habit of denying herself anything, but the events of the last few days had shaken her. The glittering surface had cracked and something that had been hidden beneath was struggling to emerge. He was drawing her to him but she resisted.

"Don't!" she said irritably.

"Why not?"

"I'm not in the mood. That will do. The caveman business doesn't go down with me."

"Oh, all right." He made an obvious effort to keep his temper. "Why am I here then?"

She lit a cigarette, noticing as she did so that her hands were shaking. "I suppose I deserve that after the way I let you behave last time."

"Darling, please don't be offended. If you knew how I've been longing to be with you again like this. Can't you be nice to me? I know you've had a hell of a time and I want to make it up to you. What made you go to the vicarage?"

"I went to get Bertie's things—partly. You attended him these last few weeks and you saw him—afterwards. I suppose there's no doubt in your mind? It was a clear case of suicide?"

His face changed slightly. "None. What do you mean exactly?"

"Well, the police don't seem quite sure about it."

"Don't they? They seemed quite satisfied at the inquest as far as I could see."

"There was nothing definite," she said eagerly, "nothing that could be called evidence, but a detective from Scotland Yard came to see us afterwards."

"Really? And what did he say?"

"Well, he was very hush-hush. I promised not to repeat anything."

"Quite right, of course," said Clowes, smiling, "though I don't suppose he would tell you anything that mattered. Those chaps know how to keep their own counsel. Frankly, I can't imagine what they're driving at, and I'm sorry if it means raking it all up and distressing you."

"Never mind me. If Bertie was murdered I want whoever did it to be punished."

He stared at her, startled and incredulous. "Murdered? What mare's nest have they got hold of? The thing's impossible. Who could have done it, and how?"

"I don't know," she said faintly. "I suppose one alone couldn't but if there were several against him—I've read of lynchings—" She covered her face with her hands. "Bertie—" she said indistinctly. "It's too horrible!"

He put an arm about her and this time she did not resist.

"It sounds fantastic to me," he said. "I can't believe it, but I presume they've something to go upon. Suppose you tell me all about it."

She fumbled for her handkerchief. "Oh dear—I can't do that. The Inspector only told me bits. He said that since Bertie came to the vicarage he had joined a gang of dope smugglers and that probably some of the other boys belonged to it too. He thinks that lately they have become involved in something more serious. I gathered that it was a jewel robbery and that somebody had been killed, and that Bertie had got frightened and wanted to back out, and so he—" She caught her breath. "And so, to avoid exposure, they killed him. That's what the Inspector thinks."

"It sounds highly improbable to me," said Clowes. "I know all those boys, you see. I was at the vicarage this afternoon just before I came along here. Williams has a whitlow and I have to dress it. They're young rotters, I admit, but they're quite incapable of organised crime. They haven't the necessary brains."

"The Inspector thinks they are led by an older man and simply carry out his orders."

"Not the poor old vicar, I hope."

"There's nothing to laugh at," said Jocelyn indignantly.

"I'm not laughing," he said, "it's no laughing matter, God knows. Your Inspector ought to leave the force and take to writing thrillers. Seriously, Jocelyn, does he suspect anyone in particular?"

"I don't know," she said doubtfully. "He said it must be some-one who is familiar with this neighbourhood and who either owns or has the use of a powerful car. Then he got quite excited. He said—it's haunted me ever since—he said—"Think of a brain with-out a heart, a keen, cold, cunning brain whose motives are the love of power and the greed of gain. If a black mamba were loose in Sussex woods it wouldn't be more dangerous."

"I didn't know policemen went in for metaphor and hyper-bole," said Clowes. "I'd like to kick the fellow for upsetting you like this. What the hell does he mean by being so eloquent? Darling, you don't really believe this absurd story, do you?"

"You're as bad as father," she said.

"So he didn't convince Lord Bember?"

Jocelyn sat up, took a mirror from her bag and began to dab at her nose with a powder puff. "Father's a politician. They're frightfully good at not believing what they don't want to believe. He's been ashamed of Bertie for years because the poor boy was weak and silly and funked things, and now he wants to forget him. Father doesn't count in this, but I do. I thought perhaps you might help me. I'm all alone."

"My dear," he said, in a moved voice, "I'll do what I can. But—what about your fiancé, Mr. Kafka?"

She was silent for a moment. Then she said in a hard voice, "That's over. I broke it off last night."

"I see."

There was a pause. Jocelyn lit another cigarette and smoked feverishly. She glanced now and again at her companion's face. He was staring thoughtfully at the fire. At last he said in a low voice, "He's been down here pretty often to see your brother. He was here—that night. He didn't arrive until after the tragedy though. At least, he said he had a breakdown—"

She turned on him. "You needn't go on. I've been through all that. It's—it's possible, but I can't believe it."

"My dear child," he said, "you were peeved with me when I pooh-poohed the whole thing and now, when I try to make a guess at this super-criminal you bite my head off. I must say you're hard to please."

"I'm sorry," she said. "I know I'm irritable, but my head's aching rather badly. I couldn't sleep last night."

"I could see that when I met you in the village," he said, "And I've brought something along that will give you the rest you need."

"Thank you. You're good to me, and I'm a little beast, and I shall never be different. I'm like the Inspector's black mamba. I haven't got a heart."

"May I kiss you before I go?"

"If you like," she said wearily. Her lips were cold, her body rigid as wood in his arms.

"Wait a minute," he said. He went into the kitchen and came back with a little grey fluid in a glass. She was sitting where he had left her on the settee. She drank obediently.

"Now go to sleep." He arranged the cushions under her head and covered her feet with a rug. "Good-bye, Jocelyn."

She answered drowsily, "Good-bye."

Already her tired eyelids were closing. He put another log on the fire and made some other arrangements. Then he left the house, closing the doors very carefully so as not to disturb her, and, mounting his shabby bicycle, rode away.

Chapter XXII
MATERIAL EVIDENCE

MARTIN had just come in and was in the library with his brother when the housekeeper, slightly flustered by all these comings and goings, announced "The gentleman who was here before, and another gentleman," and ushered in Inspector Collier and Sergeant Duffield.

Collier introduced his companion.

"We've come down to see what more we can pick up at this end, Colonel Drury. As regards the rifling of the shop in Elmer Passage and the disappearance of old Borlase we're practically certain that the gang young Vaste belonged to arrived on the scene when the job had been done. They'd planned their coup for the same day as the others. It was a good day because it was early closing and the char left at noon and wouldn't be back before Friday morning. Vaste's crowd had inveigled the daughter away, probably by offering to sell old books or furniture at the house where she was to be detained, and, incidentally, saved her life. The Russian crowd wouldn't have spared her if they'd found her on the premises and she'd made any resistance."

"You are sure the others were Russians?" asked Stephen.

He had raised himself on his cushions to listen. There was a tinge of colour in his hollow cheeks.

"Well, there was a tramp steamer from Odessa at the adjoining wharf at the time, unloading her cargo of timber. Her papers were in order, but she carried an unusually large crew, and she cleared off in a hurry a week after Borlase disappeared. The wharf adjoins the derelict yard at the river end of Elmer Passage. The river police did some dredging for us thereabouts and brought some broken bits of furniture and torn strips of black and white linoleum up from the mud. The linoleum was stained and the stains have been analysed and tested and are undoubtedly blood stains. The old man's body hasn't been found and I doubt if it ever will be. It's either gone out to sea with the tide, or they've taken it with them to drop overboard when they get far enough out."

"Poor little Anne," said Martin. "I wonder if they found the jewels somewhere about the place. It's possible that Anne's aunt hid them before she died."

"The Eye of Nero," murmured Stephen. He was lying back now, his own eyes closed. Collier glanced at him rather doubtfully before he spoke.

"The trouble is that without a body we can't prove a murder. Or at any rate some fragments of a body. And we're not concerned officially with the whereabouts of the jewels."

"Aren't you?" said Stephen. "They were the *fons et origo mali*. The emerald. Whatever possessed the Tsarina, poor soul, to choose that accursed stone to be part of her daughters' dowry? It had a name for ill luck. Loathsome thing."

"You've seen it, Colonel Drury?"

"Once, at the last Court ball before I left Russia. The Tsarina was wearing it as a pendant. It's magnificent, of course. Like green fire. It must have been re-cut since Nero had it. Did it magnify then, or reflect"—he spoke half to himself. It was apparent that he lived more in the past than the present. Sergeant Duffield cleared his throat. In his opinion they were wasting time.

"It's queer," said Collier thoughtfully, "they're just bright bits of glass to me, apart from their market value: but some people have a passion for them. Well, I won't deny that they've a bearing on our case, but our job is to find the man who took Anne Borlase up to the quarry and left her. If we can get him the Eye of Nero may be at the bottom of the sea for all I care." He looked at his watch. "We're going on to Clumber Place for a little game of Hunt the Thimble. Would you care to come with us, Martin? Can you spare him, Colonel?"

"Of course," said Stephen.

"Clumber Place?" said Martin. "How will you get to it?"

"Through the village I suppose. There's no other way, is there?"

"I was an ass not to think of it before," said Martin eagerly; "the park adjoins the end of our garden. It's a mile or more from the house and very overgrown—"

"But we could cut across from here and no one would be any the wiser? A good idea. Is it a high wall?"

Martin nodded. "Ten feet or so. But you won't have to climb. There's a communicating door. It hasn't been used, of course, for donkey's years. I didn't even know of its existence until yesterday when I was trimming the shrubs. It's right behind a clump of elder and hazel bushes. We've always left the end of the garden wild and we weren't even allowed to play there as children because there's an old disused well somewhere about and they were afraid we should fall in, weren't they, Stephen?"

"Yes," said Stephen. "I did know about the door, I think, though I'd forgotten it. I fancy it must have been put there nearly a hundred years ago when the Leeson who had Clumber Place in those days married a Drury. But it's boarded up, I fancy, and it would take you some time to break it down."

"Never mind," said Collier. "No need to damage the property. I don't think we shall find a ten foot wall an insurmountable barrier. Good-bye for the present, Colonel."

They went out by the french window opening on the lawn. Mac followed them half way down the garden, snuffling with excitement, and then, hearing his master's whistle, turned obediently and trotted back to the house.

"I've got a step ladder," said Martin. "It's out in the field. I've been giving the roof of the shed a coat of solignum. I'll fetch it."

He ran off. Collier turned rather quickly to his subordinate.

"We'll have a look at this door in the wall."

They forced their way through a mass of bushes.

"Some of these branches have been broken down lately," said Duffield.

"That was Martin probably. Must have been," said Collier rather absently. He was examining the door. It was lichened and moss grown but there were no boards nailed across it, and when he looked closer he saw that the lock and the hinges bore traces of recent oiling. His eyes met Duffield's.

"Let's get out of this," he said. When they had regained the path he added, "Not a word of this before young Martin. Here he comes."

Martin came hurrying up to them with the ladder. "Sorry to keep you waiting," he panted. "Chickens are such asses. They thought I'd come to give them their feed and it took me ages to shoo them back into the run."

With the aid of the ladder they got over the wall easily enough and dropped into the undergrowth on the other side. A few feet away from the wall the ground was clear though rotten with beech mast, and they struck through the belt of beeches whose smooth grey trunks soared grandly up into the sky, in the direction of the house.

"It's over there," said Martin, pointing, "but you won't see it until we get nearer."

"You've been this way before, Martin?"

"No. But I know the lie of the land. It's densely wooded. What are we looking for here, Collier?"

"I hardly know. But when I searched the house before it was after dark and I had only my electric torch. There may be something"—he was purposely vague and Martin, seeing that he was unwilling to talk, said no more.

They approached the house from the back and crossed a grass-grown stable-yard flanked by a row of loose boxes and a large coach-house to the kitchen entrance.

"There's one odd thing about this place," said Collier as they stood by while Sergeant Duffield manipulated the lock. "I've circularised the principal house and estate agents and not one of them has got it on their books. They had it formerly but it was taken off two years ago. They understood that it had been sold by private treaty. The former owner has died since and we haven't succeeded in tracing the present one. However, we're acting legally. I've got a search warrant." The door swung open and they passed into the dark cold stone-paved scullery.

"Duffield, you can do the servants' quarters and report to me," said Collier. "I'm going upstairs. You'd better come with me, Martin."

Collier began by opening all the shutters in the ground floor rooms. The light of day revealed traces of occupation. They found the scattered straw and a brown army blanket behind the pile of empty packing cases in the room in which Anne had been imprisoned two weeks before, with a biscuit tin still containing two or three biscuits, a cup, and a broken thermos flask. In the adjoining room the dusty boards were littered with cigarette ends and matches. Martin was given the job of picking them up while Collier, who had been carrying what looked like a despatch case, produced the necessary paraphernalia for photographing fingerprints. He had been careful not to touch any doorknobs, turning them with a pair of pincers.

"You've got all the cigarette ends? Good. Put them in this box." He peered at the draggled collection for a moment.

"Very interesting. At least three different brands. Look at this only half smoked, chewed up and thrown away. And this. Nerves. Very significant. Well, Duffield?"

The Sergeant seemed excited. "This used to be an asylum, didn't it, Inspector?"

Collier looked at Martin, who nodded. "I believe it was called a home of mental cases. There was some scandal about the death of one of the patients. It was hushed up, but the place was closed down soon after. It was a long time ago."

"If you'll come down to the basement I'll show you something."

They followed him down the dark service stairs and he showed them a door in the long passage leading to the back entrance. "The pantries, servants' hall, and wine and coal cellars are all on the left. On the right there was only this one door and it's concealed in the pitch pine panelling so that you would hardly notice it. It opens with a spring. Quite simple really."

"Duffield was in an architect's office before he joined the police," said Collier. "What's this?"

As the door opened they peered into the rayless gloom within.

"No windows. No communication with the outside world. You have your torch, Duffield?"

Collier switched on his own. The white ray travelled slowly over the walls. They appeared to be hung with some greyish striped material with a bulging, uneven surface. Much of it was torn, eaten by rats and riddled by moth and hanging in fragments.

"Mattresses," said Collier, "the padded room. But," his voice betrayed his disappointment, "look at the dust on the floor. It would show every footprint. The fellows we're after didn't know about this bolt hole. Just as well. They'd have made some devilish use of it. That stuff on the walls would deaden all sounds. Come along, Duffield. We'll try upstairs."

"Rather a set back?" ventured Martin. He had expected he knew not what from their discovery of the hidden room.

Duffield, he noticed, seemed cast down, but Collier was more philosophic.

"Bound to get a few," he said. "I'm not really worrying now that the girl's safe. We'll get our friend, Mr. X, sooner or later, and his accomplices. He must know we're on his tracks and his only chance is to do nothing to attract our attention."

"You really think that?" said Martin rather uncertainly. "I fancied from what you said you feared he might do something to Anne Borlase."

"He won't get the chance," Collier's tone was confident, "the matron's been warned, and I've got two men from the Yard watching the nursing home. No unauthorised visitors admitted. Now we won't talk for a bit, if you don't mind."

He had examined the tessellated pavement of the hall. As he stood looking up the well of the stairs his lean face was unusually grim. He drew Duffield's attention to some long smears on the dusty floor.

"Something heavy has been dragged along here."

They went up as far as the first landing. Collier examined the banisters and uttered an exclamation.

"Look here! All the dust has been rubbed off the stair rail. And here—" He stooped and picked up what appeared to be a small fragment of fibre. "Someone sawed through the rope here. The knife slipped and scored the wood of the banister. No finger-prints, I fear, but we'll powder this surface and use my last two plates."

Martin stood by while the two detectives got on with their work. Their footsteps echoed with a hollow sound through the empty house. Collier turned to him before long.

"We've got as much as we can expect in the way of information from Clumber Place. More. I've got a very clear print of two fingers and a thumb on this stair rail. It's lucky I had a plate left. I think they will prove to be those of Lord Herbert Vaste."

"Young Vaste? Good Heavens! But—"

"That tableau in the church tower was camouflage. The overturned chair and all the rest of it. You told me that yourself."

"I?"

"You and Loftus both said the body was cold though the lanthorn in the vestry was still hot. You didn't go on to draw the obvious conclusion. Vaste died elsewhere, and his body was carried to the church. A darned risky business, but it would not have suited the gang to have him found here in what had been their headquarters. He probably came here unknown to the others, hoping to rescue the girl, and was caught in the act. Come along. We've done all we can here."

They followed him silently, and all three breathed more freely when they were outside. Martin, especially, was white under his tan.

"He was terrified when he spoke to me at the study window the night before. Poor chap. I wish I could have done more for him. I—I don't like to think of what he must have gone through before he ended it. If only he had told me who the man he called the chief was!"

"Yes," said Duffield, "it's a pity the poor young chap didn't spill a bit more while he was about it. Though you mightn't be here now, Mr. Drury, if he had."

"Do you mean that we were overheard?"

"I think it very likely. Luckily for you he hadn't said enough to make you very dangerous. The invitation to supper at the vicarage was meant to keep you where they'd know what you were doing. Very clever, but they didn't know I was on the case too. That's where they slipped up. It's the old story. Piling one crime on the top of another to hide the first. You'll want to be getting back to the Dower House, Martin, I suppose?"

"Well, it's about time the birds were fed, but if there's anything I can do—"

"Nothing more at present," said Collier. "I've got to do some telephoning, and you're not on the telephone, worse luck. I may look in later in the day. You'll be about?"

"Yes. May I tell Stephen what you've found this morning?"

They had returned across the park by the way they had come. They climbed the wall that divided the park from the Dower House garden without much difficulty, though the ladder had been left on the other side. Collier and his companion got into their car, which they had left in the drive, while Martin went in to his brother.

"Where shall you phone from, Inspector?"

"The nearest A.A. box. It's only a couple of miles away. Well, Duffield, out with it."

Sergeant Duffield glanced from the lean brown hands grasping the steering wheel to the rather set face of his superior officer.

"The Drurys are friends of yours."

"Well—I knew Colonel Drury when the war was on. We were in the same battalion for a while. I hadn't seen him or heard of him since until I came down here in connection with this case. I hadn't met the boy, Martin, before. But they're all right, Duffield."

"The younger one seems straight enough," said Duffield slowly, "but I'm not so sure about the Colonel. He didn't want us to take that short cut to Clumber Place. That door's been used lately. Who oiled the hinges and the lock?"

"Not Stephen Drury. The poor devil can't move a yard without crutches."

"Are you sure of that, Inspector?"

Collier turned to stare at his subordinate and nearly ran the car into the ditch. Duffield gasped. "For God's sake mind your steering! I'm applying one of your own rules. Take nothing for granted."

"All right," said Collier. "Go on talking. I'll listen."

Thus encouraged Duffield resumed. "Well, of course he looks magnificent lying there like a crusader on a cathedral tomb, but I couldn't help thinking you couldn't have a better bit of camouflage than a reputation for helpless invalidism. Mind you, I'm not suggesting that he's just an ordinary crook. With him it might even be that queer passion for precious stones you were talking of. I thought I noticed a glint in his eye. He said he hated that emerald. But—who knows—"

"Rot!" said Collier. "Why, it was they who called in the Yard. If we round up the gang it will be thanks to them. I'll admit that door in the wall is worrying me a bit, but not because I imagine they're privy to it. Here we are."

He drew up by the roadside and entered the telephone box.

Duffield remained in the car. Two fields away a team of horses was ploughing. Steam rose from the horses' flanks and there was a flash of white wings as the gulls rose and came back to the freshly turned furrow. Beyond the sere autumn woods rose the long line of the Downs. Two or three cars passed, but the two C.I.D. men were in mufti, and no one noticed them.

Collier came out of the box with the air of a man in a hurry, ran across the road and sprang into the driving seat.

"What's the time? Getting on for one? Sorry, but we've not time for lunch. I made my report to the Yard and they put me on to Chief-Inspector Cardew. He says Kafka rang up an hour ago from the old man's place in Regent's Park and wants to see me if I'll call as soon as possible. Sounds as if he meant to come clean. We'll see him first."

"You think Maurice Kafka knows more than he's told the police?"

"I think it highly probable. Why do we live in a country where one has to be so damn civil to unconvicted murderers, Duff, my boy? A spot of third degree is indicated, but it's not to be thought of. If we laid a hand on the ingenious Mr. X, save in the way of kindness, we should be hounded out of the Force."

"Unless he resists when we arrest the bloke," said Duffield soothingly. "You can knock him out then, you know."

"Let's hope I get a chance," said Collier, swerving to avoid a kitten that had run out of a cottage gate. "When I think of the way that wretched boy was hounded to his end, and the death he had devised for the girl—for sheer callousness this chap would be hard to beat. I've got to catch him," he said, half to himself.

"You may catch him indirectly, through the dope smuggling."

"I believe they've cut that out since they got into this mess."

Soon after half-past two they reached their destination, and were shown by the ex-prize fighter butler into the waiting-room with its immovable furniture and its Flemish burgher. After Rubens, or, as its present owner maintained, by Rubens over the mantelpiece. Collier, looking up at that broad countenance, with its innumerable wrinkles and deep-set, brilliant black eyes, thought he saw a likeness to the great art dealer himself. The door opened as the thought passed through his mind and old Kafka waddled in and took his place at his writing table.

"Good afternoon, gentlemen."

"Good afternoon, sir." Collier hesitated. He had assumed that it was Maurice who had wanted to see him. Had he been mistaken?

Israel Kafka enlightened him.

"That other"—he pointed a stubby finger—"that is another policeman, eh?"

"My colleague and assistant. Sergeant Duffield."

Kafka sat for a moment, staring at the green malachite inkstand on his table. He was yellower than ever and the pouches under his eyes more noticeable, and his great bulk sagged in the chair as if the spirit that informed it were weary of its task.

"I've had a bad night," he said. "A bad night. You think of things lying awake. Reputation. Reputation. I've built up my business honestly, Inspector. I've never played a dirty trick. I've never forgiven the man who tried to play a dirty trick on me. A good many have tried, but not many have succeeded. A Jew may be straight or he may be crooked, but he's very seldom a fool. Are you one of those who despise my race, Inspector? Do you talk of dirty Jews?"

"No, sir," and there was no mistaking Collier's sincerity. "I have friends—and one a very dear friend—of your nation."

Kafka smiled for the first time. "That is good. Then you are not prejudiced. When you were here yesterday I did not tell you all I knew. I dreaded the thought of being involved in some unpleasantness, and especially for the sake of my son Maurice. My son is a very fine young man, Inspector. I can remember as a little boy running barefoot in the dark alleys of the ghetto at Prague where I was born; but he is different. I sent him to a good school and then to Oxford. He will go far"—he checked himself—"but that is not what you have come to hear, eh? I must tell you then that a fortnight ago I received through the post a typewritten communication with a small cardboard box containing four very fine diamonds packed in a dirty bit of cotton wool. The letter, which was signed J.B. informed me that the writer was obliged to go abroad at a moment's notice after getting rid of most of the contents of his second-hand book and furniture shop in Elmer Passage. He asked me, as a favour, to re-stock the premises and carry on the business during his absence, to give no information to the police regarding him if they made enquiries, to keep what sum I thought fair to pay myself and hold the rest for him to be sent on later. I got a friend of mine who is a diamond merchant of Hatton Garden to value the stones. Four hundred and sixty pounds. I sent a plain van down that night with some stuff I had by me and put one of my employees, a young man I could trust, in charge. But I changed my mind about keeping the shop open, and it has been closed since that day. I did not see that it would help Borlase to run it at a loss."

"Why didn't you tell me all this yesterday, Mr. Kafka?"

"Borlase had asked me to keep the thing quiet. I did not care for the transaction. I did what he asked me."

"Was Borlase a friend of yours?"

"No. I knew him by sight, that is all. I have seen him formerly attending sales. Latterly his daughter came instead of him. It was for her sake that I was willing to do him a favour, Inspector, for that little bird, hopping about so bravely to pick up the crumbs. We talk always when we meet. She is not afraid of old Kafka." He chuckled at the recollection, and then grew grave again. "You must not blame her for anything. If there was anything crooked about their business she didn't know it."

"Why did you change your mind about informing the police. Mr. Kafka?"

"Will you have a cigar. Inspector?"

"No, thank you."

"I will." They had to wait until the cigar was lit and drawing well before he resumed. "After you had left me I thought over what you had said. I began to wish I had kept Borlase's letter."

"You didn't?"

"No. I destroyed it."

"That is a pity."

"It was typewritten and signed only with his initials. J.B. I asked myself if I had been deceived. It was certainly strange that Borlase, a man of hitherto excellent character, should disappear with his daughter. Those diamonds, too. He had never, so far as I knew, dealt in jewels. His business was small and far from prosperous. Where would he get the capital to purchase diamonds?"

"What sort of state was the shop in when your representative took over?"

Kafka touched an electric bell. After a moment the butler answered it.

"Ask Mr. Simons to come here."

Mr. Simons proved to be a sleek and well-groomed youth whom Collier had seen in the shop in Elmer Passage when he called there with Martin; proof, if he had needed proof, of the truth of Kafka's story. He looked at his employer, after one swift glance at the two men from the Yard.

Kafka's smile was reassuring. "You will answer any questions these gentlemen put to you, Simons, without reserve."

"Very good, sir."

But Simons was not able to add greatly to the sum of Collier's knowledge. He had taken a small vanload of stock from the Balham branch of Kafka's Stores and had found the shop all but cleared. He was not favourably impressed. The premises were dark, low pitched, very unsuited to modern requirements. They struck cold and damp. Yes, the floor and the walls had been recently washed and were hardly dry. There was no covering on the floor. As he had received no instructions he did not attempt to enter the back premises and the door leading to the stairs was locked.

"How did you get in?"

Kafka answered that. "The key of the shop-door was enclosed in the letter I told you of, Inspector. Is there anything further?"

"Nothing."

When Simons had left them Kafka looked enquiringly at Collier.

"And now will you satisfy my curiosity? Have you any news of Borlase and his daughter?"

Collier had been thinking hard. "You have an international reputation, Mr. Kafka?"

"Among art dealers and connoisseurs, certainly."

"You mentioned Prague just now. You have relatives and friends still in that city?"

"Cousins. Yes."

"And in Russia?"

"My wife came from Odessa. I have relatives by marriage there also. What has that to do with this matter. Inspector?"

Collier hesitated. Kafka had answered calmly and without any apparent reluctance. Yet he had been conscious that Duffield sitting by him had stiffened to attention.

"Have you ever been in Russia, Mr. Kafka?"

"Not for thirty years, but Maurice was there in the Spring. Why?"

"Do you know anything of the tramp steamer *Sonia*, flying the Soviet flag, and sailing from Odessa, who landed a cargo of timber at the Candlin Steps Wharf a month ago and left under ballast the day you took over the shop in Elmer Passage?"

"No," said Kafka.

"But those on board—the captain of that ship—might know of you?"

Kafka rubbed out the end of his cigar on the ash tray.

"That is possible."

Collier leaned forward. "That letter must have been written by someone who knew you."

Kafka's eyes, black and glittering as jet beads under their wrinkled lids, met his steadily.

"In my business, Inspector, one meets all kinds of people. I assumed that the letter came from Borlase. Why should another write as though from him and ask me to reopen his shop? Tell me that?"

"To gain time, Mr. Kafka, and to divert suspicion." Collier glanced at his watch. "Is that all you have to tell me?"

"Certainly. I hope no harm has come to Borlase and his daughter, Inspector? As I have told you I have regard for that young lady."

"I am much obliged to you," said Collier, ignoring the question. "Might I have a word with Mr. Maurice Kafka now?"

The dealer's manner changed and became more distant.

"My son is not here."

"Not here? Where is he?"

"I cannot say. He has his own friends. He comes and goes as he pleases here. In any case he could not assist you. I have not discussed this matter with him."

"Quite. But I've got to see him."

Kafka's big hands, distorted by arthritis, clutched the arms of his chair. He was like an old lion, thought Collier, fighting for his young, teeth and claws bared.

"I have nothing more to say to you. I must remind you that I sent for you and volunteered all the information at my disposal. If it is the diamonds you want I will give them to you if you will sign a receipt, eh? Yes"—as he saw Collier's lips twitch—"I am a Jew—I will not be cheated even by the police."

"I don't want the stones," said Collier patiently. "Later, perhaps. At present I want a word or two with your son."

"And I repeat that he cannot help you."

"I am the best judge of that."

"I will not have my Maurice dragged into this dirty business." Kafka rang the bell.

"Show these gentlemen out, Abe."

"And that's that," said Collier, when they were outside and the ex-pugilist butler had bolted the gate after them.

"We'd better go on to the Yard now. I've got to report to the Chief, and we can have those plates you took developed."

Chapter XXIII
COLLIER IS WARNED

On his return from Clumber Place Martin had gone straight to the library and told his brother all that there was to tell. Stephen listened without comment, and when he had done lay for a while silent.

"It comes to this," he said at last, "Clumber Place has been the meeting place and headquarters of a gang of dope smugglers. By some chance they got inside information about the Eye of Nero and the diamonds. They brought Anne Borlase to Clumber Place to get her out of the way. Another crowd got in before them at the other end, and the girl was left on their hands. The rest followed automatically. Well, not quite that. Mr. X is ingenious, Martin." He raised himself a little on his pillows. "I wonder if he knows that his second attempt to eliminate her failed? I wonder that very much."

Martin moved uneasily. "Collier's done his best to keep that business at the quarry quiet. The major and his daughter won't talk, and in the village they don't know of Anne's existence. And he's having the nursing home watched. He warned me not to go near the place in case I was followed."

"He can't be too careful," said Stephen. "Third time lucky. Mr. X might succeed—the third time."

Martin pushed his hair back from his forehead with a nervous gesture. "Don't! You sound so cold-blooded. When I think of that poor kid—it's queer. I only saw her that one afternoon she came here, but I feel I know her quite well. I think of her as Anne. I suppose it's because she's been in our minds so much ever since that day."

"You and Collier took her straight to this nursing home. Where is it exactly?"

"It's a house called St. Amory's on the London road, just outside Horsham. Collier's got two men watching it. He told me he'd taken every possible precaution."

"He'd better. Without her his case, such as it is, falls to pieces. Suppose these finger-prints he's found on the banisters are Bertie Vaste's? It proves he was there some time or other, but—what's that?"

"What? I didn't hear anything."

Mac had jumped down from the couch where he had been laying curled up at his master's feet, and rushed across to the french window. The October days were growing chilly and Martin had closed it when he came in.

He had to raise his voice now to make himself heard for Mac was barking excitedly.

"Shall I let the little beggar out?"

"No, I don't think so. If there was anyone—I can't have anything happening to Mac. Shut up Mac. That noise is no use." The terrier, foiled of his hoped-for rush down the garden to hunt for possible intruders, came back, grumbling, jumped up to his accustomed place and composed himself to sleep.

"It can't have been anything or he wouldn't have settled down again so soon," said Martin. "I'll get a spot of lunch and carry on with making those new coops."

He spent the rest of the afternoon working in the field and came back to the house at five for tea. Mrs. Clapp was just taking it into the library. Martin followed her, with Mac at his heels, snuffling importantly, his muzzle smeared with mud. His master eyed him tolerantly. "You old scoundrel, you've been digging up last week's bone. It's the night for his bath, isn't it Mrs. Clapp? "

"Yes, sir. You come along of me now, Mac."

She pulled him out from under the armchair where he had taken refuge and carried him off.

Martin poured out the tea and carried a cup over to his brother. He was wondering, not for the first time, what would happen when Mac died. Stephen's hold on life was so slight. There was so little left to him. He would miss Mac badly himself, if it came to that.

Stephen glanced up at him. "What's the matter?"

"Nothing."

The door bell rang and they heard Mrs. Clapp's and a man's voice in the hall. A moment later Collier walked in.

"Just in time for a cup of tea." He helped himself to bread and butter. "I've been up to town and back since I last saw you, Martin. I come from Bury now. Kafka's married sister has a weekend cottage there. She's abroad and has left a married couple in charge. Maurice Kafka came down to-day, but somebody rang him up about three o'clock and he went off again. I think it's just possible that he may go to Carysford Aerodrome where Outram's brother is a pilot. Duffield's gone to see. That's why I'm alone."

"Did you do any good in Town?" asked Stephen.

"Not much," said Collier, with his mouth full.

"You think young Kafka knows more than he has admitted?"

"I missed my lunch," said Collier. "I'm as empty as a drum. I'll have another slice of that excellent cake. My day's work isn't over. I'm going down to the vicarage next. It's time Mr. Henshawe's promising pupils were put through it. Then I'm due at the nursing-home between nine and ten. I promised I wouldn't be later. They seem to think the girl may recover consciousness before long."

"May I come with you?" asked Martin.

Collier eyed him thoughtfully. "It's not a bad idea. She knows you. She'd be more likely to speak than if she found herself among complete strangers. All right. I'll call for you on my way. I don't know, though," he hesitated, "that means leaving the Colonel alone here with your housekeeper."

The invalid, who had been lying with closed eyes listening to their conversation, opened them wide.

"You're not suggesting that I am in any danger?"

"How can I tell? You may be."

"Gad! That's refreshing. But why?"

"This crowd that has been after the jewels probably knows that if they reached England safely they were to be consigned to your keeping. They had reason to believe that they never came into your possession—but they can't be sure of that. Anne Borlase came down here to see you. She only brought a letter—but would they believe that if they were told it? The jewels may have been found, in which case you are perfectly safe and the gang will be concentrating their attention on the girl."

"They may be thinking she's safe too—in the quarry," said Stephen grimly.

"They may—but I daren't bank on that. As to you—you've done what I asked a few days ago, I hope, barred all the window shutters at nightfall, and bolted the doors. You're isolated here, half a mile or more from the nearest house, and shut in by woods. Anything might happen. And that reminds me. I looked at that door in the wall at the bottom of your back garden this morning. It's been used recently. The lock and the hinges have been oiled."

Martin stared at him. "Great Scott! Why didn't you say so at the time? But by whom? We haven't got a key, have we, Stephen? Hadn't I better nail a couple of boards across?"

"I thought of that," said Collier reluctantly, "perhaps, for your own safety, it would be advisable."

"But you'd rather we didn't," said Stephen quickly. "It might put somebody on his guard against us, eh?"

"That was rather my idea," Collier admitted. "I wouldn't take the risk if you hadn't such serviceable shutters to all your windows. You could stand a siege."

"They were made and fitted by the village carpenter in my grandmother's time," said Stephen. "She was a typical early Victorian female, all swoons and sensibility, and she was terrified of burglars. Don't worry about me, Collier. I rely on you to fetch Martin this evening. Mac and I will take care of ourselves."

"Good. Then I'll buzz along. I'll help with the window fastenings now, Martin, before I go. It's getting dark."

Collier drove slowly down the road towards the village. It had begun to rain and the dense undergrowth that bordered the track looked sodden and uninviting. The man from the Yard, who normally was fond of the country, found himself wishing for the cheerful glow of lighted shop fronts and glittering sky signs. Though he had done his best to conceal the fact from the Drurys he was depressed. When he had reported to his superiors at the Yard after his interview with old Kafka he had received very little encouragement.

Cardew had tapped on his desk impatiently with the end of his pencil, always a bad sign with him.

"You've got a lot of men on this case now, Collier, watching the ports and so forth, and what does it amount to? In your place I would drop your attempts to prove that young Vaste's suicide was anything more than an ordinary case of neurasthenia. And I'm inclined to think that Kafka's story has cleared up the mystery of Borlase's disappearance. In a word, he's bolted with the jewels. Shady, if you like, but there doesn't seem to be any legal owner to claim them. That leaves you the girl. You're on firmer ground there. A clear case of attempted homicide. Concentrate on that and never mind the rest."

Collier knew better than to argue when those above him were in this mood. He answered woodenly "Yes, sir. Thank you, sir," and turned to leave the room.

Cardew had stopped him. "One moment. Look here, Inspector. We have to do our duty regardless of parties, but there's no point in antagonising such men as Lord Bember and old Kafka. Any scandal involving them or anyone belonging to them would make a very unpleasant impression abroad. Sir James was saying that again only this morning."

Collier had paused with his hand on the doorknob. "Would you mind putting that a little more plainly, sir? I mean, am I to understand that this case will be dropped if their names can't be left out of it? "

"Certainly not. That would be entirely contrary to the high character and traditions of our department. But if we make a mistake, if, after creating a scandal, we did not secure a conviction, we'd be done for, Collier. Absolutely. You and I, and probably Sir James too. So for God's sake don't move in a hurry and until you're dead sure."

Collier did not make a fetish of his career, but he had worked hard in the past and had risen to his present position in the C.I.D. at an unusually early age, and he was looking forward to further promotion. Cardew's warning had startled him.

It is to his credit that it did not deflect him for an instant from pursuing what he conceived to be the path of duty. But, naturally, he was worried.

He had not realised when the game began that the stakes would be so high. He reflected, with a grim smile, that his opponents were probably in the same case. Well, it would have to be played to a finish now.

The vicarage gate stood open and he drove his car in and left it in the drive.

The door was opened by a stout, dark youth in a soiled Fair Isle pull-over who stared at him inimically.

"What do you want? The vicar's out."

"When will he be back?"

"Not until to-morrow. He's gone to a Diocesan meeting. You'd better call again if you want to see him." He was closing the door when Collier inserted his foot.

"Your name's Thompson, isn't it?"

"What of it? I don't know you."

"I am Inspector Collier of New Scotland Yard. I'd be glad of a little chat with you, Mr. Thompson, if you'll open the door a little wider. Thank you."

He entered the hall. "Why didn't one of the servants answer the door?"

"They've both left."

"So you have to wait on yourselves? Very trying. I almost wonder your parents and guardians leave you here," said Collier conversationally as he followed Thompson into the shabby dining-room.

"My people are in India."

"I see. Where are the other two, Outram and Williams?"

"Williams is up in his room. He's got a bad hand, a whitlow. I don't know where Outram is. I'm not his keeper."

"Don't take that tone with me," said Collier sharply.

"All right," said Thompson sulkily. "He may have gone for a walk. What about it?"

He stood lounging against the mantelpiece, with his hands in his pockets and a cigarette in his mouth. Collier, looking at his slack mouth and sullen eyes, was conscious of a growing distaste. He had to get something out of this cub. How was he going to do it? He might succeed by shock tactics. He pushed a pile of battered textbooks to one side and sat on a corner of the table facing his subject.

"I'm going to be perfectly frank with you, Thompson. I'm going to tell you all I know about you. If, when I've done, you will fill in the blanks, you may come out of a very nasty mess with a whole skin." He broke off to light a cigarette.

"I don't know what you're talking about," growled Thompson.

"Wait. You were expelled from your public school when you were sixteen. You had to be removed from a coaching establishment at Wimbledon. You've been here ever since. Not a very hopeful beginning, but that's not our affair. Since you came here you've become a member of a dope smuggling gang. Outram and Williams are in it too. You've been getting the stuff from Outram's brother, who is an air pilot at the Carysford Aerodrome which runs a bi-weekly service to the Continent, and from agents in Southampton and Shoreham. You boys have acted as go-betweens with them and the distributors in London. It was exciting, and it supplied you all with ample funds. But a few weeks ago your—shall we call him your organiser?—planned a little jewel robbery as a side line. He had heard—it doesn't matter how—that the Tsarina had sent a packet of precious stones to England for safe keeping a few weeks before the Imperial family were removed from the Tsarskoe Selo to Siberia. The woman to whom they had been entrusted died a few days after her arrival, and nothing more had been heard of the jewels, which included a famous and historic emerald which had formerly belonged to the Empress Catherine. Your friend assumed that the stones had been hidden in certain premises—I don't want to make mysteries—in the shop of the dead woman's brother. To make a search of these premises easier the old man's daughter was inveigled down here while some of you were sent to induce the old man to assist you. That was a fortnight ago last Wednesday. The shop was closed at midday and remained closed until the following Tuesday, when it was reopened for one day only under entirely new management. The former owner has not been seen since, but fragments of linoleum and shattered bits of furniture that had been part of the stock have been recovered from the river and tested for bloodstains."

Thompson opened his mouth and shut it again without saying anything. His muddy complexion had faded to a sickly pallor. It was apparent to Collier that he was badly frightened.

"Now I'm giving you a straight deal, Thompson, so I'll tell you now that I don't think the old man was murdered by your little lot. No. There was a rival syndicate after the stones, and they got there first. You were left with the girl on your hands. *The girl on your hands.*"

Collier stopped as if he had no more to say and sat staring at Thompson, who looked anywhere but at him. There was a tense moment of silence. Thompson raised his head at last.

"This is all Greek to me, Inspector. What girl? Where? I'll bet you haven't a vestige of proof of—of anything."

Collier was watching him. "You think you're safe since that night Martin Drury had supper here, the night Vaste hanged himself, don't you?"

"You can't blame any of us fellows for that," said Thompson, rather too quickly. "Drury can bear witness that we were here in this room with him all the time. We were all here when the bell rang. We were all damn sorry about it if it comes to that. Vaste was a soppy young fool, but no one disliked him."

"Bullies don't necessarily dislike their victims, Thompson. I happen to know why you were expelled from Hurtles. But we'll leave that aspect of the case for the moment. I'm going to tell you what happened that afternoon. Vaste did not mind dope smuggling and other forms of dishonesty, but he'd had a nervous dread and hatred of violence. The other members of the gang, including the leader, discovering this, forced him to take a principal part in your first unsuccessful attempt to murder the girl by pushing her over the cliff beyond Beachy Head. She fell on a ledge and was rescued the following morning, but you got her back again. It was necessary to dispose of her, and once again Vaste was to be forced to take a part in the horrible business. On the afternoon in question he was told to meet your leader at Clumber Place to receive his instructions. Now what comes next is guess work on my part. Did he go there before the appointed time, hoping to remove her into a place of safety, and fail to find her? Or did he meet the chief and plead in vain for mercy? That may be made clear later. What I do know is that he hanged himself from a stair rail on the second landing at Clumber Place rather than take part in what had been planned. And if he were my son I should find some comfort in that." Collier lit another cigarette, his merciless eyes on the haggard face opposite.

"As you pointed out just now you and Outram and Williams all have an alibi. Martin Drury can prove that you were all here during the time that the body must have been moved from Clumber Place to the church tower, since it must have been done after dark, that is to say not before about seven o'clock and the moment when, all the preparations having been made, the producer of the grimmest farce ever staged could ring up the curtain. That's why I should advise you, for your own sakes, not to let anything happen to Martin. That point has already occurred to you perhaps? The instinct of self-preservation."

Thompson licked his dry lips.

"Who told you—all this?"

"Never mind that at present. The show wasn't over. The producer had to carry on with the next act. The girl was drugged. She had been pushed into a sack. The mouth of the sack was tied with a length of the same cord Vaste had used. The car in which they had both been brought from Clumber Place was left in the lane here while the driver was busy in the church. When he had finished there he ran back to the car and was off before the exploring party had left the vicarage. You know his destination, Thompson?"

"No. I—I haven't the least idea what you're talking about. I—I assure you."

"All right," said Collier. "There's a chalk quarry two miles out of the village that is used as a rubbish dump for three parishes. The girl was left where the cart loads of rubbish would fall on her from a height of thirty feet. An unusual solution of the ever-recurring problem of the disposal of the body. Sit down if you want to, Thompson."

Thompson sat down. He looked green. Collier watched him closely. It seemed to him probable that the details of the transaction had not been known to all the members of the gang. It was apparent that Thompson had suffered a severe shock. But was he horrified at what had been done, or merely by the fact that the crime had been discovered? Collier leaned towards him and his tone grew more persuasive.

"Now I may be wrong on points of detail, but in the main I know I'm right, and the whole story is going to be proved sooner or later before a jury. Now's your chance, Thompson. You tell me what I want to know and you'll be let off easily when the time comes."

"King's evidence," muttered Thompson.

"I'm giving you the chance I should have given Outram or Williams if either of them had opened the door just now instead of you. And you can take it from me that they'd have jumped at it."

The wretched boy sat huddled in his chair, his restless fingers, yellow with nicotine, pulling at his lower lip.

"What do you want?" he said at last.

"There's an older man running this show of yours. I called him the producer just now. Who is he?"

"I can't tell you that."

"You'll have nothing to fear. You can come away with me now. You'll be protected. I can promise—" Collier looked up, startled by a sharp rapping on the ceiling. "What's that?"

Thompson jumped up. "It's Williams. I expect he wants something. Excuse me for one moment."

He hurried out of the room. Collier, after a momentary hesitation, followed him, but he had to get round the long dining-room table to reach the door and Thompson was already on the floor above when he entered the hall. He stood for a moment listening. He thought he heard a car starting in the lane. He crossed the hall in three strides, wrenched open the hall door, and looked out. His car was standing where he had left it. He closed the door and ran up the stairs. Thompson was just coming out of Williams' room.

"It's nothing much," he explained. "He wants me to put a kettle on the gas ring. The doctor said he was to steep his bad finger in hot water at intervals. I was just going to do it when you arrived."

Collier was not entirely convinced. "Why couldn't he put a kettle on himself?"

"The poor chap's feeling rotten. I offered to do it."

"The good Samaritan, eh? I'll just have a look at him while I'm up here."

"All right. Do. Convince yourself that I'm not lying," said Thompson.

Collier glanced at him quickly. He was undefinably uneasy. Had he somehow lost the initiative in the last few minutes? What had passed between the two young men during those few seconds they had been alone together? He opened the bedroom door and went in.

Williams was lying on his bed, fully dressed, but minus his shoes, propped up with pillows and cushions gathered from the chairs, and smoking a cigarette. He looked pale and his left hand was bandaged.

"Hallo!" he said, "I thought I heard voices. Who's your friend, Thompson?"

Thompson answered. "No friend of mine. A detective from Scotland Yard."

"Oh Lord!" said Williams.

"Look here," said Collier briskly, "you're both very young, and that will be taken into account. Tell me who your chief is and I can promise you won't lose by it."

"Will you give us ten minutes to think it over?" suggested Thompson.

"I can't let you out of my sight."

"That's O.K. with me. Just time to smoke a fag." He turned to Williams. "Let me have one of yours, old bean."

Collier watched him as with shaking hands he struck match after match. Had he been wise to allow an interval for reflection. Were they, for some reason, playing for time?

"I can't allow you more than five minutes," he said.

"Oh, very well."

Collier remained on his guard, standing with his back to the door and his right hand in his coat pocket. As a matter of fact he was unarmed, but they were not to know that. He noted that Thompson dropped his pose of not understanding what he was talking about and that Williams had tacitly admitted his complicity. "If I had Duffield with me," he thought, "I'd take a chance and arrest the pair of them now." And yet—could he in this case take chances? Cardew's warning recurred to him. He must play for safety. Downstairs he had felt that he was making progress. Thompson's resistance was crumbling. But since he had come up to Williams' room Thompson had regained some of his confidence. He was shaking with nerves but he was no longer at a loss. It was as if he had received instructions and was carrying them out.

Collier thought hard. The vicarage was an old house and solidly built. When he had been in the dining-room with Thompson the door had been shut. Would he have heard anyone moving about the place if they had been careful to make no noise. He glanced at Williams' stockinged feet and wished again that he had not come alone.

"Was there anybody up here with you just now, Williams?"

"Nobody."

Was he lying? Possibly. Collier looked at his watch. "Time's up."

Thompson ground the end of his cigarette in the marble top of the washstand and flicked some ash out of a crease in his soiled pullover. For an instant his eyes met the eyes of Williams.

"Right oh," he said. "Carry on."

Collier restrained his impatience with an effort. "You know well enough what I want," he snapped. "The Head of your gang. Come. Is it Maurice Kafka?"

There was an odd breathless silence. Thompson broke it.

"We've sworn not to tell. But—look here. You promise to let us off if we help you?"

"I'll do what I can."

"Shall we, Williams?"

"I suppose so."

"Then—if you go to Clumber Place now you'll get him. But you'll have to be darned quick about it. You came in a car?"

"Yes."

"You'll have to step on it."

Collier hesitated. Clumber Place. He had meant to ask the Chief Inspector to send down a couple of men to occupy the house, but Cardew's acid comment on the number of men he was employing already had checked him. The idea of visiting that ill-omened house, standing solitary in its enclosing woods, alone and after dark, did not appeal to him.

"All right," he said. "I'll run down the village first and get the local bobby to come with me."

"Then you'll miss your man," said Thompson. "I'll tell you why. I was to have reported to him this evening. I was just about to start when you turned up. He told me he shouldn't wait for me in any case after half-past seven, and it's twenty six minutes past now. If he said he won't wait, he won't. But don't let me urge you on. It might be a bit dangerous meeting him like that. You'd be safer two to one."

"It won't pay you to play any tricks on me, Thompson."

"I know that. You've got four minutes."

"Oh hell!" Collier dashed out of the room and down the stairs. The front door slammed. The two young men looked at each other. They heard the car start and gather speed. Williams rolled off the bed and reached for his shoes. Thompson took out his handkerchief and wiped his face.

"I—I half wish we hadn't," he said.

CHAPTER XXIV
CLOSING IN

MARTIN laid down his book. "I can't read," he said, "what's the use of trying? He's late."

Stephen had been as conscious of the passing minutes as his younger brother, but he was more used to inaction.

"What time did he say?"

"He was to be at the nursing-home between nine and ten. It's twenty past eight now. Normally it would take about half an hour to drive to Horsham. It isn't safe to go much over thirty along these winding lanes."

"You are ready?"

"Yes. I'd better ask Mrs. Clapp to bolt the door after me, hadn't I? She wasn't in the kitchen just now when I looked in."

"She's gone down to the village, Martin. She went before Collier left us, just after clearing away the tea. She asked me this afternoon if she might spend the night with her married niece. She's ill again and she sent up one of her children with a message. I told her she could. She'll be back in time to get breakfast."

Martin looked worried. "Why didn't you tell me before? I wouldn't have agreed to go with Collier. I don't like leaving you absolutely alone here."

Stephen smiled. "I've got Mac. And I can hobble as far as the door and push the bolts."

The clock on the mantelpiece struck the half-hour.

"Collier was going to the vicarage. Anywhere else?"

"He didn't say. I don't think so. He hoped to scare those chaps into telling something, but I think he depends chiefly on what the girl may say when she regains consciousness."

Martin put another log on the fire and listened for a moment.

"He'll ring the bell, of course. We're bound to hear. Every night since we found her in the quarry I've woke up thinking of it. I mean, the moment when Collier opened the mouth of the sack and we saw her head, her brown hair all smeared with dust and her poor little face as white as paper. I—I thought she was dead, Stephen. And I looked up at that great shelving bank of rubbish and knew what would have come crashing down on her defence-less body if she'd been left there a few hours longer. Ghastly. I'll never forget it as long as I live."

He stood with his back to his brother, gripping the mantel-piece with both hands. "I didn't think such things were possible," he muttered.

"Collier feels as strongly about that as you do. Almost too much perhaps. He may slip up through being over keen. I don't like his being so late."

"Neither do I. He's got all the threads in his hands. If anything happened to him—"

"The Yard wouldn't let go, Martin. It doesn't pay to damage a policeman. The professional criminals know that well enough. But—I wish he'd come."

They waited, neither uttering a word, while the clock ticked away another five minutes. Then Martin turned to face his brother. "Ten to. I can't stand this, Stephen. I'll get out the car and run down to the vicarage, I can't miss him. He's bound to come back the same way. But you'll have to come into the hall, old chap, and bolt the door after me."

Stephen reached for his crutches. "All right. I'll be at the door by the time you've got the car out of the shed."

Martin did not offer to help him. He knew Stephen preferred to be left to make his slow and difficult way unembarrassed by well-meant supervision. Even Mac, though he watched every step, was careful not to indicate by excited barking, that, in his opinion, the distance between the invalid's couch and the front door might be more quickly covered. It was reached at last. Stephen leant for a moment against the wall, breathing heavily after his exertions. Why had not Martin brought the car round? Mac had run out and was scuffling joyously under the laurels. Martin came round the house from the shed and joined his brother in the porch.

"Come inside," he said hurried. "Come in, Mac, you old scoundrel."

Mac came back reluctantly. Martin shut the door. "The car's been put out of action, Stephen. There isn't a drop of petrol left in the tank and all I had in store has been poured away. Not only that. The tyres have been slashed."

"When?"

"Any time since I came back from my round this morning. I haven't been near the shed since. I never thought of locking the door. Anyone could slip up by the back path from the gate unnoticed. Luckily I've got my old push bike in the scullery. I was mending a puncture this afternoon."

Stephen's sunken blue eyes gleamed approval. "Carry on," he said. "I wish to God I could come with you. For Heaven's sake don't let the thought of me cramp your style. If there's anything amiss Collier may need you. Don't think you need hurry back to relieve my anxiety. I shall be anxious, of course, but I can wait. Good luck."

"You'll bolt this door. You won't do anything rash—" urged Martin.

It seemed an absurd thing to say to that broken giant, upheld by sheer will power. He knew only too well that the physical effort he had just made must have sapped his little store of energy.

Yet there was an unaccustomed ring in Stephen's voice that reminded Martin of the man he had been, the wonderful brother he had boasted about long ago at his prep. school. And so—

"You'll be careful," he pleaded.

"You old hen with one chick, I will. Better bring your bike through the house. Good-bye, Martin."

The night was still and very dark, with a fine drizzle of rain. The little gleam of light from Martin's bicycle lamp travelled along the road before him like a will o' the wisp. He had been considerably startled by the damage done to his car. He was angry too, for the money he had spent on it had been hard earned. He should have locked the shed, of course, but the door was not fitted with a lock. The incident showed that the gang knew that he was a possible source of danger to them, and that they were particularly anxious that he should not go out that night. The ground dipped sharply here to a hollow where the road was crossed by a shallow stream. Martin rode through it and pedalled hard up the opposite slope. After that it was all down hill to where the road forked, one way leading past Clumber Place and the other on to the vicarage, the church, and the village. The vicarage gates were open and he rode straight up the drive, propped his bicycle against the stucco pillar of the porch, and rang the bell.

The door was opened by Outram.

"Has Inspector Collier been here?"

Outram looked queer, Martin thought. There were patches of red on his cheek bones and his eyes were unnaturally bright. He stared at Martin as if he had not understood his question.

"Who's he?"

Martin bit his lip. Was he being indiscreet? Perhaps, after all, Collier had changed his mind and had not come to the vicarage.

"Well, a friend of mine. Has anybody called this evening?

"I really couldn't say. I've been out down the village to buy stamps. I'll ask Thompson." He vanished and reappeared after a moment. "Thompson says a man called and asked for Mr. Henshawe. Thompson told him the vicar wouldn't be back to-night, but he insisted on waiting. After about half an hour he got sick of it and went. Perhaps that was your friend."

"Didn't he give any name?"

"I'll ask Thompson," said Outram, who seemed to be in an unusually obliging mood. He went back to the dining-room, closing the door after him. Martin, standing in the porch, heard the subdued murmur of voices. He was uneasy. Perhaps he had done wrong to come. Collier would blame him for interfering. But he had gone too far now to draw back.

Outram came back. "No name. Sorry, old thing, and all that."

"Oh. it's all right, thanks," said Martin. His chief desire now was to get away, and Outram showed no desire to detain him. Martin wheeled his bicycle down the drive. He had not decided on his next step. If Collier had called at the vicarage and left after half an hour he had had ample time to return as he had promised to the Dower House. Had he gone up to Crossways?

He had told Martin just before he left him that Lady Jocelyn was coming down. "She wants to help," he had said, "and it may stop one earth for the fox." Martin had disapproved. "I don't think a girl ought to be mixed up in this if there's danger." And Collier had nodded. "You're probably right. But do you know any way of keeping that young woman out of anything if she wants to be in it?" And Martin had agreed that it might be difficult. And so—"I'll see if she really has come down," thought Martin as he reached the gate, and, mounting his bicycle, he rode away.

Williams, watching from an upper window, called down to the others.

"He's turned to the left."

It was still raining and the village street was deserted. Only a few lights showed here and there in cottage windows, and the blaring of a loudspeaker was audible in the bar of the Red Lion. When he reached Crossways he saw from the lane that all the windows were dark, but since he had come so far he would make sure that there was nobody there. He rode up the new gravel drive cut through the heather and gorse bushes that surrounded the house and tried the garage. The door yielded to a touch and he saw Jocelyn's red two seater inside. He went on to the house and rang the bell and knocked. At last the lights in the living-room went up, and he heard uncertain steps in the entrance lounge and Jocelyn's voice, curiously high and strained.

"Who's that?"

"It's me. Martin Drury."

"Oh—are you alone?"

"Yes."

She opened the door. He looked at her quickly as he went in. She was clinging to the doorknob, apparently for support. Her little face was chalk white under the paint and her eyes seemed enormous. Martin was shocked by her appearance. Instinctively he put out a hand to save her from falling.

"What's the matter?"

"I don't know. I feel rotten. I've been asleep and I had bad dreams. Have you been knocking long?"

"About ten minutes."

"As loud as you did just now?"

"Yes."

"Good Heavens. I must have been sleeping like the dead. But I've hardly closed my eyes for a week. Martin, be nice to me." He put his arm about her and half carried her into the living room where he made her sit down in one of the deep armchairs while he turned on the electric fire. "You're cold. Your hands are like ice. Perhaps you ought to have some tea," he said doubtfully.

"Presently, perhaps. Give me some brandy to go on with. I feel like nothing on earth."

There was a row of bottles and ingredients for cocktails in the sideboard. He brought her what she had asked for. She shut her eyes and sipped it slowly while he stood by. He noted that she had been sleeping on the settee. The shoes she had kicked off were lying near with the rug that had covered her. She opened her eyes, gave him the empty glass, and pushed her tumbled black curls back from her forehead with a weary gesture.

"Are you feeling better?" he asked anxiously.

"Yes. Better now. You're a good sort, Martin. What's the time?"

"Twenty to ten,"

"Gosh! Then I've been dead to the world for five solid hours. And if you hadn't roused me with that infernal hammering—

There's an engine thudding in my head. My bag's over there, darling. You'll find a bottle of aspirin. That's right. Now—" She made an evident and rather pathetic effort to pull herself together. "What have you come about?"

"I hoped to find Inspector Collier. He was to call at the vicarage and then come back to us, but he hasn't come back. I'm getting worried about him."

"Can't he take care of himself? He looks solid."

"Yes, but—I don't know what to do," Martin confessed. "He was to have been at Horsham between nine and ten. The girl, you know. Did he tell you about her?"

She clasped her head with both hands. "Did he? Yes. He said Bertie died because he tried to save her from the others. Is that true, do you think, Martin?"

"Y—es. Look here, may I use your phone? And have you a telephone directory?"

"Of course. You'll find it in the hall."

She sat after he had left her leaning her aching head on her hands. He came back presently.

"I rang up the nursing home. He hasn't turned up. And they say she's beginning to struggle back to consciousness. He might get something from her now."

"You know her, don't you?" said Jocelyn dully. There was a piston rod working in her head. Thud. Thud. Thud. She could not see anything clearly.

"Yes. She brought Stephen a letter. I say, will you lend me your car?"

"What for?"

"To get to Horsham. They may let me see her without Collier. I can but try. She might tell me things."

Jocelyn pressed the palms of her hands to her aching eyes. Fireworks, she thought. Golden rain. But something deep down fought against the pain.

Chapter XXV
ANNE SPEAKS

Martin was about to press the night bell at the nursing home when a man emerged from the shrubberies and a light was flashed in his face.

"No use, sir. No visitors allowed here."

"Are you one of Inspector Collier's men?"

"I am."

"Is he here now?"

"Who are you, sir?"

"I'm Martin Drury. The Inspector was going to call for me to-night and bring me here. But he never turned up so I came along."

Apparently his bona fides was accepted for the plain clothes man's tone changed and he became almost confidential.

"The matron was expecting him over an hour ago. My job's to see that no unauthorised person gets near enough to the patient to harm her. You might ring that bell, Mr. Drury. Maybe they know more than I do inside. The Inspector may have rung up."

Martin obeyed. A grey-haired woman in nurse's uniform opened the door a few inches without taking off the chain.

"Who is it?"

The plain clothes man answered. "It's all right, madam. This is Mr. Drury who was to have accompanied the Inspector to-night. Have you had any message from the Inspector?"

"Not a word. It's most unfortunate because the patient has regained consciousness and she would probably be able to answer any questions that were put to her. But, of course, we don't know what to ask, and we are afraid to fatigue her unnecessarily. I've been waiting, hoping every minute that he would arrive, but really I can't wait much longer. In her weak state she can't be left too long without nourishment."

"Well, you needn't wait for the Inspector for that."

"She'll have to have her medicine immediately after, and when she's had that she must not be disturbed on any account. The doctor's trying a new ingredient. His instructions were explicit."

"I see. Well, I suppose he can see her to-morrow. She'll be a bit stronger, too, once having turned the corner."

"I didn't say she'd turned the corner. The doctor doesn't say—but between you and me, I'm afraid this may be the final flicker."

Martin, standing by, bit his lip hard, Anne had been so much in his thoughts.

The detective rubbed his chin uncertainly. He was more worried than he cared to admit by Collier's non-appearance. He knew that the Inspector believed that Anne Borlase's life was in danger just so long as she was the sole possessor of information that might lead to the arrest of the leader of the gang that had kidnapped her. He would be running a risk if he acted on his own initiative instead of merely following out the duty assigned to him, but. under the circumstances, he decided that he must take it. He would be for it at the Yard if he let an opportunity for getting a statement from an important witness for the Crown slip. Probably, he reflected sourly, he would be for it in any case. The consequences of the Inspector's absence would be visited on his subordinates. In this he was less than just to Collier, who never shirked his share of responsibility.

"In that case," he said, "Mr. Drury had better see her with you and me present, madam. I'll take down anything she says, and you can witness her statement and her signature if she's able to sign."

"Very well." She took off the chain and admitted the two men to the hall. She turned to Martin. "I suppose you really are Mr. Drury? The Inspector has made me quite nervous."

"I'm afraid I haven't a card," said Martin, "only these." He took one or two letters and receipted bills from his pocket-book and proffered them. The detective coolly intercepted them and looked them over before he handed them back. "That's all right, Mr. Drury. My name's Pollard, by the way."

The lights in the hall and on the stairs were heavily shaded. The house was very quiet. The other patients were, presumably, asleep. Only the nurse on night duty sat on the landing, wrapped in a shawl and reading a novel. She looked after them curiously as they passed.

The matron paused with her hand on the knob of a door at the end of the passage on the first floor. "I've given her one of my best rooms," she whispered, "though I haven't yet heard who is paying for her. But never mind that now. Will you please ask as few questions as possible, Mr. Drury, and be careful not to excite the patient?"

"All right," murmured Martin, but his heart sank. What was he going to say to Anne? Collier would have known. He, and he only, had all the threads of the case in his hands.

He glanced appealingly at Pollard. "I don't quite know—I hope I don't make a mess of it."

Pollard's fervent, "So do I, sir," was hardly encouraging.

The nurse who had been sitting by Anne's bedside rose as they entered and went out of the room. The matron bent over the patient and addressed her with the brisk cheerfulness that is considered the right tone to take with the sick and dying.

"Feeling better, my dear? That's right. Here's a friend, Mr. Martin Drury, come to see you for a few minutes."

She made way for Martin who stood awkwardly enough, gazing down at the wan little face on the pillow.

She gazed back at him at first with a little frown of perplexity and then with a faint smile of recognition.

"Of course," her voice was very weak, a mere thread of sound. "Colonel's Drury's brother. You were feeding the chickens in the field. You were both—so nice to me. After that"—her smile faded and fear dawned in her eyes—"have I been ill? Bad dreams—"

"You're all right now." he said quickly. "They are all your friends here, taking care of you."

"I went down to Sussex and they locked me up in a room. They had nothing to sell really. It was all lies. Was that a dream?"

Martin sat on the chair Pollard pushed forward for him and took her thin little hand in his strong young grasp.

"No," he said. "But don't be frightened now. It's all over."

"Where's my father? Is he here?" Her eyes moved about the room searching for him.

The matron came to the rescue.

"He isn't here now."

"Is he safe?"

"Yes." lied Martin. She was in no state to hear the truth. Besides, there was still a chance that old Borlase was alive.

"Look here. Anne, could you describe those men who kept you shut up?"

"Yes. I think so." They all waited anxiously while she collected her thoughts, groping pitifully in the confusion of her weakened mind. "The one who drove the car. He was stout and thick-set with a dark, ill-tempered face. Like a bull, I thought. Quite young. He drove me from the station. There were others. I heard their voices, but I only saw the one with the bandaged head."

"The bandaged head?" echoed Martin.

Pollard was writing busily in his notebook.

"Yes. He wore a sort of hood of white linen with holes for his eyes. He said he'd had a motor accident."

"Did he speak to you?"

"Oh yes. At first he pretended, but later he told me they wanted the jewels Aunt Mary brought over from Russia. He seemed to think they were hidden in the shop. Then he asked me if I had taken them to Colonel Drury. I told him I'd only taken a letter from a Russian girl the Colonel had been fond of. I didn't want to tell him anything." Her voice shook. "I'm sorry. He made me. I had to say how Aunt Mary died, and how I found the letter sewn in the lining of her dress so long afterwards. I don't know if he believed me. He frightened me." Her wasted fingers were trembling. "Don't let him get me again."

"No, no."

Pollard intervened. "Was he tall or short?"

"Not short. Not specially tall."

"Would you know him, do you think, without his linen mask?"

"I don't know."

"Did you notice his hands?"

"He wore gloves."

"Damn him," growled Pollard. "He thought of everything."

"That's enough," said the matron firmly. "She must have her supper now, and then rest."

Anne had closed her eyes. She opened them again as Martin gently released her fingers. "You'll come and see me again, Mr. Drury?"

"Yes, Anne." The matron was putting her signature as a witness in Pollard's notebook. Neither of them were looking towards the bed for the moment. Rather shamefacedly Martin lifted the girl's hand to his lips. He felt a fool, and yet it was what he had been wanting to do all along. "I'll come again to-morrow," he mumbled. Getting out of the room was an anticlimax. His ears were burning, but he felt fairly certain that Pollard had not noticed anything. Martin glanced back from the threshold. The matron was pouring some whitish substance from a little covered saucepan into a feeding cup. She set it down carefully on the little table by the bedside and uncorked a bottle of medicine.

Martin followed Pollard past the night nurse, still reading on the landing, down the stairs to the dimly-lit hall below.

"The Inspector will be disappointed," said Pollard heavily.

His own disappointment was obvious. "He's been banking on getting a description of the man from her. I wonder—" The telephone just at his elbow rang sharply. "Maybe that's him now." He took off the receiver. "Hallo . . . yes . . . yes . . . Good Lord!" He dropped the receiver, thrust the astonished Martin out of his way and went charging up the stairs, three steps at a time. The nurse on the landing stood up hurriedly, dropping her book in her agitation as he tore down the passage to the room he had so lately left.

CHAPTER XVI
THE UNKNOWN QUANTITY

STEPHEN Drury made his slow and painful way back to the library. His back was aching rather badly as the result of his unaccustomed exertions but he had still some arrangements to make before he could lie down and rest. He had to take something from a drawer in his bureau and slip it into his right hand coat pocket. That done he unfastened the shutters that covered the french window opening on the garden and unlatched the window itself before he hobbled over to his couch, laid his crutches down within reach, and settled down to wait.

Mac had watched his master's every movement with a bright enquiring eye, waiting also for the moment to come when he could jump up to his place and go to sleep, but the unlatched window intrigued him. He trotted over after Stephen had left it to scratch at the frame and whimper uneasily. The night outside pressed against the uncurtained glass. Mac came away with his tail between his legs, leapt on to the couch and lay down with his head on his paws and his ears cocked to listen.

Stephen looked at him doubtfully. Would it have been better to shut him up in the adjoining room? He wished that he had, but he had expended all his available energy. He could not face the prospect of walking so far and back again. And the expected visitor might be arriving at any moment now.

The minutes passed but they did not seem long to him. After seventeen years of inaction, of what, to a man of his adventurous spirit, had been a living death, he had been given an active part again. It would be a brief one, he knew, but he thanked the Fates for it nevertheless. That the police, in the person of Collier, the Inspector in charge of the case, would not have approved only added spice to the anticipated adventure. He had had to depend for so long upon others for everything that he had developed a secret craving to do something, anything, off his own bat. It was this that had impelled him to withhold a part of his confidence even from Martin, whom he loved. Martin was a good fellow, but inclined to fuss.

Stephen had had his couch moved back that afternoon, alleging a draught, to a place where it could not be seen by anyone looking in at the window. He had turned out his reading lamp, and the room was lit only by the fire burning on the hearth. It was silent but for the ticking of the clock, and the silence was still unbroken when one half of the french window moved slowly outward.

"Come in, won't you," said Stephen, laying a restraining hand on Mac's collar as he felt the hackles rising along the old dog's back, "and shut the window after you. I get chilled so easily lying here."

He switched on the reading lamp and tilted the shade so that the light fell on the intruder.

He saw a man of medium height, wearing a raincoat buttoned up to his throat. His head and face were completely masked with white linen bandages.

Stephen smiled. "What? Has the purveyor of accidents fallen into one of his own little traps? No, of course not. Camouflage, eh? Very ingenious, but rather conspicuous."

"Easily removed," said the visitor drily. "Why was this window left open?"

"To save you time and trouble."

"You expected me?"

"I knew you would want to search the Dower House sooner or later. It was the obvious thing to do. If the packet of precious stones entrusted by the Tsarina to the countess Nadine, and by her to her old English governess Mary Borlase to bring over to this country was not lost on the way or hidden in the shop in Elmer Passage there was a possibility that it had come into my possession. I wish you'd tell me how you came to hear of it."

"Look here, Drury, are you playing for time? Is this a trap? I warn you that you're for it if you play any tricks with me."

"No tricks, I assure you. I'm alone in the house. My brother has gone to look for Inspector Collier who failed to turn up. If he does return you will have ample notice and can leave as you came, by the window."

"Thank you. I'm not worrying about the Inspector. He's had a nasty smash. Something went wrong with the steering gear of his car and he ran into a tree. A bad business. I'm afraid he's done for, poor chap. Unfortunately, as it happened in the grounds of Clumber Place nobody knows about it."

"Except you."

"Exactly."

Stephen was silent for a moment. Then he said, "He's my friend. But the Criminal Investigation Department isn't a one man show, Mr. —Mr. X. You aren't out of the wood yet. You criminals aren't as clever as you think yourselves. You're so groovy. This accident stunt. You're overdoing it. But of course nothing is going according to plan now. You're just hitting out wildly."

The visitor kept his temper, but there was an edge to his voice when he answered. "Not so wildly as you think. There won't be any evidence—or, rather, there won't be anybody to give evidence—to-morrow."

"A holocaust?" said Stephen lightly.

"I could shoot you now, Drury, but I won't if you're reasonable. You know what I want. The jewels. The diamonds and the Eye of Nero."

"If I must I must," said Stephen slowly, "but will you tell me how you first heard of them? Satisfy my curiosity."

"Certainly. A Russian sold me the information. He was a footman at the Tsarskoe Selo and paid by the Revolutionary Government to spy on the Tsar and his family. He overheard the Tsarina giving her instructions about the stones to the daughter of Count Sariatinski. When he mentioned your name as the recipient of the packet I pricked up my ears. I knew something about you. I knew you had been at the Embassy at St. Petersburg before the War. I thought it was worth investigating. Unfortunately he must have blabbed to someone else about the same time. Whatever the police may think, we didn't ransack the shop in Elmer Passage or murder the old man. That's what put us in the soup. But for their damned interference we shouldn't have had all this trouble."

"Too bad," said Stephen ironically.

"That's enough from you, Drury. We're wasting time. The girl brought you the stones then? The little liar. She swore she hadn't."

"She didn't. A packet came by post many years ago. A sealed packet with a half sheet of note paper scrawled over in pencil. *Keep this. Don't tell anyone. Letter following from—*" Stephen broke off. He could not bring himself to utter Nadine's name before the other. "I put it in my bank. Later, when I was discharged from hospital and had come home for good I took it out again so as to have it ready. It's in that safe over there."

"The diamonds and the emerald?" There was a ring of uncontrollable excitement in the other's voice.

"I don't know."

"What do you mean?" he said roughly.

"The packet was sealed."

"And you left it like that? Gad! Drury, I don't know if you're superhuman or subhuman. But I'm not sure that I believe you. Hand over your keys."

"And if I refuse?"

"I shall take them."

"Very well. Don't come any nearer. Catch." He took a bunch of keys from his coat pocket and threw them. The other caught them and went down the room towards the safe. "I expect you're surprised that I trust you not to shoot me in the back," he remarked. "You see, I happen to know that the pistol you keep in the top drawer of your bureau is not loaded."

Mac, rigid under her master's hand, received some message telegraphed from Stephen's brain through his nerves, and responded with a sharp defiant bark.

The intruder spun round. "Damn you!" he snarled. "Keep that dog of yours quiet or I'll silence him for good."

"All right!"

"Hell! it's a combination lock."

"Yes. The key's for the inner door."

"What is the combination?"

Stephen gave it, his quiet voice expressionless.

The other laughed jeeringly. Mac had startled him and his temper was getting frayed. "Easy, aren't you?" he said. "I wonder how you got your reputation as a dare-devil, Drury. *Sans peur et sans reproche* and all that rot. I thought I'd have a lot more trouble persuading you. Have you developed a yellow streak since you've been lying here, or was it always there?"

He glanced round as he spoke at the recumbent figure just beyond the circle of lamplight that lay between them. Stephen was laughing.

"My dear Mr. X, I'm simply shaking with fright. It's more than a streak, I assure you. I'm yellow, as you phrase it, all over."

The stranger's head, formless and horrible in its enveloping white linen mask, turned quickly towards the door. He listened for a moment before he answered.

"I don't much care for your tone. But Mr. X is good. You can go on calling me that."

"Thank you. I intend to. I wonder why you're mixed up in all this. Dope smuggling's a filthy business. Maltreating defenceless girls is even worse."

"That's enough from you. But, if you want to know, love of excitement, and love of power." The outer door of the safe swung open.

Stephen raised himself a little on his pillows to watch him as he tried one key after another into the inner lock.

The long raincoat effectually concealed his figure and his hands were gloved. Nor did his voice betray his identity, for he had spoken throughout in a falsetto that was evidently assumed. He had not succeeded in maintaining his pose of cynical indifference. As he stooped, fumbling over the keys and swearing under his breath it was obvious that he was greatly excited. This, no doubt, was one of those moments he lived for. Stephen remembered a recent conversation with Collier.

"You care a lot for these stones?"

The other answered curtly. "Yes. I am—rather keen. I want the emerald." The second door was open. He flashed his electric torch into the inside of the safe and thrust in his arm. "Brown paper and blue seals?"

"Yes."

He came back into the circle of lamplight to examine the seals.

"The letter N and a coronet. That would be your little countess, eh?" He broke the wax and tore the wrapping off the little cardboard box without waiting for a reply.

The lover of Nadine, watching him, bit his lip until the blood came. It sickened him to see the thing her hands had touched pawed over by this brute, but it had to be borne. Why. oh why had he not made sure that his pistol was loaded. It had been a few days ago. He had gone through one of his bad days since. Had Martin found it and unloaded it, fearing that he might yield to an impulse to end his life? It was possible. But how did this other know?

The intruder had ripped off the lid and was turning over the contents of the box. "There are no stones here." He turned swiftly on Stephen with a threatening gesture, and Mac, whose bright eyes had been fixed unwinkingly upon him, tore himself free and sprang at him. Stephen cried out in a panic,

"Don't touch him. He can't hurt you. His teeth are all gone."

But Mac had already been hurled against the bookcase by a savage kick. He lay still for a moment and then, recovering himself a little, made a feeble effort to crawl back to his master. Mr. X walked deliberately over to him and fired at the small shaggy body. Mac whined once, tried again to move in the direction of the spinal couch that was the centre of his little world, rolled over, and lay still.

Stephen controlled himself with a violent effort. The other was still raging. "That's what you get for trying to put me off with rubbish. I suppose you hoped I'd carry off the box without looking at it. I'm not such a fool."

As he spoke he hurled the box and its contents into the fire. The dry petals of long withered roses shrivelled instantly.

The packet of letters lasted longer, the edges curling up as the flames touched them. A long curl of silky black hair fell into the hearth.

Stephen's voice when he spoke sounded strange in his own ears. "I never knew what was in the box."

The other came over and stood by him, staring down through the holes in his linen mask at the beautiful worn face.

Stephen stared back at him unflinchingly.

"Where are the stones, Drury? I've got to have them."

"All right. Look under my pillow."

"Ah—"

As he bent over him Stephen's hands went up with the lightning quickness he had learned long ago in the boxing ring, but not to strike. A blow was not possible without any weight behind it. He could only grip his enemy by the throat.

The other had been over-confident and was taken by surprise. The rug slid away under him and he fell heavily, striking the back of his head on the polished boards and dragging Stephen after him.

After the end of their fall the silence was unbroken but for their heavy breathing. For a minute or more Stephen felt the body on which he lay threshing to and fro like a wounded snake trying to get free. Then its struggles weakened and ceased.

CHAPTER XVII
NIGHT WORK

THE post office at Ladebrook was kept by a woman, who eked out her exiguous Government salary by selling sweets and tobacco and groceries over the counter adjoining the cage in the corner of the dark little shop from which she dispensed postage stamps and postal orders. During the summer months, when hikers passed through the village, there was also some sale for picture postcards of the post office itself, a sixteenth-century cottage with a thatched roof and a flight of stone steps leading up to the shop door.

Miss Pringle, the postmistress, who had gone to bed as usual at ten, was roused from sleep some time later by a persistent though not very loud knocking below.

Miss Pringle looked out of the window of her tiny bedroom over the shop. The night was dark but she fancied she saw something lying on the step below.

"Who is it? Is there something on fire?"

A man's voice answered. "Let me in. I want to ring up—"

"At this hour? Come again in the morning!"

"I'm a policeman," said the voice.

"Nonsense," said Miss Pringle vigorously. She was convinced by this time that this was some practical joke of the young gentlemen at the vicarage They had played her tricks before.

"You're not Jimmie Deane. I'll tell him about you to-morrow. Disturbing people like this. It's disgraceful."

"Deane's dead, poor chap. He was with me. A car smash—"

Somehow the voice carried conviction this time. Miss Pringle snatched a tweed coat from the hook behind the door and ran downstairs, only pausing to light the gas in the shop before she unbolted the door.

The door opened inwards and Collier fell in with it and sprawled at her feet.

"It's all right," he gasped, for the little post-mistress had not been able to repress a cry of alarm. "I'm afraid my arm is broken, and it feels as if a couple of ribs were stove in, but there's nothing serious."

"I'll get some brandy." She darted into the living room behind the shop and returned with a tea cup half full of neat spirit.

"There." She knelt on the door and propped him up while he sipped and choked. "A car smash, did you say? And Deane with you? At this time of night. I don't know what we're coming to, I'm sure." A sudden doubt assailed her. What if this was a preliminary to a hold up? "I warn you there are three men in the house, and a shot gun—"

Collier sat up. "Better soon," he muttered. He must not give way now.

"If your arm is broken it ought to be set. I'll ring up Doctor Clowes. He's the only one now that Doctor Brewer is away and Doctor Lucas is ill," she babbled, "but I don't know if he'll be back. He gets such a lot of night calls. As far as Horsham. He was saying it's lucky he has a motor cycle as well as a push bike. Whatever's wrong now?"

Collier was struggling to his feet. "The phone. Quick." He reached the instrument, hobbling round the counter to get to it and wincing with pain at every step, and took up the receiver. Miss Pringle, following him, stared at him with mingled compassion and respect. He was so torn and battered, so smeared with mud and blood. Yet the blue eyes gleamed indomitable in that white face and his method of addressing the Exchange would have made Miss Pringle's hair stand on end if it had not already been imprisoned in curling pins. He was so masterful. Like the he-men in the Pictures, she thought.

He glanced round at her while he waited to be connected.

"The others sleep soundly," he remarked.

"What others?"

"Didn't you say there were three men—"

"I live alone," said Miss Pringle with dignity.

Collier was sufficiently recovered to grin at this admission.

"I see. Run up and get some clothes on," he advised in the paternal tone he had adopted in his uniformed days. "I don't want you to catch a cold, and I'm afraid you won't be able to go back to bed just yet. I'm going to ring up the head-quarters of the county police and they'll be sending along quite a lot of men. They'll come here. Rather an invasion. I hope you don't mind. You deal with His Majesty's Mails. This is His Majesty's business."

The little woman drew herself up. "I hope I shall never fail in my duty, Mr.—"

"Inspector Collier."

"Inspector. I'll get the fire going."

As she hurried on her clothes in the room above she could hear his voice at the telephone but she could not hear what he was saying. What could have happened? She dressed in record time, dragged the curlers out of her short grey hair, and ran down again to relight the fire and put a kettle on the gas ring. "For," she said to herself, "whatever it is they'll be glad of tea."

Another idea occurred to her. She had a limited but, within its limits, a well-ordered and efficient mind. She took a basin of water and a clean towel into the little overcrowded shop where Collier, having finished with the telephone, was sitting in her own chair behind the counter. His head had fallen forward on his breast but he roused himself as she came in.

"What is it? Oh—yes. I suppose I am a ghastly object—"

"Don't you move," said Miss Pringle. "I'm going to sponge your face and hands. And what you've been doing to get yourself in such a mess beats me—"

"That's very kind of you." He submitted to her ministrations. She had removed most of the caked mud and blood and was trying to remember the whereabouts of a roll of lint she kept for possible cut fingers when two cars stopped in the road outside and somebody knocked peremptorily on the shop door.

"Will that be the police?"

"Yes."

Miss Pringle opened the door and in a moment the tiny shop seemed to be full of men.

A tall man in a braided uniform approached the counter.

"I am Superintendent Pannett, of the County Constabulary. Are you Inspector Collier?"

"Yes. You'll excuse my not moving. I'm afraid I'm rather a crock. Never mind that for the present. There's no time to lose. I'm down here investigating a case of attempted murder. You've heard something about it. The Yard notified your Chief Constable. You must not think I'm poaching. It started in London."

"That's all right. You look pretty bad. A nip of brandy—"

Collier smiled faintly. "Better not. I've had some. Must keep sober. I'll just tell you what happened this evening. Three of the young men who are staying at the vicarage here are implicated in this business. I had a straight talk with one of them. I wanted to get at the ring-leader. He finally told me I'd find him at Clumber Place. You know it. An empty house, no caretaker. Well away from the road. They've been using it as their headquarters. I was alone, having sent my sergeant off on another trail, but I happened to meet the village constable in the lane just after leaving the vicarage, and I asked him to accompany me. The park gate was unlocked. I—I had an idea that I might be too late and I accelerated up the avenue. Half way up something happened. The next thing I knew I was on my hands and knees in a mass of undergrowth twenty yards from the road. I suppose I remained there about five minutes. I was dazed by the shock. Then I remembered Deane, and I started crawling back to the car. I saw it presently. Though it had turned right over the headlights were still on. Somebody was moving round it, stooping to examine it more closely. As he crossed the road he stopped to light a cigarette. He struck two matches before he got it going, shading the flame with his hands, and I had a clear view of his face. He did something to the trunk of a tree and then crossed over and repeated the same performance with another tree. It was too dark to see but I felt fairly sure that he was detaching a length of cord or possibly of wire. He then returned to the car and succeeded in turning off the headlights. After that I heard the dead leaves rustling under his feet as he passed quite near me. I waited a bit longer and a motor cycle came down the avenue from the direction of the house, swerved round the overturned car, and left me to it."

"One moment." said the Superintendent. "You saw this man's face. Would you know him again?"

"It was Doctor Clowes."

"What? You are not suggesting—"

"Nothing, at present." said Collier. "I'm only stating the facts. I went on crawling until I emerged from the undergrowth on to the road. It was pitch dark under those trees but I had my torch and fortunately the bulb was unbroken. I switched it on and I saw what he had seen. A man's hand protruding from under the car. I touched it and felt for the pulse. No use. Poor chap. If only he hadn't met me in the lane—"

"Oh dear," said the little postmistress pitifully, "and him with such a nice young wife and three little ones."

"It's a bad business," said the superintendent, "but if you ask me, Inspector, I should say Doctor Clowes' presence on the scene was purely accidental. He was probably on his way home from seeing a patient and hearing the crash came along to lend a hand if required."

Collier did not answer immediately. He was leaning forward, his bruised and battered fingers gripping the edge of the counter.

The Superintendent watched him anxiously. Miss Pringle ran into the back room and came back with a laden tea tray.

"I'm sorry I haven't enough cups for everybody."

"We don't need it," said the Superintendent. "Give him some and have a cup yourself, ma'am."

Collier sipped the hot liquid gratefully. When he resumed his voice was firmer. "You may be right, but I daren't take any risks. I rang up the nursing home where Miss Borlase is a patient when I got here. The first thing, before I called you. I blame myself for not having realised that Clowes would be visiting patients there in the absence of Doctor Brewer. I have to regard him, provisionally, as a suspect. The sooner he explains himself the better. Let me think—"

He sat frowning, making an obvious effort to concentrate. The superintendent rubbed his chin uneasily. The C.I.D. men were very clever and all that, but this one had met with an accident.

"Addled his brains," thought the local man, "all very well, but we shall get into a hell of a row if we run about arresting people without warrants for the Lord knows what."

"Look here. Inspector," he said, not unkindly, "you're all in, as the Americans say, and no wonder, after what you've been through. If you try to carry on in the state you're in you'll be doing something you'll regret afterwards. Let me ring up the ambulance. If you've a bone broken it ought to be set without any more delay. And then a good night's rest in a comfortable bed—"

Collier waved away the well-meant advice. "Presently. I can't let go yet. He'll slip between our fingers if we don't look out. How many men have you brought?"

"Seven, in two cars."

"Good. Send two—I say, you must forgive me for giving orders. Don't take offence, Superintendent, for God's sake. Lives are at stake."

"All right," said the other.

"Good. Send two men to Clumber Place to verify what I've just told you. they must look at the trees. If wire was used it probably cut into the bark. They ought to find traces. You'll need more men and a jack to lift the car off poor Deane. That can be done later. Send three to fetch Clowes here. They can tell him there's been an accident and the injured man is in the post office. No more than that. As a doctor he's bound to come. You understand?"

The Superintendent nodded. He could see his way to do that. He went into the roadway with his men and gave them their instructions. "And be careful with the doctor. I haven't seen or heard a particle of evidence that he's done anything wrong. You be civil to him, see?"

"But we're to bring him, whether or no?"

"Oh, he'll come."

Collier heard the murmur of their voices outside and could make a pretty good guess at what was being said. He realised that he was still virtually alone, holding up the case as Atlas held up the world, on his bowed and weary shoulders. He was in no state to face Clowes and wring the truth from him, but it had to be done.

The shop door bell jangled as the Superintendent re-entered, stooping to avoid knocking his head against the lintel.

"What you need—" he began.

Collier opened his eyes. "There used to be a chemist off the Shaftesbury Avenue in the days when I was attached to a West End division," he said dreamily. "He used to mix a pick-me-up for his women customers. They get dead tired, poor souls, especially on wet nights. I tried it once, out of curiosity, and nearly jumped over the roof. Potent. That's the word. I need one now—but I'll have to do without it."

He closed his eyes. Miss Pringle looked enquiringly at the Superintendent who shook his head significantly.

Collier opened his eyes again. "There's just one thing," he said. "Don't let Clowes touch me. Promise."

The Superintendent, who had by this time made up his mind that his colleague was not in full possession of his faculties, adopted a soothing manner. "Yes, yes. my dear fellow. Don't worry yourself."

Collier stared at him for a moment. "I mean it," he said curtly. He turned to the little postmistress. "You heard. He's not to come near me." Some instinct prompted him to add. "I trust you." before he fainted.

CHAPTER XVIII
STEPHEN'S SHARE

"How dare you!" the matron was flushed with indignation as she faced Pollard across her patient's bed. The shattered fragments of the medicine glass he had knocked out of her hand lay at her feet.

"I'm sorry," the plain clothes man was still rather breathless. "The Inspector's orders. He rang up just as we got down to the hall."

Martin had followed Pollard into the room. Anne's frightened eyes turned to him appealingly. "Mr. Drury—what's the matter? What does it mean?"

Martin sat down in the chair he had vacated only a few minutes earlier. He did not know what to say to reassure her since he was as ignorant as she was of the reason that had sent Pollard pelting up the stairs again, but he took her hand and held it tightly.

Pollard, after one glance at them, beckoned to the matron to follow him to the other end of the room. After a momentary hesitation she obeyed.

"I require an explanation," she said sharply.

He nodded. "That's right. You were going to give Miss Borlase a new medicine?"

"No. The same. Well, possibly there was a fresh ingredient. The doctor brought it along when he came."

"What doctor?"

"Doctor Clowes. He's acting as locum while Doctor Brewer is away. Doctor Lucas has been attending this patient, but he's laid up."

"So that this was Doctor Clowes' first visit?"

"Yes."

"Inspector Collier's instructions are that Miss Borlase is not to take any medicine prescribed or made up by Doctor Clowes."

The matron reddened. "The Inspector must be mad. He takes too much upon himself. I take my instructions from the doctor in charge—"

"Not in this case," said Pollard. "I said instructions. If you must have it, madam, the word is orders. If you decline to carry them out I've no option but to remain in this room and see to it myself."

She gazed at him for a moment without replying. Pollard saw that her anger had abated and was quick to take a more persuasive tone.

"It won't hurt her to go without medicine for a few hours," he said. "You can give her any nourishment or stimulant you think advisable. The Inspector rang up from Ladebrook post office and he seemed to be in a bit of a hurry. He didn't explain and I know no more about the whys and the wherefores than you do. I don't know a thing about this doctor, for or against. I never so much as heard his name before."

"He doesn't practise as a rule," said the matron. "It's just to oblige Doctor Brewer, who was ordered a long sea voyage. He's quite a young man and I understand he's engaged in some form of research work. If he was one of our regular visiting doctors nothing would induce me—"

"Naturally. Of course not," said Pollard, who saw that he had gained his point. He resisted an impulse to mop his brow. He disliked heated arguments with women. This one had proved more amenable than he had dared to hope at first.

"I'll take charge of the bottle," he remarked. "If you've any paper and sealing wax I'll fasten it up securely in your presence."

"Very well. It's all most extraordinary, but you take the responsibility. You've given me no choice. I can only hope all this excitement hasn't harmed my patient."

She turned back to the bed. Martin signalled to her not to speak. Anne was asleep. He tiptoed out of the room and Pollard and the matron joined him in the passage.

The matron smiled at him. "You have a soothing effect, Mr. Drury."

Martin flushed. "I'm coming back in the morning," he said. "Was there anything wrong with the medicine?"

The matron had hurried off to her own room to get string and sealing wax. Pollard repeated what he had heard over the telephone. Martin turned rather white.

"Clowes? And the Inspector rang up from Ladebrook post office? That's queer. Clowes is a friend of Lady Jocelyn's. I know he's often at Crossways when she's down there for week-ends. Why, he was fetched to the church to see young Vine, He gave evidence at the inquest. Oh, it's impossible. There must be some mistake."

"That's as may be. sir. I've told you all I know."

"Yes, quite. I think I'll get back to my brother."

"What's your number, sir, in case the young lady should ask for you? You seem to have a knack with her, if I may say so."

Martin groaned. "We're not on the telephone unfortunately. I'll run over the first thing to-morrow."

They shook hands and Martin ran downstairs and let himself out. It was still raining and the darkness was profound. He had to give most of his mind to driving Lady Jocelyn's car, but at the back of his mind his thoughts were busy with the latest development. He did not care much for Clowes. He had resented the young doctor's brusque manner when he came to visit Stephen but he had seemed pleasant enough when they met later in the village. It had never occurred to him that he might be involved with the gang. And yet—his position gave him certain facilities. And in one respect he filled the bill. Though he had only been living in the little home he had taken on the outskirts of the village for a little over a year he probably knew more of the neighbourhood than many of the natives. During the past summer he had explored the Downs and the Weald pretty thoroughly, sometimes on foot and sometimes on his old push bike, but always with his collecting box on his shoulders. Was it moths or mosses? Martin, who had met him occasionally on his rounds, had not troubled to enquire.

Martin had closed the gate when he left the Dower House to ride down to the vicarage. He got out to open it and drove in. He was thinking now chiefly of Stephen, Stephen waiting, with his iron patience, for news of the outside world to be brought to him. He knocked sharply twice, and, then, after an interval, three times. It was the signal they had agreed upon. He would have to allow his brother five minutes to traverse the distance from his couch in the library to the front door. He listened eagerly for the dragging foot-steps and the accompanying patter of Mac in attendance on his master. He lifted the flap of the letter box and called through it.

"It's me, Stephen."

But the silence within remained unbroken.

Martin's heart seemed to miss a beat. The window shutters had all been bolted and the doors made fast. Helpless as he was Stephen had surely been safe from any attack from outside. But there was a possibility that the unusual exertion and excitement had been too much for him. He called his brother by name more loudly than before. There was no answer. It was strange that Mac had not barked. Mac surely must have heard him. He decided to go round to the back of the house and knock on the library window.

If necessary he could get in through one of the windows upstairs. There was a ladder locked up in the tool shed, and he had the key with him. But when he came round the corner of the house he saw that a ladder would not be needed. The french window of the library was wide open and the inner wooden shutters he had been so careful to close were folded back against the wall. The room itself was lit by the shaded reading lamp and the last glimmer of a dying fire.

Stephen Drury was lying face downwards on the door beside his couch.

Martin heard a cry and did not know that he himself had uttered it. He raised his brother in his arms and saw that he still breathed. He slipped a cushion under his head before he laid him down again and ran into the dining-room for brandy. When he returned Stephen's eyes were open.

"Mac," he whimpered. "My little dog. He killed Mac. I tried to choke the brute, but I must have fainted before I finished him off. Just my luck. He isn't here, is he?" He tried to raise himself and sank back with a sigh.

"There's nobody here. Wait a minute."

Martin bent ever the dog where he lay in a pool of blood. His lips were trembling. Mac, who had meant so much to them both. His eyes were dim with tears as he stared down at the little body. He brushed them away impatiently.

"Stephen—he—he isn't dead. Perhaps there's a chance—" he was tearing his handkerchief into strips. "What happened? Why was the window open?"

"I opened it. I hoped someone would come. I waited, and a chap in a mask turned up. I had my old army pistol. I thought it was loaded—but he knew better."

Martin's jaw dropped. "Oh Lord!"

"You unloaded it, eh? Recently?"

"Well, Clowes advised me to when I met him the other morning in the village. He said you seemed depressed, and it wasn't wise—"

"Clowes, eh? That's interesting. Bring Mac over to me. Martin."

"All right. I'll get you back on the couch first and he can lie in his usual place. He's very weak, poor old boy. He's lost a lot of blood. The bullet went clean through the fleshy part of his shoulder. We'll pull him through."

"There," he said presently, when he had settled them both to his satisfaction, and Mac was feebly licking his master's hand.

"What was the beggar like?"

"He wore a mask of white linen. A hood covering his head entirely."

"Collier rang up the nursing-home to warn them against Clowes not an hour ago. He called there this evening and prescribed a new medicine for Anne. We were only just in time to stop her from drinking it. I'd been to the vicarage and on to Crossways. Lady Jocelyn was there. She lent me her car. You oughtn't to have done this, Stephen. He might have killed you. It was a frightful risk."

"I must have left my marks on him," said Stephen with satisfaction. "His beastly neck ought to be black and blue for some time to come. Why has Lady Jocelyn come down again?"

"With some idea of helping Collier. She's broken off her engagement. She looked ill and desperately unhappy."

"Hardly surprising."

Martin had closed the window and fastened the shutters. He made up the fire, and fetching a cloth from the kitchen, mopped up the blood on the floor.

"Jocelyn isn't a bad sort," he said. "She's had a rotten upbringing. Lord Bember may be a brilliant orator and all that, but he can't have shone as a father. She did what she could for her young brother. She was fond of him."

"Did you ever meet Bember's secretary, this fellow Kafka?"

"I've seen him about the village occasionally with Jocelyn. A good looking chap. One of the quiet sort. She talked and he listened. How's the old dog now?"

Stephen was gently stroking the shaggy grey head. "You've got to live a little longer. Mac." There was a catch in his voice.

He was silent for a moment,

"You might close the sale, Martin."

"What? Did that crook—"

"Naturally. That's what he came for. He thought I might have the doings. I wasn't sure myself—"

Martin stared at him. "What do you mean?"

"I've had a small sealed packet in my possession for about sixteen years. A message in pencil was scrawled on the inner wrapping, asking me to keep it safe and to say nothing to anyone until I received definite instructions. The last words were *The rest follows by hand.* I think now that Mary Borlase posted it when she reached London and before she went to her brother's house. The jewels remained in her possession. Almost certainly she hid them somewhere about the place. I kept the packet entrusted to me in the safe. I had to give up the key and the combination to our Mr. X. He thought he'd got the diamonds and the emerald. Especially the emerald. But the contents were of no value—to him. Will you look in the fender. Martin? There's just a chance—"

Martin obeyed. After a moment he came back to his brother. "Only this," he said gently.

Stephen took the long curl of silky black hair and placed it very carefully in his pocket-book. After another pause he resumed. "The brute lost his temper then and snarled at me, and Mac went for him. He kicked the dog across the room and then shot him. Thank God he was too blind with fury to shoot straight. I made up my mind then to strangle him if he came within my reach. I've still got the use of my hands. He dragged me over on to the floor on top of him and I suppose the effort was a bit too much for me."

"I wish you'd told me and Collier about the packet," said Martin.

"The habit of reserve grows on one, Martin. Besides I was almost certain the contents were what they proved to be. I—I can't talk about Nadine even to you."

"I understand."

"I wonder where he got to," murmured Stephen.

Martin was closing the window shutters. "I'm going to search the house now," he announced.

"Better reload my revolver and take it with you. Though I don't think you'll find anyone. What will you do after that?"

"I'd like to drive down to the village. Collier rang up the nursing-home from the post office. He ought to be told what's happened here. But I don't like leaving you again."

Stephen smiled. "I'll stay put this time."

"You'd better."

CHAPTER XXIX
THE MARCH OF NEMESIS

DOCTOR Clowes entered the little post office briskly, stooping as the tall Superintendent had stooped to avoid knocking his head against the lintel. He had apparently been roused from his slumbers, for his usually sleek hair was ruffled and he was wearing a coat over his pyjama jacket. "Well," he began, "where's the—" he broke off as his restless brown eyes caught sight of the detective from Scotland Yard, who was still sitting behind the counter, white-faced, and with his left arm in an improvised sling, and his own colour faded perceptibly. It was apparent to them all that Collier's presence there was as unsuspected as it was unwelcome. The Superintendent, who had been gloomy, brightened. Perhaps, after all, there was something in the Inspector's theory. He signed to one of his men to stand with his back to the door by which the doctor had entered.

"It's like this, sir," he began. "There's been an accident to a motor-car in the avenue of Clumber Place. One of the occupants was killed, and the other was thrown clear. You see him here. Inspector Collier, of the Criminal Investigation Department at the Yard. The other man, I'm sorry to say, was the village policeman, James Deane. Is it a fact that you were passing at the time?"

"Along the road, do you mean?"

"No. That you were in the grounds."

"Certainly not. I know nothing whatever about it."

"Where were you between eight and nine this evening?"

"Let me think. I called at the vicarage. One of the vicar's pupils has a poisoned finger which needs frequent dressing. After that I went home. I read for a while and went to bed early."

"Your servant can corroborate that?" said Collier speaking for the first time.

The doctor was answering readily enough now. "I'm afraid not. I have a woman in to clean Tuesdays and Fridays. For the rest I wait on myself. I'm sorry you've had such a nasty smash, Inspector. I see your friends here have rendered first aid. I suppose I have been fetched out of bed to do what I can for you?"

He advanced towards the counter and set down his bag.

"Oh, there you are, Miss Pringle," he said genially, "I didn't notice you at first. Quite an invasion, isn't it. I can't examine you here, Inspector."

"I don't want you to. Thanks all the same," said Collier blandly.

"No?" His eyebrows went up. "Then may I ask why I have been brought here?"

Collier did not reply immediately. He was convinced in his own mind that the face he had seen by the momentary light of a match by the overturned car was the face of Doctor Clowes, but he realised that his unsupported statement would not be enough. Proof. How was that to be obtained?

"You dressed in a hurry, doctor?"

"Yes My overcoat and a pair of slacks over my pyjamas, as you see. I thought you might be in urgent need of my services," said Clowes drily.

"I see. Very good of you." He stared at Clowes' hands which were encased in leather gloves. "You remembered your gloves. Do you always wear them?"

"Nearly always. A doctor has to be careful of his hands."

"But you can't—" Collier checked himself. He remembered now. The hand that struck the match was certainly bare. No doubt the right hand glove had been removed to take the pulse of that other hand that had protruded from under the body of the car. The headlights had been switched on afterwards. Collier smiled. There would almost certainly be irrefutable proof.

"I wonder," he said, "if you have any objection to having your finger-prints taken by the police?"

"I certainly should. I am not a criminal. You have nothing against me."

"That's all right," said Collier easily. "We can get dozens of excellent prints, no doubt, at your house, for purposes of comparison with any we may find on my car. Nearly always wearing gloves isn't enough, doctor."

"You can't enter my house without a warrant."

"No."

"Well, I'm going home now anyway," said Clowes.

He turned towards the door but the constable who blocked the entrance did not move.

"I'm afraid we shall have to detain you for a few hours," said Collier.

"'Rather a high-handed proceeding," said Clowes, with white lips. He appealed to the Superintendent. "You leave it all to this man from London. Surely you have some say in the matter. You have no right to keep me here. The police can't ride rough-shod over the public in this country. You'll live to regret this."

The Superintendent had been thinking the same thing. He was far from easy in his mind. But he was not in the habit of yielding to bluster, and Clowes had made an unfortunate impression.

"He's a twister," thought the Superintendent. So he answered stolidly. "The Inspector's in charge. I'm lending my support."

"Oh, very well." Clowes made a not very successful effort to regain his usual rather jaunty manner. "You'll discover your mistake in time, I suppose. I can afford to wait for an apology. I—" he did not finish his sentence. A car had stopped in the road. One of the policemen on duty outside opened the door a few inches.

"Mr. Drury to see Inspector Collier. He says it's urgent."

The Inspector's weary face lighted up. "Let him in."

Martin looked at Clowes, but the doctor was choosing a cigarette from his case and did not meet his eye. He crossed over to the counter. "I've something to tell you—"

Collier nodded and got stiffly to his feet. "In the other room. Will you come with us, Superintendent? You will await us here, doctor."

"It appears I have no choice," said Clowes sourly.

Miss Pringle's tiny sitting-room was more comfortable than the shop. A fire was burning in the grate. A white-faced clock ticked cheerfully on the mantelpiece between a pair of spotted black and white china dogs. It was ten minutes past two. The Superintendent closed the door and the three men sat down. Martin was staring at Collier. "I say, you look all out. What happened? Why didn't you call for me?"

"Never mind that now," said Collier. "I want your story if you've got one."

Martin complied, describing his call at the vicarage, where Outram could tell him nothing, his visit to Crossways and his borrowing of Lady Jocelyn's car to drive to Horsham. He told them what had happened at the nursing home, and of Stephen's struggle with the masked intruder. The two policemen listened with rapt attention. When he had done Collier groaned.

"Some people have all the luck. He had Mr. X there, in his hands, and he let him go. Don't misunderstand me. Martin," he said quickly as the young man reddened at what he imagined to be an implied criticism of his brother. "He did wonders far more than he should have attempted alone in his state. If only he'd confided his plan to me. He might have been killed. But he can't have damaged Clowes as much as he thought he did or he'd show the marks."

"That's true," said the Superintendent. "But Clowes has his coat buttoned up to his throat, and a muffler under that."

"The colonel gripped him by the throat?"

"Yes, and fell off his couch on top of him before he lost consciousness. If it's Clowes I wonder he can speak. His neck must be badly bruised. Stephen's pretty helpless at getting about but he hasn't lost his grip."

"Wait a bit," said Collier, "by his own admission Clowes went to the vicarage this evening to dress young Williams' finger. Let's assume that he was there when I called. I interviewed the other boy, Thompson, in one of the ground floor rooms. Our conversation may have been overheard. It's a possibility. Williams rapped on the ceiling after a while and Thompson went up to him. I followed but not quick enough. If the doctor was there I fancy there would have been time for him to tell them to send me on to Clumber Place—which they did very cleverly—and get off himself to fix up his little gadget in the avenue. I heard a car starting up in the lane. The question is would he have had the time after I saw him examining the overturned car, and assuring himself, as he thought, of my elimination, to go up to the Dower House and have the encounter you have described with Colonel Drury, and get home after it and go to bed. Frankly, I doubt it."

"Do you mean that we've gone too far with Clowes?" asked the Superintendent anxiously.

"No. We've got him for what he did to-night. If he doesn't swing for the murder of poor Deane I'm a Dutchman."

"That sounds like my men come back now," said the Superintendent. He opened the door into the shop. "Is that Milsom and Cludd?"

"Yes. sir."

"Report to me in here."

Two constables in uniform entered and the elder stood forward as spokesman.

"We proceeded as directed and found the gate of Clamber Place open. We found a small four-seater car overturned half-way up the avenue. The marks on the road surface indicated that it had turned round and dashed against a tree before turning turtle. The body of a man was pinned under the car. We managed to jack her up sufficiently to get him out and identify him as Police Constable Deane, stationed at Ladebrook. Carrying out instructions we examined the trees on both sides of the road and found fresh marks on the bark of two that faced one another that looked as if a wire might have been fixed round the trunks at a height of four feet from the ground."

The superintendent, with something definite to work upon, was brisk and efficient.

"No trace of the wire?"

"No, sir."

"It must be found. There must have been thirty feet of it at least. And, probably wire-cutters. Cludd, you will go now to Doctor Clowes' house and see that no one enters it until I come. I shall get a search warrant and go through it myself in the morning." Cludd saluted and went out. Milsom remained by the door, awaiting his orders. The superintendent turned to Collier. "I shall ring up for an ambulance to fetch Deane's body and somebody will have to break the news to his wife."

"Perhaps Miss Pringle would do that," suggested Collier.

Pannet brightened. He had been dreading that job. "I'll ask her." He looked at Martin. "Do you want police protection up at your place, Mr. Drury? I can spare you one of my men."

"Thanks, but I hardly think it's necessary. I fancy Mr. X has shot his bolt as far as we are concerned."

The Superintendent nodded. "All right. Just as you like. Though the Inspector has the last word. It's his case, though I'm dealing with this bit of it." He glanced inquiringly at Collier, who was shovelling more coal on to the fire. "I don't see what more can be done before the morning, do you?"

"Well, I'd like two of your fellows to keep an eye on the vicarage. Those three boys must be shaking in their shoes, though they've brazened it out so far. I want them to remain where they are for the present. If it's Clowes they're afraid of they may come clean when they hear he's under arrest."

"The leader of the gang is the man who wears the linen mask," said Martin. "Anne Borlase saw him wearing it. Her description and Stephen's tally. The masked man is Mr. X."

"Phew," said the Superintendent. "It is hot in here. What made you pile on the coal, Inspector? There was a good fire before."

"Shall I open the window?" said Martin.

Collier stopped him. "No. Wait a minute. Can we have Clowes in here, Superintendent? I'd like to ask him one or two questions."

"Certainly."

The Superintendent spoke to Milsom. "Ask Doctor Clowes to step in here for a moment."

Clowes came in without any apparent reluctance. He teemed to have gained confidence in the interval that had been allowed him to reflect on his portion. It remained to be seen whether that confidence was well founded.

"Sit down, doctor," said Collier, indicating the only available chair which he had pushed forward himself to face the fire. "Have a cigarette."

"Thanks. I'll smoke my own. When are you chaps going to realise that you're exceeding your powers? You'll get into no end of a row for this. I shouldn't be surprised if it doesn't end in a Royal Commission. You'll both lose your stripes."

Nobody replied. He glanced round him at their grave faces.

"That's all right, doctor," said Collier, "we'll do any worrying that has to he done about that, and, meanwhile, we'll get on with our job. First of all it's my duty to warn you that anything you may say can be used in evidence against you. On the other hand"—he broke off—"I was going to say that the police would bear in mind any assistance you gave them, but, candidly. I don't think they will after what has happened to-night."

"I see." Clowes had listened to this with a smile on his face, but it was a stiff, set smile that deceived nobody. "You can't be surprised after that if I lie low and say nothing. Am I to be kept up all night? If I mayn't go home you must provide me with a bed somewhere else. I'm tired—and boiling hot," he added irritably. "This room's like an oven." As he spoke he tugged at his muffler and unbuttoned the top button of his pyjama coat—"what the hell are you all staring at me like that for?"

Collier answered for them all. "Looking for something that isn't there. All right, Superintendent. You can take him away with you. Miss Pringle said I might spend the night on her sofa here. I'd be glad if you'd lend me a car in the morning and a man to drive it. I must get back to Town as soon as possible."

When Martin went out of the shop Clowes was already in the first of the two police cars, sitting at the back between two plain clothes detectives. There were lights in Deane's cottage a little farther down the street where the little postmistress, escorted by a large constable, was breaking the bad news to the wife of the dead man; but the other houses were in darkness. The villagers were sleeping peacefully, unaware of the march of Nemesis. Martin yawned unrestrainedly as he climbed into his borrowed car and let in the clutch. He needed sleep just then more than anything in the world, and there was already a glimmer of light in the sky to the east, and, under the deep thatched eaves, a drowsy twitter of half awakened birds.

Chapter XXX
PORTRAIT OF A GIRL IN GREEN

Israel Kafka, always an early riser, had finished his frugal breakfast of rolls and coffee and was examining a print he had bought at a sale with a magnifying glass when he heard voices in the hall. He laid the glass down with a slight frown. He had had a restless night and was not feeling quite himself.

The ex-prize-fighter brought in a card on a salver.

"Lady Jocelyn Vaste, sir."

"Did you tell her that my son was not at home?"

"Yes, sir. She asked for you."

"Tell her I'm not well," but Jocelyn had followed the servant and was already at the door. A hurried make-up betrayed lines of fatigue and her eyes were heavy, but her green beret was pulled on at its usual rakish angle and she was wearing a green frock under her mink motoring coat. The old man bowed, but he did not offer to shake hands with her. She might have the decency to wear black for her brother, even if he was a waster, he thought.

"Won't you sit down?"

"Thank you." Jocelyn looked about her. She had been only once before to the famous art dealer's house. On the night before her engagement to Maurice was announced she and her father had dined there with the old man and his son.

"What a lovely room!"

"Yes. I have many beautiful things. In a long life I have acquired much. And to what do I owe the honour of this visit?" She realised that Maurice must have told him that their engagement was at an end. The black eyes, so like and yet so unlike those of the younger man, were frankly inimical. Brave as she was she flinched a little.

"You hate me?"

"On the contrary," he said smoothly. "But—since you are not going to marry Maurice I hardly expected to see you again. I am a little puzzled."

His face reminded her of a Buddha carved in ivory grown yellow with age. She leaned towards him. "Please, Mr. Kafka, I haven't driven up from Sussex to talk about myself. I'm awfully unhappy, but never mind that now. It's Maurice. I—I want him to be warned. I—" she covered her face with her hands and added indistinctly, "Whatever he's done I want him to be warned."

"Warned?" said Kafka. "About what?"

She lifted her head. "I don't know how much you know. It's the police. If you know where he is will you tell him? Perhaps he could hire a plane or something and get right away."

"You do not know Maurice," said his father, "if you imagine he has done anything wrong. I, in my seventy years—I may have been greedy, grasping, unscrupulous. A dirty old Jew, Lady Jocelyn. I have sometimes—not always—deserved to hear those words on Christian lips. But Maurice is different. That is why I have told him often he would never succeed in business. If he had been born poor he would die poor. He is too proud, too—" be added something that she did not understand. "That is Yiddish. The word I want is fastidious. That is why, if you will forgive me for saying so, I wondered that he chose you."

Jocelyn was not offended. This stark candour appealed to her.

"I know," she said. "I must have seemed frightfully unsuitable to you. But one doesn't choose the person one falls in love with. It's just a rather ghastly accident as a rule. Thank you for listening to me. If you'll pass on what I've said. That's all I ask. And at once, please." She stood up. "I'll be going back to Berkeley Square now."

"One moment. You drove up from Sussex this morning?"

"Yes, I started at seven. I'm half dead. Good-bye, Mr. Kafka."

"Good-bye," he said. She thought his voice sounded kinder.

"He loves Maurice," she reflected. That was only natural. Not many fathers cultivated the ironic detachment of Lord Bember. The man servant with the broken nose was waiting in the hall to show her out. He even came out with her into the road and closed the door of the car for her after she had climbed into the driving seat.

Berkeley Square. Her father and stepmother would be still in Paris and she would have the house to herself. That was one comfort. She would have a hot bath and go straight to bed. Steady now, steady, she told herself as she steered through the traffic. This was the last lap. Soon, quite soon now, she could relax.

Martin Drury, arriving at Crossways with her car soon after six as she was pottering about in her dressing-gown, boiling the kettle for a cup of tea, had been full of news. He had told her of Clowes's arrest and seen her first blank incredulity turn to horror.

"But—he was here last night. I told him—lots. He—I was so lonely and miserable. I let him—Martin! Can't I trust anyone?"

"He's only one of the crowd, Jocelyn. He isn't Mr. X."

"Martin, he gave me some stuff last night to make me sleep. It made me sick. You remember how hard it was to wake me when you came round a bit later." She stared at him, wide-eyed. "Was he trying to poison me?"

"Why should he?" Martin argued. "He probably made the stuff a bit stronger than he need have done with the idea of keeping you quiet. People react so differently to dope."

She had abandoned the attempt to get herself some kind of breakfast, and was sitting, her shaking hands tightly clasped in her lap. Martin made the tea and poured out two cups.

"I can do with some," he explained. "It was nearly four when I turned in. An hour and a half's sleep isn't much use. I feel like a chewed rag, but I had to come round early. I've brought back your car, but if you don't want it I'd like to go to Horsham in it."

She sipped her tea. It was very hot. "Horsham? Oh, that girl you told me about. The girl whose aunt brought the Tsarina's jewels to England. You've taken quite a fancy to her, haven't you?"

"I like her," he said.

Jocelyn set down her cup. "Well, I can't let you have my car because I'm going back to Town in it, but I'll give you a lift as far as Horsham if you like." She looked at her wrist watch. "I'll dress now. I shall be ready in twenty minutes."

She had dropped him at the nursing home and driven on alone. Afterwards it had occurred to her that she might have waited to hear how the other girl was. But she was not really interested. Jocelyn's benevolence did not extend to young women she had never set eyes on. She was, if anything, annoyed with Anne. She had got Martin. Let her be satisfied with that. And then, with a kindlier impulse, "Poor little thing. I'm a selfish greedy pig," thought Jocelyn bitterly as the car slid gently to a standstill by the kerb.

The butler admitted her. She stopped to speak to him

"Tell Miller to take my car round to the garage. I shan't be going out again to-day. I'm awfully tired and I'm going straight to bed."

"Very good, my lady."

Jocelyn went straight up to the bathroom and turned on the hot water tap. "I might as well be clean outside," she thought wearily. Thank God she had not let Clowes kiss her again last night. Life was foul. She remembered how a clever and amusing woman of forty had once said to her, "My dear, peace comes when you can honestly say that you get more comfort from a hot water bottle than a lover." Had she nearly reached that stage? She dropped a handful of bath salts into the water.

"I'll go right away," she thought, "and—and become a nun."

She got into the bath. The water was deliciously warm.

Meanwhile Inspector Collier, who had made an even earlier start, had arrived at New Scotland Yard and been called to the Chief's room to make his report. The telephone had been busy during the night and he was hardly surprised to find Sir James with Cardew.

"You've got me out of my bed an hour before my usual time, young man," was his greeting. "What's wrong with your arm, eh?" he added as he noticed the sling.

"Broken last night, sir, when the car I was driving overturned."

"Careless driving?"

"A wire across the road, sir. A trap, and I fell into it. Unfortunately the village policeman who was with me was killed."

"Ah yes. The Chief Constable rang up. They're handling the business. Any proof?"

"A certain amount. I saw a man on the spot directly afterwards and identified him. He's under arrest. They searched the scene of the accident and found some matches and a cigarette that had been dropped and trodden into the ground. They were going to search his house this morning."

"Who is he?"

"A young doctor who settled in the neighbourhood rather over a year ago. He didn't practice. He was supposed to be engaged on research work, but he's been acting as locum for the local G.P. lately. His name is Clowes, Henry Clowes. He's got an Edinburgh degree."

"Did you suspect him of being a member of this gang*"

"No, sir I didn't. I ought to have smelt a rat when he gave the evidence he did at the inquest on Lord Herbert Vaste. He must have known the boy had been dead more than an hour when he saw him. If he'd been on the square he would have drawn the attention of the police to the point."

Sir James lit a cigarette. "You may be right about Vaste. Inspector. I gather that your theory is that he hanged himself in the empty house that has been used as the gang's headquarters at some time during the afternoon rather than carry out another attempt to dispose of the girl they had been keeping there, and that his body was subsequently carried to the church so that it might be found there?"

"Yes, sir."

"Nasty piece of work the fellow must be who planned that," murmured Sir James. "Was it this man Clowes?"

"Anne Borlase recovered consciousness last night, sir. Colonel Drury's young brother was there and Sergeant Pollard, who has been watching the house. She told them that the man she saw wore a white linen mask. He wanted to know the whereabouts of the jewels. She couldn't tell him as she didn't know. Her recollection was confused. She'd been kept under the influence of drugs, of course. I rang up the home while they were there. It was after I had seen Clowes. I suddenly realised that he was probably locum there too. As a matter of fact he wasn't. But he must have heard yesterday that the girl was there. He went and told, the matron that he was taking over the case. I was just in time to warn them not to let her have any medicine he prescribed. Pollard got hold of the bottle for analysis."

He went on to describe Stephen Drury's struggle with his masked visitor.

"When Martin returned to the Dower House he found his brother lying on the floor where he had fallen. His assailant had vanished. What became of him? I think myself that he had a car and that he got clear away."

"You think he's the head of the gang? The brains?"

"Yes."

"Clowes?"

"I don't think so. Clowes may have been his right hand man. It's somebody who has been able to inspire a kind of perverted hero worship in his followers. Those boys at the vicarage have been loyal to him. We've picked up three fellows who have been smuggling dope from the East, the first mate on an orange boat, a chap who keeps a bird shop in Portsmouth off the Hard, an unemployed waiter. We know enough now to break up the gang, but I don't want to catch the sprats and let the whale go. Whale. A whale's a Christian to him. He's more like a shark or a devil fish."

"You don't think they murdered the old man who kept that second-hand furniture and book shop, the father of the girl?"

"No, sir. They inveigled the girl away with the idea of raiding the shop in her absence. I don't think they intended murder, but the Russians from the timber boat were before them. After that there could be no drawing back. If they let her go she'd accuse them of killing her father. They were bound to get rid of her. They put it off as long as they dared."

There was a pause. Sir James walked to the window and stood there drumming on the pane. The telephone on the desk rang and Cardew took up the receiver.

"Yes . . . yes . . ." He rang off. "Reports from the men who are watching Mr. Kafka's house, sir. Mr. Kafka has not returned, but Lady Jocelyn called twenty minutes ago. She's just left. She's driving herself in the car in which she went down to Sussex the day before yesterday. She's being followed."

"They haven't left off watching the house, I hope," said Collier. "No."

Sir James turned back abruptly. "Where's young Kafka, do you know?"

"He went to Berkeley Square on Tuesday night. Lady Jocelyn was alone there as her father had returned to Paris immediately after his son's cremation at Golder's Green. She rang me up after he left and told me she wanted to help the police to find out the whole truth concerning her brother's death. She was very excited.

I gathered that she had broken off her engagement. She suggested that she should return to Ladebrook for a few days I agreed. I didn't think she could help much. My idea was to reduce the number of unoccupied houses in the neighbourhood. Crossways had been used before as a bolt hole. She went down on Wednesday. I meant to look her up, but I hadn't time. Kafka, meanwhile, had done what I rather expected him to do, and gone to the weekend cottage of his married sister at Bury, about eight miles off. He is a frequent visitor there and comes and goes as he pleases. I went to the place with Sergeant Duffield. The housekeeper told me that soon after his arrival he had had a telephone message from, she thought, his father, and that he had left again immediately. She had been in the next room while he was answering the telephone and fancied she had heard Brighton mentioned. We went on to Arundel, where Duffield hired a motorcycle at a garage and went off in the hope of picking up the trail, but he had no luck."

"I've met young Kafka," said Sir James. "A good looking chap. Very quiet."

"A dark horse," said Cardew.

"He did exceedingly well at Oxford. His post as private secretary to Lord Bember is only a method of marking time. He'll probably stand for Parliament himself eventually. I wonder he's remained with Bember as long as he has. He's supposed to be a difficult man to work for. A bitter tongue. But of course if he was involved with young Vaste—"

He looked at Collier who answered the look rather than the words. "He went down to Ladebrook the day Lord Herbert put an end to himself. He says his car broke down. He's no real alibi for that afternoon or evening."

"We've got to be absolutely certain before we move another step." said Sir James, and he spoke with the utmost gravity. "Old Kafka is a great man in his own way. He's immensely rich and very generous. He bore the cost of the rebuilding of St. Ursula's. He bought that Rembrandt five years ago and gave it to the nation. He doesn't parade his benefactions. He's done more in that way than the general public realises. And he's immensely proud of his son. Heaven only knows how he'll react to this."

"He's in it. sir."

"What do you mean—in it?"

Collier repeated what Israel Kafka himself had told him of his taking over the shop on Elmer Passage.

"He swears that he did it to oblige old Borlase and his daughter. He thought they'd got into financial difficulties. I believe he was telling the truth and that for once in his life he'd been made a dupe."

"By his son?"

"No. By the men on the Russian boat who ransacked the shop, killed old Borlase, and, for all we know, got away with the jewels. They'd cleaned the place up and probably they thought that if they could induce Kafka to take it over they'd divert suspicion from themselves to him. They may be business rivals not unwilling to do him a dirty trick. He did take it over. He's got a lot of second-hand furniture and antique shops all over London. But the young fellow he put in reported that the position was inconvenient and the business moribund, and he closed down after twenty-four hours, keeping the key to hand over to Borlase if he ever returned."

"You think that's all as far as he's concerned?"

"I do."

"But how much does he know now? Will he try to shield his son? I tell you he won't take this lying down. Why did Lady Jocelyn go to see him this morning—" He broke off as the telephone bell rang again. Cardew handed the receiver to him.

"It's for you, Sir James."

"Hallo. . . . Yes, speaking. Who? Oh, Mr. Kafka. Yes. Oh, I'm usually here about nine. One of the world's workers. What? Oh, that's very good of you. I—look here—I think I must ask you to wait a day or two. Then, if you care to renew your offer, I think it will be better. If you wish, of course. I shall be here."

He hung up the receiver and looked round at the others.

"That was Israel Kafka himself speaking from his house in Regent's Park. Lady Jocelyn left him, as we know, about ten minutes ago. He's losing no time."

"What did he want, sir?"

"He wants to give five thousand pounds to police charities."

"Gosh!" murmured Collier.

"It's rather touching, I think," said Sir James. "It's too naïf to be offensive. He's got the wind up all right. I temporised, and he said he was coming round to see me."

"Well, he can't buy the C.I.D.," said Cardew.

Sir James smiled at his indignation. "No. But the attempt to do so is instructive. It shows to what lengths he is prepared to go—" He broke off to answer another telephone call. "This is for you. Collier. It's from the man who's watching Lord Bember's house in Berkeley Square. Lady Jocelyn has just gone in and her car has been taken round to the garage by the footman. I think I'd have a word with that young lady before long, Inspector. It looks to me as if she's trying to double-cross you. Wait and see old Kafka first. They are bringing him up here now."

"Very good, sir."

Sir James lit another cigarette. "It's all very well, Collier. Maurice Kafka may be your Mr. X. but how are you going to prove it?"

"I can prove it all right if I can lay hands on him before the marks on his throat have time to fade," said Collier grimly.

"By Jove, I forgot that. And when you've got him—if he is the man—will every member of the gang be accounted for?"

"Yes. Young Vaste told Drury it was called the Council of Ten, and the man who keeps the bird shop in Portsmouth said the same." He brought out his notebook. "Outram, Thompson, and Williams, young Vaste's fellow pupils at Ladebrook Vicarage, Outram's airman brother, the shopkeeper, the first mate, and the waiter, and, of course, Clowes. That makes nine."

"And not one of them have squealed?"

"Well, in a way. They all say they're only obeying orders and disclaim responsibility. I think those chaps down at Ladebrook are the inner ring. It's worth noting that though they are all bad eggs they are all what they call well connected."

Cardew snorted. He had very little use for blue blood. But Sir James groaned. "I know. The Outrams are an old family. The General is very much respected. The Stourfield Outrams—" he stopped as a young policeman opened the door and Israel Kafka appeared on the threshold.

"Good morning, Sir James. It is good of you to receive me so early."

Cardew, who had not seen him before, was impressed in spite of himself. They all felt the impact of his personality. This was a man accustomed to make swift decisions and to take big risks. He crossed the room, breathing stertorously and leaning heavily on his stick, and sank into the chair Collier brought forward for him.

"Thank you, young man. I know your face. Ah, you came to see me the other day."

"You have something to tell us, Mr. Kafka," said Sir James.

The old art dealer's vast bulk was immovable, but his black eyes turned towards the speaker. "Nothing. If you thought that you misunderstood me. I fancied you had, and that is why I came myself. I wish to contribute—"

Sir James held up his hand. "One moment, Mr. Kafka. I must ask you to wait. If, later on, you care to renew your offer, we shall, of course, be very grateful. We are very anxious to get into touch with your son. Can you tell us where he is?"

Kafka had learned facial control in the auction room. He was used to being watched. He continued to stare blankly at his interlocutor. "Maurice? He went down to my daughter's cottage at Bury. I had been going to a sale at Hassocks but I didn't feel well enough to I rang him up and asked him to go in my place. There was a set of Chippendale chairs. He's not a bad judge of Chippendale. I have not heard from him since and he has not come home. He probably spent the night in Brighton."

"I see. Thank you. You are expecting him back?"

"Yes. On the other hand he might run over to the Continent. He is needing a change. He has had—how do you say—one upset."

Kafka's faint foreign accent was becoming more marked. He was beginning to betray symptoms of tension.

"An upset? What was that, Mr. Kafka?"

"His engagement. It was broken off. That is all." He looked round at the three faces as inexpressive almost as his own.

"I tell you. I tell you. I am his father. He could not deceive me. He would not try—"

The bell was ringing again. "Excuse me," murmured Sir James.

They waited while he listened.

"He has not gone abroad, Mr. Kafka. He has just entered Lord Bember's house in Berkeley Square."

CHAPTER XXXI
INSPECTOR COLLIER'S WATERLOO

JOCELYN had had her bath and gone back to her room when somebody knocked at her door. "What is it?" she asked irritably.

"It's me, your ladyship, Lambert. Could I speak to you?"

"All right. Wait one minute." She took the first frock that came to hand from her wardrobe, a dark red silk, and slipped it over her head, passed a comb through her thick mop of black curls, and was ready.

Lambert was standing just outside. He had been with Lord Bember ever since Jocelyn could remember, but he never presumed on the fact. Efficient and imperturbable, he was a model of discretion. To see Lambert's rosy cheeks faded to a mottled grey and his hands trembling as he lifted them towards her was as shocking to Jocelyn as it might have been to see the moon fall from the sky. It was a portent of the end of all things. Unconsciously she caught at the door knob for support.

"What's the matter, Lambert? Don't look at me like that."

"My lady, did you hear that noise just now?"

"Do you mean a sort of—I thought it was a car back-firing or a burst tyre."

He shook his head. "It was in the house. In the study, the little study, my lady. The room Mr. Kafka uses. I came up as quick as I could and tried the door. I couldn't get in. It's locked."

She stared at him. "What do you mean? There's nobody in the house but me, is there?"

"Mr. Kafka came twenty minutes ago, my lady. He said it was to fetch his things away. It—it was while you were in the bathroom. After a bit I let him go up to the study. He said he wouldn't be long. And now—I don't know what's happened, but he didn't answer when I called him."

Jocelyn's face was as white as paper. She brushed by him and ran down the stairs to the door below. The room in which Maurice had worked was on the left. She tried to turn the door handle.

"Maurice! Maurice!" There was no sound within. She turned to Lambert, who had followed her. "We'll have to—" the rest of the sentence was drowned by a loud knocking at the hall door.

"Shall I go, my lady?"

"Yes. See who it is."

She leaned against the wall, her eyes closed. She felt faint and sick. She heard men's voices below and heavy foot steps.

She burst out crying, her hands before her face.

A hand was laid on her shoulder. She lifted tear-drowned eyes and saw Collier's face, drawn with anxiety. "Pull yourself together." he said. "What has happened? We know Maurice Kafka is here. His father is below."

There were other men with him, stalwart men with grave, intent faces. Jocelyn tried to control her trembling lips.

"I—I didn't know he was here. Lambert told me just now. I—we heard a shot."

Collier and Cardew exchanged glances. "Try a key from one of the other doors."

Lambert intervened. "That's no use. They're all different."

"Then we must break the door down. Fetch a poker."

Another minute and Collier had thrust his sound arm through the splintered hole in the upper panel and had turned the key in the lock. They all crowded into the room after him.

The secretary's room bore traces of his occupation. There was a typewriter under a black cover on the writing table. The book shelves were filled chiefly with works of reference. A large framed photograph of Lady Jocelyn stood where he could see it when he lifted his eyes from his work. A long-legged doll dressed as a pierrot leaned against the frame and seemed to leer down with a ghastly inhuman smile at the body lying between the writing table and the door. An automatic lay on the carpet close to the clenched right hand

Jocelyn went forward and knelt beside it. She was remembering her dream of the lips that had grown cold as they pressed hers.

"Maurice—"

The eyes were not quite closed. She could see a rim of white through the thick black lashes. The window was shut and a cloud of bluish smoke still filled the room. Collier and an older man were bending over him.

"Through the chest. But he's still breathing. Ring up for the ambulance. There's a doctor next door. Get him at once. Look out, here's his father."

Israel Kafka had been slow in mounting the stairs, but he had reached the landing at last. All made way for him as he entered the room. He sank heavily into the chair placed for him where he could watch his son's unconscious face.

The doctor, an elderly man, came in carrying his bag. He unbuttoned the wounded man's coat and waistcoat and slit open his silk shirt with a pair of surgical scissors.

Jocelyn moaned a little as she covered her face with her hands. Somebody—it was Collier—helped her to her feet and made her sit down. "It's the blood," she whispered.

"I know. Be brave."

"Well," said Israel Kafka at last in a dead voice.

The doctor glanced up at him. "You are his father?"

"Yes. Will he live?"

"I can't be certain. I think he may. I think so. If he is to be moved it had better be done now, before he regains consciousness."

The police ambulance had arrived and four men were waiting on the landing with a stretcher. Kafka turned to Sir James, who had come with him but had taken no part hitherto.

"I may have him?" he said.

Sir James asked him to wait while he spoke to Cardew. The Chief-Inspector was conferring with Collier a little apart.

They both looked round as the Commissioner joined them.

"Kafka wants to take his son home. What about it?"

Cardew looked worried. "That's all right, sir. The fact is—" Whatever it was it seemed to stick in his throat. "Collier's been on the wrong tack. Utterly mistaken. He may as well face it now. Young Kafka isn't the man we've been after. We both had a good look at him just now when the doctor was examining him. There isn't a mark of any kind on his neck."

"That's torn it," said Sir James ruefully. "We've forced our way in here and broken down a door. Lord Bember will be furious. It's a mercy he's in Paris and not likely to walk in on us now. And old Kafka will never forgive us. But—wait a bit—why did Maurice shoot himself?"

"Lady Jocelyn turned him down," Cardew reminded him.

"I see," said Sir James slowly. He turned to the younger man who had not yet spoken. "Do you agree, Collier?"

"I'm afraid I don't," said Collier. "I'll tell you why afterwards, sir, if you don't mind waiting downstairs for a moment after they've taken young Kafka away, and then returning here."

Cardew turned away impatiently, annoyed by what seemed to him sheer obstinacy. Why couldn't the fellow admit that he had dropped a brick of the largest size?

Sir James acquiesced, but coldly. "Very well. I'll hear your reasons." He went back to Kafka. The stretcher was being carried out under the doctor's supervision.

Collier, rather white under his tan, for he realised that he had been snubbed and that there were worse things in store if he failed to justify himself, crossed the room to where Lady Jocelyn sat. It must be strange to her, he thought, to be completely unnoticed, but she was not thinking of herself.

"Lady Jocelyn," he said gently. "This has been a fearful shock to the old man. I wonder if you could bring yourself to go back to Regent's Park with him. I think he would be glad of your company."

"No, he wouldn't. He hates me."

"I don't think he is the man to hate what his son loves."

She looked up, startled by such directness. "Oh—"

He was thinking that her natural pallor became her. She looked younger and softer with her cheeks unrouged. She would need friends—if he was right.

"You don't mind my saying—"

"Not a bit. I always trusted you. Inspector." Her eyes sought his, asking for reassurance. Her voice dropped to a whisper.

"Then you've changed your mind? You don't think now that Maurice—"

"I was misled," he said, "by appearances."

"Thank you," she said.

He looked after her as she crossed the room to where old Kafka was slowly struggling to his feet. Sir James took one of his arms. Jocelyn took the other. They went with him to the door, but there was not room for all three to pass out together. Sir James released the arm he held and stood back. Jocelyn still clung to the old man's sleeve.

He turned his head in his slow fashion and his dark, unfathomable eyes searched her face.

"You—you came to warn me. There is something in all this that I cannot understand."

"Mr. Kafka," she said humbly. "Please—please let me go home with you. I—I shan't be in your way."

"Why?"

"To be near Maurice."

He stared at her a moment longer. His face changed slightly.

"Very well," he said, "my dear."

They left the room together. The hall door was open. As they went down the stairs Jocelyn could see the stretcher being lifted into the waiting ambulance. In the hall Lambert helped her into a fur coat. She rejoined Kafka on the threshold and this time he took her arm. His chauffeur was standing at the foot of the steps. The ambulance had started. The old man and the girl entered the huge glittering car and were driven away.

Inspector Collier drew a long breath of relief. The decks were cleared for action.

CHAPTER XXXII
MR. X

THE little group of errand boys and idlers, attracted by the unwonted spectacle of an ambulance outside one of the largest

houses in the square, was dispersing, prompted by the monoton-
ous "Pass along there, please," of the constable on the pavement.

"What was it, officer? A case of scarlet fever?"

"That's right. And you'll catch it if you hang about here breathing in the microbes. Pass along, will you."

Lambert, the butler, still held the hall door open. "You're going
now, aren't you?" he said.

Collier looked at him. "Not just yet."

The butler closed the door with evident reluctance. "You were
glad enough to see us just now, Lambert."

The old butler answered with dignity. "I was. But now that the
poor young gentleman has been removed there's no reason for you
to stay. I'm answerable to his lordship. He won't be best pleased
over that broken door, though I admit it couldn't be helped."

He started perceptibly as Sir James came out of the dining
room followed by Cardew. "I beg your pardon, gentlemen. I quite
thought you were gone."

"Not yet," said Sir James, "but I overheard what you were
saying to the Inspector and I quite agree. Our presence was necessary, but if we remain any longer Lord Bember might be justified
in complaining that we were abusing his hospitality. You can say
what you have to say at the Yard, Collier."

"I beg your pardon, Sir James, but I am afraid it must be said
here. That is to say, upstairs, in the secretary's room."

Sir James' eyes narrowed. "You have some good reason for
this, Inspector?"

"Yes, sir."

The butler intervened. "I can't allow you upstairs again,
gentlemen. This isn't my house. If you like to step into the dining-
room—"

"The dining-room won't do at all," said Collier. It was noticeable that his confidence grew as the old man servant maintained
his attitude. "You can accompany us, Lambert. Lead the way."

Cardew glanced at Sir James, prepared to assert his authority
at a hint from the Commissioner, but Sir James avoided his eye.

Lambert turned to them imploringly. "I can't prevent you—but—I've been thirty years in his lordship's service, but he'll not forgive me for this. I shall lose my place."

"I hope not," said the Commissioner. "I will explain to Lord Bember, if necessary, that you could not help yourself." But he did not look forward to making that explanation.

Collier was already half way up the stairs to the landing. Lambert, seeing that there was no alternative, went up after him, and the two high officials from Scotland Yard followed. To their surprise Collier did not walk directly into the study but stopped to feel in his pockets.

"I turned the key in the lock," he explained, "and brought it along with me. I was the last to come out. Here it is."

They went in. The room was as they had left it, with only one trace of what had so lately happened there, a small dark red stain on the plain fawn-coloured carpet. Collier turned to the Commissioner. "Won't you sit down, sir? What I have to say may take a few minutes."

Sir James shrugged his shoulders, and took the chair in which old Kafka had sat. "Very well," he said, not unkindly, for he had a liking for the young Inspector, "don't beat about the bush."

Collier took the hint. "It's just this," he said rapidly. "Duffield lost sight of young Kafka yesterday. We know now, through his father, that he attended a sale at Hassocks. Presumably he spent the night at an hotel there, since we combed the Brighton hotels without success, he drove up to Town this morning and came straight here to fetch away his personal belongings. Lambert here admitted him. A few minutes later he heard a shot, and, hurrying upstairs, found the study door locked on the inside and failed to obtain any answer when he knocked. He fetched Lady Jocelyn and we arrived almost at the same moment." Collier walked over to the writing table and called their attention to a little pile of books and a few untrained photographs and snapshots. "Doesn't this look as if he really had begun to collect the few articles that he valued here? What induced him to stop in order to shoot himself? It doesn't make sense. I know the Chief-Inspector says it was because she had turned him down. I don't think that would be a sufficient motive in Kafka's case. From what I've seen of him he's neither a weakling nor a quitter. If he had been Mr. X he might have taken that way out when he realised the game was up—"

Cardew could contain himself no longer. "Are you suggesting that it was an accident? He was clearing out the drawers and forgot that the pistol he had kept there was loaded. I agree that is quite possible, but why keep us here to listen to you?"

Collier turned to him. "Did you notice the bullet hole in his coat? I'll confess I didn't observe it very closely at first. I was more interested in seeing if his throat showed any traces of rough usage. But when I was satisfied on that point I looked again. There was no sign of scorching. Another point. Kafka's right hand was clenched and the pistol was lying three inches from it. If he had dropped it before he fell it would have been nearer his feet. If he was still holding it—well he wasn't—it wouldn't roll or slither any distance on this thick carpet. Kafka didn't shoot himself. Somebody shot him. And that somebody afterwards placed the pistol where we found it in the hope that we should assume that the wound was self-inflicted."

"The door was locked on the inside," said Sir James. He looked at the butler. "Is there any other exit?"

"None, sir."

"That settles it. I think," said the Commissioner. "The window was closed."

"But there's another door in the further wall. One of those doors fitted into the panelling that they were so fond of in the eighteenth century, isn't there, Lambert? I made a note of the windows on this floor when I was in the street just now seeing off the ambulance, and there's one at this end unaccounted for."

The butler moistened his lips. "That's right, Inspector. It's just a little drawing-room. There's a camp bed in there. Mr. Kafka slept there sometimes, not often, when there was a big debate on at the House and his lordship wanted him to stay late. But you have to pass through this room to get to it."

"It's that space between the two bookcases. isn't it? I don't see any handle?"

They all looked at Lambert, who neither spoke nor moved.

Sir James stood up. "Show us how it opens," he commanded.

"It's a sliding door. It runs very easily if you push it," faltered the butler.

The door slid away behind the bookcase as he spoke and Collier passed into the dressing-room, closely followed by Sir James and the Chief-Inspector. The room was very small and simply furnished with a camp bed, a washstand, a chest of drawers with a shaving mirror and some brushes on it, and a large wardrobe.

Collier stared hard at the bed. "The housemaid here doesn't know her work," he remarked. "The sheet is crooked and badly tucked in. Perhaps she was in a hurry. Or perhaps it wasn't the housemaid. It's very close in here. Shall we go back into the other room?" His eyes conveyed a message. Sir James, who had opened his mouth to speak, shut it again, and Cardew, who had been about to do the obvious thing, refrained.

They passed out again through the doorway in the panelling and found the butler leaning against the bookcase.

"What's the matter with you, Lambert?"

"Nothing, sir." He swallowed hard. "If you're satisfied perhaps you'll go now?"

"Presently," said Collier. He seemed to think that the old man might be deaf, for he raised his voice. "We haven't looked inside the wardrobe yet. We shall have to do that before we leave. Would you like a drop of brandy, Lambert? You don't look at all well."

Lambert tried to speak but only uttered a smothered cry. Collier caught him as he stumbled and lowered him gently to the floor.

"Let him lie flat for a bit," he said. "He's an old man and he's had more than one shock lately. I'm sorry I had to press him so hard, but it couldn't be helped." He looked at the Commissioner. "We'll go back in there when you give the word, sir."

Sir James's wholesome colour had faded somewhat. He had begun to understand, but Cardew was still frankly bewildered.

"I don't—" he began.

Sir James signed to him to be silent. "Now," he said. Once again Collier led the way into the dressing-room, but this time he went straight to the wardrobe. His right hand was in his coat pocket. He opened the door with his left. Something heavy fell out and rolled over at their feet.

It was the body of a man wearing a brown Jaeger dressing-gown over blue silk pyjamas. It exhaled a rank odour of bitter almonds. The muscles were still twitching, but after a moment all movement ceased.

"Who—who is it?" asked Cardew hoarsely.

Collier was silent. Sir James answered. "Lord Bember."

Cardew caught his breath. As it happened he was the only one of the three who had never seen Lord Bember in the flesh; but pictures of him often appeared in the daily and weekly papers. He recalled one, taken not long ago, on the steps of the registrar's office with his second wife. He recognised the harsh, predatory features and the jutting jaw. The lips, foam-flecked, were drawn back in what seemed a merciless caricature of the rather wolfish smile known—and dreaded—by his opponents in the law Courts, and. of late years, in the House. He had been shelved when he was given a peerage. They had feared him more than they trusted him. For all his hard metallic brilliance they had suspected a flaw, and, it seemed they had been right, since here he lay, having died the death of a rat in a trap, there was a white silk scarf wound about his neck. Collier, bending over him, loosened it and pointed to the black bruises on the swollen throat.

"Let's go back to the study," said Sir James abruptly. "I can't breathe in here."

They went back, and Collier, coming last, closed the sliding door. Lambert had recovered sufficiently to struggle to his feet and was in his former place, leaning against the bookcase.

Sir James answered his unspoken question. "We've found him. He's dead. Prussic acid. You knew he was there, of course?"

"Yes, sir. He told me not to mention it."

"Not to mention it is good. However, I'm not blaming you, Lambert. Only you must tell us all you know now."

"It isn't very much, sir," quavered the old man. "His lordship came home last night very late, between one and two. There was nothing in that. He kept very irregular hours. But I heard him coming up the stairs, hoisting himself up like, step by step, and I was afraid something had happened so I went down to him, and he seemed in a bad way. When I asked him if I could do anything he shook his head and pointed to his throat. It seemed as if he couldn't speak. I asked if I should get a doctor and he shook his head again and his eyes were angry so I didn't dare to say more. He wouldn't go to his own bedroom but lay down on the bed in Mr. Kafka's dressing-room. I asked him again if I could fetch him anything and he wrote what he wanted me to do on a sheet of notepaper."

"Have you kept it?"

"No, sir. I wasn't to let the servants or anyone know he'd returned. We all thought he was over in Paris with her ladyship. I was to come through the study at intervals to see if he wanted anything, but all he needed then was rest. So I left him. I was a bit bothered when Lady Jocelyn came back this morning, but I didn't suppose she'd go into the study since Mr. Kafka wasn't there. Then, when he came, I didn't know what to do. I made an excuse and ran upstairs to ask his lordship how I was to proceed, and he said, 'Let him come up, but don't say I'm here.' After that, gentlemen, I know no more than you what happened."

"We shall have to wait for Kafka's account," said Sir James, "meanwhile, what do you say. Collier?"

"Kafka was collecting the odds and ends he meant to take away with him. He heard a movement behind him and turning saw the sliding door open and his employer levelling a pistol at him. Lord Bember fired, and saw his man drop. Probably he had realised that discovery was certain if he waited. There were some of Kafka's belongings in the dressing room and when he had done here he would be going in to collect them. The shot must be heard and he hadn't much time. He locked the study door on the inside, wiped the pistol and laid it by Kafka's right hand and hurried back to the dressing-room and his bolt hole in the wardrobe. There was a chance that we should be satisfied. If I had left the study door unlocked he would have slipped out while we were downstairs."

"Near enough," said Sir James. "You get full marks for this business, doesn't he, Cardew."

Chief-Inspector Cardew acknowledged the fact without rancour. After all Collier had been his protégé and his discovery.

"This is going to make a big splash, sir."

Sir James frowned. "It mustn't. I'll have to see the Home Secretary. I don't say we could have let him go scot free. But he's paid in full."

He glanced at Collier. There were some things that could not be put into words. It was fortunate that the Inspector had realised the wisdom of giving their quarry time to escape by the only way left open, the way of death.

He turned to the butler. "I hope the family will be able to rely on your discretion, Lambert."

The old man answered with dignity. "Yes, sir. I never was one to talk. I shan't begin now."

Sir James reflected. "I think the best way would be to give the other servants a holiday on board wages. Let them go this afternoon. I will arrange for the body to be removed during the night. If newspaper men get wind of anything and come to ask questions you can say that Mr. Kafka shot himself by accident. Lord Bember, so far as you know, is abroad."

"Very good, sir. What about Lady Jocelyn, sir?" Sir James smiled faintly for the first time. "I don't think you need worry about her, Lambert. I think she will be staying with Mr. Kafka's father for the present."

"Yes, sir."

Sir James lit a cigarette. "Have you any question to ask Lambert before we go, Collier?"

"One, Sir James. You've spent half your life in Lord Bember's service, Lambert. You were with him when he married his first wife and when his children were born. Was there, in your opinion, anything unusual in his relations with his son? We know he was a hard man."

"He was a hard man," said Lambert, "but in his cold care-less fashion he was proud of Lady Jocelyn; proud of her looks and proud of her spirit. But poor Master Bertie—Lord Herbert. I should say he was different, soft and slack and easily daunted, and from the first his lordship despised him. Despised him and hated him."

Was it their fancy or had the air of the room grown colder?

The Commissioner shivered. "Unnatural," he muttered.

The old man servant's faded blue eyes met his. "It seemed so," he said, "but there'd been trouble in the house before the child was born. We servants didn't rightly know what it was but we heard raised voices behind closed doors and we noticed that one gentleman who used to come often when the master was away on circuit didn't come no more. Mrs. Vaste died when the baby was only a few weeks old. If she hadn't I sometimes wonder what would have happened. Mr. Vaste, he wasn't sure at first, but I think that as the boy grew up so unlike him he made up his mind that he couldn't be his, and—God forgive him—vented his jealousy and his bitterness on the innocent child."

"I see," said the Commissioner thoughtfully. "One thing more. Did Lord Bember, to your knowledge, collect precious stones?"

"I couldn't say, sir, but it's quite likely. He had locked drawers in his bureau in the library and kept stuff there that he used to gloat over in secret. He had what you might call underhand ways, sir. He liked to laugh alone. A bad sign that, sir, I always think."

"You are quite right. Lambert. We must be going now. We shall take this key. Get rid of the servants and await further instructions."

Later on, in his own room at the Yard, when various machinery had been set in motion, Sir James returned to the psychological aspect of the case. "Clowes will be convicted for the manslaughter of Police Constable Deane, and the rest of the gang will get rather shorter terms of imprisonment for smuggling dope. It's been a fairly thorough clean up after all, thanks to you, Collier. When did you guess that Lord Bember was Mr. X?"

"Not until I saw that Kafka could not be the man who had been half strangled a few hours before by Colonel Drury. Then all the pieces in the puzzle fell into place. It had been obvious that poor young Vaste was the victim of an almost insane hatred. Who hated him, and why? He was nobody's rival. He seemed in a general way so harmless. In his determination to ruin the boy body and soul Mr. X risked the failure of his plans. As to the gang itself, the Council of Ten, it satisfied his craving for excitement, it gave scope for the ugly streak of cruelty, the love of power." He checked himself, flushing. "I beg your pardon, sir. You asked me what I thought. I'm talking too much."

"No," said the older man. "We nearly took you off the case at one time. But you handled it remarkably well. And you are right. The whole thing hinges on the warped mind of one man. The others, left to themselves, would never have touched this Russian jewel business. They were his creatures throughout. Well, I've been in touch with the powers that be, and it's all settled. No scandal. A plane accident in mid-channel. The pilot will be picked up. Poetic justice, eh? He was fond—too fond—of arranging accidents. I wonder if, when the assessors go through his stuff for probate, they will find the Eye of Nero."

"I don't think so," said Collier. "You remember, sir, that old Kafka received four diamonds for his services? I fancy the Eye of Nero has returned to Russia. Much good may it do them."

"They say green is unlucky," said Sir James, smiling, "But it's meant a step up for you."

THE END

Printed in Great Britain
by Amazon